SEARCHING FOR YOUR SONG

SARA WETMORE

Print ISBN: 978-1-7376429-6-1

Ebook ISBN: 978-1-7376429-7-8

Book cover design by 100covers.com

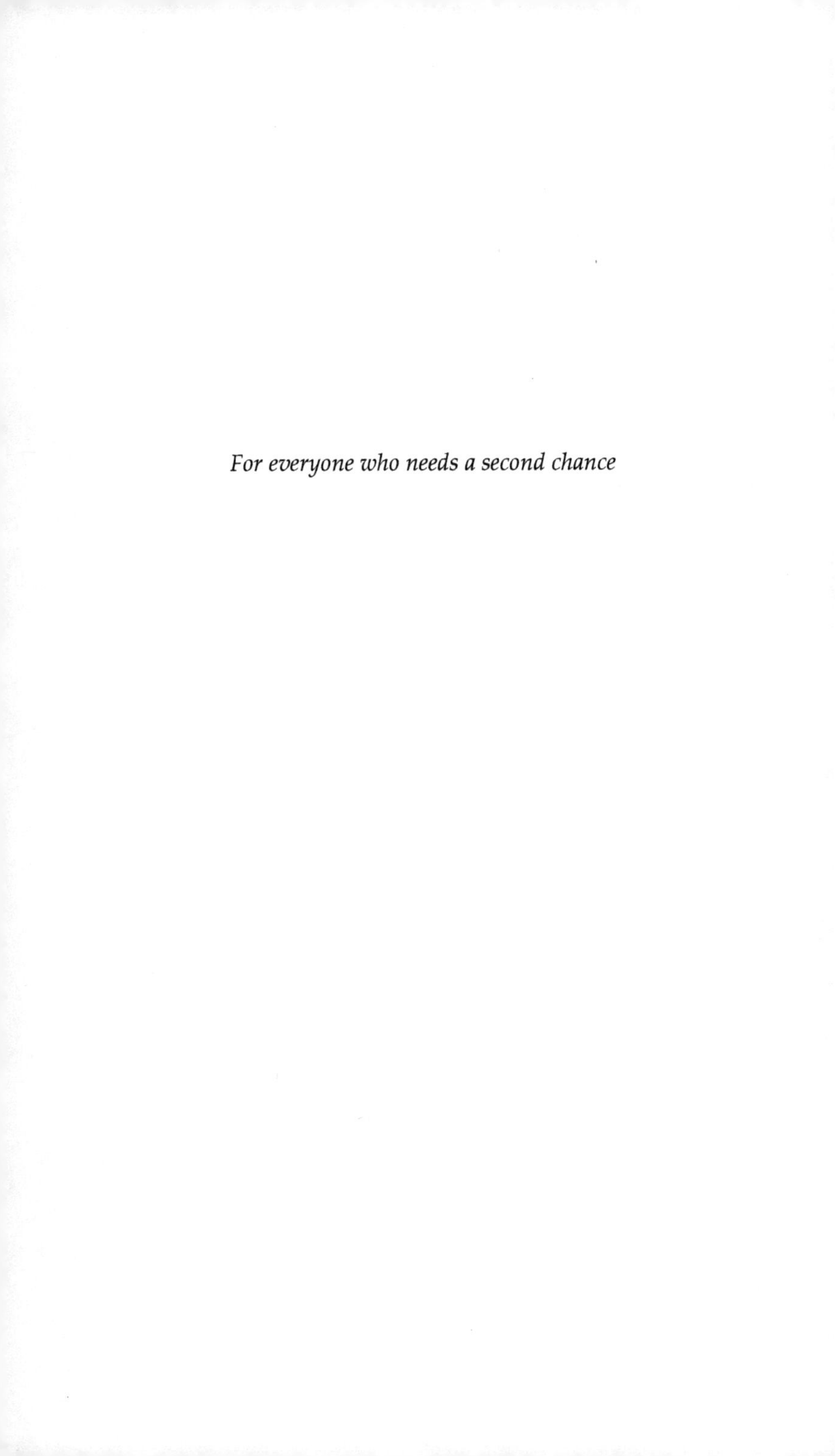

For everyone who needs a second chance

CHAPTER
ONE

LOLA

JULY 10, 2022

I love waking up early. It is one of the many simple pleasures in my day that brings me joy. When my alarm goes off at 4:00am, I'm not distressed; there's no need to panic, there's no need to rush. I've got plenty of time and a job that I am devoted to waiting for me.

I suspect I am crepuscular, much like the whales that I study. I am energized by the twilight hours just before sunrise and after sunset. Whales prefer this time because it is safer to communicate without being heard by predators – such as the J, K, and L pods of orcas in the Puget Sound – because the water better absorbs the sound, probably because there is less human-caused interference. That is what I hope to solve, establishing environmental law preventing noise pollution not just in the waters of Washington, but globally. I've studied for this nearly my entire life, and now I am getting close to obtaining the data I need to make a more compelling case, if I could only secure more funding to follow their migration routes. It doesn't pay much, but I am powered by purpose. Always have been.

My studio apartment in Kirkland is not far (at least by Seattle standards) from the Shilshole Bay Marina, where my employer, The Whale Conservancy, docks our research vessel.

This grants me at least a few hours of the morning to do what I wish, and what I wish is to settle into my routine: brush teeth, make coffee, eat overnight oats, read a chapter or two of a book, shower, get dressed, and head out the door.

Similar to waking early, I also like arriving early. I do this for a multitude of reasons, but primarily, it's simply that being early lessens my anxiety. As a late-diagnosed autistic adult, the more I can do to ease my anxiety, the better. Routine helps with this. I don't do well with change, which is why I cling to the predictable.

When I finally arrive at the marina, no one else is there; it's just me, the rising summer sun, and humpback whales breaching in the water. While I can't see the humpbacks from the marina, I know they are out here. That's one thing I can always count on. That is, after all, why I am here.

Brandon, my fellow researcher at The Whale Conservancy, is late as usual. Lateness drives me crazy, but at least when it comes to Brandon, I know what to expect. We've done this hundreds of times before: we load up the boat with our equipment, such as the hydrophones that we use to measure sounds in the ocean and their acoustic impacts on marine life, and I drive us out into the Puget Sound to collect data and make observations. Then, we head back to the dock, eat lunch, and meet at the office to analyze and transcribe the data into neat, little talking points. We do this four days a week, and every day it is the same. Brandon doesn't seem to mind. For this, I am so appreciative.

As we load the boat, I can tell there is a heaviness in Brandon. He seems bothered by something, but it's probably not my business to ask. Still, he drags his feet and moves so slowly that I fear we'll miss the morning activity out on the ocean.

"Come on, slow poke," I gibe. He cracks a smile as he carries the last of the equipment onto the boat. "Ah – there's the Brandon I know."

His foot snags on the side of the boat as he climbs in, causing him to nearly drop the hydrophones. He catches himself though, saving the gear from crashing into pieces on the deck.

"Sorry," he stutters, clearing his throat. "I got it though. It's all good."

Is it all good? It doesn't seem like it. Something is up, and it pains me to not know things. I eye him suspiciously as he sits down and rubs his neck.

"Okay, if you say so," I say.

I pull the boat away from the dock and drive it out into the water. He doesn't say another word until we are well within the Puget Sound. We putter slowly, as everyone should as they enter the whales' habitat, before I turn off the motor entirely. As we coast along and bob among the waves, I begin preparing the hydrophones to drop into the water, but Brandon just sits there wringing his hands.

"What would you do – you know, for a living – if you didn't have this?" he asks.

The question stops me in my tracks.

"I don't know," I say. I am dead serious. "This is all I've ever wanted to do. Why do you ask?"

He avoids my searching eyes and squirms a little in his seat.

"Brandon, do you know something I don't?"

He lets out a deep sigh.

"Nothing is final yet. Maybe I shouldn't even say anything."

I fold my arms and stare at him even harder. Whatever information he is holding back, I need to know.

"Dude, just tell me," I plead.

With a sharp inhale, the words come tumbling out.

"Dawn told me that our project has lost funding," he says. "The development team has been trying to secure the money we need for months, but no one will donate and no one in D.C. seems to care. A bunch of heartless idiots."

"You've gotta be kidding me," I whisper. Bending forward, I grab my knees and fight for breath.

Brandon jumps up from his seat and stands by my side, rubbing my back with sympathy.

"Hey, hey," he says calmly. "It's okay. It's going to be okay."

I snap up and walk toward the port side. As I stare at the stillness of the water, I am struck by an incredible pang of grief. I could lose this. I could lose all of this.

I want to yell at him, as if it were his fault, but I know it's not. It's both no one's fault and everyone's. If only people knew how crucial the project was – how if we don't protect the whales, the entire food chain in the ocean will destabilize, disrupting the food supply for other species, including humans. It's not just about the whales. It's about balancing a global network of aquatic and terrestrial ecosystems.

And it's about my job, too. I've dedicated my entire life to this. It's literally all that I know. Without it, everything I have worked so hard to build will come crashing down. I'd have to move in with my sister, Ruby, or worse – move away from her and my dad, Tino, entirely.

I shake out my hands and turn towards Brandon.

"How long do we have?" I ask.

He looks down at his feet. "I don't know. A couple of months?"

"Okay," I say.

"Okay?"

"There's still time to save this. We just need to think of something."

It's funny how well I seem to handle big setbacks like this. Give me a minor inconvenience and I have a full blown meltdown. Give me an actual crisis and I rise to the challenge, immediately trying to come up with solutions. The way my brain works makes little sense, but at this moment, I am glad it's able to function at all.

"How are we going to fix it?" Brandon asks. "Dawn has tried everything."

"Really, Brandon? Everything?" I say sarcastically.

"What could we possibly do that she hasn't already?"

I ponder this for a moment. I don't doubt that Dawn has fought tooth and nail for our research, but there is only so much that The Whale Conservancy can do, especially here in Washington.

"Everyone here is so damn obsessed with the three resident orca pods because that is all they hear about. I know they are important, but no one seems to care about the humpbacks because no one is talking about them," I say.

Brandon's eyes light up.

"So, we need to spread the word," he agrees. "But how? Even if we got one article published, it could take months to raise the money, if we get any at all."

He's right. This isn't as simple as a press release or a magazine article. People hardly read these days anyway, and there's no guaranteeing that writing a story would motivate anyone to donate to our cause.

"What we need is to get a lot of affluent people in one confined space, where they are forced to confront the issue," I say.

"Like a fundraiser?" Brandon asks.

"Better," I say. "Like a gala."

He grabs my hand tightly, grinning wide.

"Lola, you are a genius!" Then, his grin disappears and he drops my hand. "But do we know any rich people? Famous people? I sure don't."

At the very mention of famous people, a wave of painful memories comes rushing back.

Oscar wasn't always famous. Before he started that band, he would play songs on the guitar for me and only me. Even now, when I hear his band on the radio, I feel a little betrayed, like this thing that he used to only share with me now belonged to everyone. But really, it was me that betrayed him. That's why things fell apart.

When I found out I was pregnant our senior year of college, I didn't tell him. I had just been accepted to the marine biology program at the University of Oregon. We would be following different paths regardless, and I... I didn't want to change course or be left alone with his child. Not while he chased his dreams and I missed out on mine.

I know it wouldn't necessarily play out how I had envisioned, but I couldn't take the risk. I should have told him about the pregnancy, about the subsequent abortion, but ultimately, I still believe I made the right choice – for both of us. Instead, I buried my secret, and when we graduated, I packed my things and moved to Eugene without so much as a goodbye.

Now, he plays his guitar for stadiums full of adoring fans.

And I study the creatures that captured my heart long ago, when I was just a little girl with her nose in a science book.

In the end, we both got what we wanted. Didn't we?

"Lola," Brandon says, waving his hand slowly in front of my eyes. "Are you alright? You look like you're going to be sick."

I blink in quick succession and shake out my hands.

"Yeah," I exhale. "Sorry, I just..."

"Do you know someone?" he asks, trying to mask his hopefulness.

My eyes catch his and his brow is twisted with curious sympathy.

"No. No, I don't."

"Then let's get to work, eh?" Brandon chuckles. He gives me a playful shove before crossing the deck to fuss with the hydrophones.

We spend the rest of the morning recording whale songs and other acoustics. The humpbacks occasionally jump or spyhop to view our little boat above the rippling surface. It seems they are as curious about us as we are about them. Well, me at the very least. Brandon likes his job well enough. He loves marine life. But he would much rather be surfing a wave than sitting silently on the quiet, steady water, waiting for a chance to lock eyes with a gentle giant. Not like me.

We see a whale swimming along with its calf, and my heart drops into the pit of my stomach, remembering all I lost to be here, all that I gave up. All the while, Brandon has no idea. Oscar has no idea either. He probably just thinks I stopped loving him, and that hurts just as much.

I loved him once.

But I suppose I love this more.

"Whoa! Did you see that little guy?" Brandon exclaims, pointing in the water.

My eyes dampen with gleeful sorrow.

"Yeah," I say. "It's beautiful."

And it is. Every time.

CHAPTER
TWO

OSCAR

JULY 10, 2022

"Oscar!" Madison yells over the din of the party. "Is that Shane Silver?"

Her voice is sweet, but the syllables slur together ever so slightly.

I know what she is doing. She does this everywhere we go, as if someday my introductions will induct her into the A-list celebrity circle. I suppose I'm just not influential enough – to get her into a Marvel movie, at least.

"I don't know. Is it?" I lie. I squint my eyes in his direction. Try to really sell it. A sharp intake of breath and I am bracing myself for the favor to follow.

"Come on, babe. Introduce me!" She grabs my arm, starts pulling me in Shane's direction.

Deep down, I lament the fact that she is an up-and-coming actress and not an aspiring songwriter. I could actually help with the latter. People assume that all famous people get along with other famous people, but when it comes to most of them, I cringe at the conversation, the same ten humble-brags that seem rehearsed and reek of money. So little of them care for the art for which they most likely became famous. Each word is a flex, a stepping stone to boast about their latest vacation, their latest purchase, their latest exploit. Me, Jacob, and Tyler never made this adjustment to our speech. Music has always been the focus. Fame happened entirely by accident.

After crossing the crowd in this rooftop bar, Madison drops my arm and nods toward Shane Silver. I sigh and lightly touch his arm to get his attention, readying myself for the dance I wish I never knew.

"Hey, Shane. How are ya?" I say. Cringe. Cringe, cringe, cringe.

"Oh, hey, man. Oscar Kelly, is it?" he asks. He's right, but I hate how he phrased it as a question when he is at *my* band's afterparty. A power play.

"The very same," I laugh. "Can you believe this party?"

"It's nuts, man," he says. "Seattle is such a cool city."

We can agree on that. Seattle is great; not only is it where we chose to end the North American tour, it's also where Jacob and I grew up. Seattle is home. But Shane doesn't care about any of that, so I keep it simple and play his game of fame-chicken.

"We always end our tours here," I say. "Can't beat this view."

I look out over the skyline, but I see Shane's head turn toward Madison.

"No," he says. He looks her up and down, eyes ravenous and his mouth practically drooling. "No, you cannot."

Madison is gorgeous. Blue eyes, long blonde hair, and even longer legs. She is by all standards what we would call "Hollywood hot." But often, I wish she hadn't gotten all that surgery to fit that ideal. It seems like every few months, she is getting a new procedure: Botox injections, lip fillers, a nose job. She was pretty before all of that. Now she looks more dolllike than human. Still pretty, but in the same way that I can appreciate a perfectly straight line: perfect, but completely lacking in any characteristics that make it unique. To me, it just looks like every other straight line.

"Hey," Madison says in her most sultry voice. She outstretches her hand to shake Shane's. "I'm Madison Elm."

Shane is immediately more invested in his conversation with her than he is with me, maybe because he can feel my insincerity, or maybe because he doesn't want to bed me. Madison is much better at this than I am. Some people were just meant to be famous. She is one of them. Not me.

Shane lifts her hand to his lips, kissing it lightly. I roll my eyes. Yes, this bothers me, but I know she is flirting and using her beauty to advance her career. Just more reason that I find all of these people so disingenuous. Madison has shown me this firsthand.

"Madison Elm," Shane repeats, still holding her hand. "What do you do, Madison Elm?"

"I'm an actress," she says proudly.

"Is that so?" Shane is flirting back while I stare daggers into his skull. He catches me giving him a dirty glance, but seems unperturbed as he turns back toward Madison. "Come. I want to hear all about it."

His hand meets her lower back, guiding her to the edge of the roof so they can talk alone. As they walk away, Madison turns around and shrugs at me, a signal that she's saying, *Sorry, I gotta do what I gotta do.* And I get it. I won't resent her for it. But it does make it seem like she is using me to get ahead the same way she uses everyone else. She is a shark, and I am a bloody carcass in the water.

I look around and see many familiar faces, but none that I would call friends. All of these self-absorbed people gathered in one spot, not to celebrate our music or our tour, but to congratulate themselves on their own successes, constantly belittling each other if one person appears more successful than themselves, always keeping score.

I want none of that. I was actually more happy before our band, The Unadored, took off. But I am grateful that it has allowed me to make music my livelihood. Not every artist gets that lucky.

Come to think of it, the last time that I remember being truly happy was when I was in college – when I was with Lola. We would sit on the campus lawn. She always had her head down, drowning in schoolwork, while I just messed around with my guitar.

Sometimes, I would try to get her to smile by playing that song by The Kinks. I'd look at her and feel the warmth of sunlight on my skin, though if truth be told, it seemed as though the warmth was coming from within instead. And then my brain couldn't resist singing the words: *I'm not the world's most passionate guy, but when I looked in her eyes, well, I almost fell for my Lola. Lo-Lo-Lo-Lo-Lola.*

She would crack a smile, likely more sick of the song the more times I played it, but that look always made me feel like a hundred times the rockstar that I am today. She was the only one that I wanted to impress.

But then one day, we graduated and she was gone. No reason, no explanation. I don't think she even said goodbye.

This broke me. All I could do to save myself from the deep depression that I felt was to pour all of myself into music. Jacob and I would binge-write songs for months on end, until one of our songs started gaining steam online. With just over 250,000 people who streamed that first single, we were ecstatic. We thought that would be the height of our musical careers, until I got a call from some suit in California that wanted the rights to use the song in an upcoming movie. Of course, we said yes, but to our surprise, it wasn't just *in* the movie. It was in the *trailer*. More people heard that song than we could have ever imagined. Fast forward nine years, and here we are: on a rooftop in our hometown celebrating the close of our seventh world tour.

All the while, I wonder what Lola thinks about that, if she thinks about me at all. I don't know where she is or what she is doing, but wherever she is, I am sure she is making a difference. Must be nice to have that kind of purpose.

"Hey, Oscar," Jacob says, handing me a fresh, fruity drink. "Madison ditched you again, huh?"

"That's showbiz, baby," I say. I take the drink from him and sip from it speedily.

"You shouldn't be alone at your own party," he laughs, but his tongue is tinged with pity. "What's going on?"

I am alone so much more than at this party, but I don't know how to tell him that.

"Do you ever wish we did something else? Something that – I don't know – is a force for good?" My gaze drifts toward the horizon, my ears to the sounds of the city and the sea.

"Music is a force for good," he says. "But I think I know what you mean. You want to do charity or something? We can do that, you know."

"I don't know what I want," I sigh and look around the party. "This all feels so…"

"Hollow?"

"Yeah. That."

"Well," Jacob begins, "We aren't recording for a while. Take some time to do something for others while you're here. Or go somewhere else. Build schools in Africa? I don't know."

Jacob is right. We do have some time to kill. I need a project: a selfless project.

"What about whales?" I blurt out without even thinking.

Jacob nearly chokes on his drink.

"Oh no, buddy. Don't go down this road," he says. "You're not going to find her."

"What?" I protest. "I still know a lot about them because of her. At least I think I do."

"You're not going to convince me that you don't have any ulterior motives here," Jacob says. "But I guess it isn't me you need to convince. It's yourself."

"Despite what you think, I care a lot about whales. Sure,

maybe that's because of Lola, but my heart is in it, you know?" I down the rest of my drink. "When I think about that cause, I feel…"

"Sentimental," Jacob interjects.

"I suppose so," I acquiesce.

Jacob musses my hair and laughs.

"You have always been such a sap, dude."

"Rather be a sap than a passionless pragmatic," I joke. "You should get back to the party. No need to waste all of this on me. I'll be fine, I promise."

"You sure?" he asks.

"I'm sure. Thanks for the drink."

"No problem, my guy," Jacob says, clapping me on the back. "Hey, maybe tomorrow you should research some nonprofits to get involved with, see if that helps. Now, if you'll excuse me, I'm going to go find Tyler."

I give him a sarcastic salute. It seems like one of us is always trying to track down Tyler. In fact, I am beginning to think I should do the same.

I look around the party to find any familiar faces: Tyler, Madison – or hell, even Shane.

Everyone is missing, hidden from sight.

I move through the crowd, scanning everyone's faces as they smile and give me a passing congratulations. But none of them are the faces I am seeking. Why is it every time someone goes missing, it's both Tyler and Madison?

It dawns on me that they must be together. Briefly, I consider it an affair, but then I remember. Immediately, I make my way to the restroom.

When I open the bathroom door, I see both Tyler and Madison hunched over a creased hundred dollar bill.

"Oh, hey!" Tyler perks up. He nods toward the money.

Madison takes another bill, rolls it up, and sniffs white powder from within the crease. She stands upright, sniffing a few more times, before sashaying across the room and closing the door behind me.

"Shh… come on, babe," she says, draping her arms over my shoulders, but my body is rigid. I bite the inside of my cheek and glance at Tyler.

"It's alright, man," Tyler says. "Just give me a second."

He replenishes the powder and snorts it through a rolled bill, as well. Setting the tainted money on the counter, he shakes out his entire body like a wet dog before wailing like one, too.

Tyler and Madison are both staring at me intensely, and I can feel my heartbeat quicken, adrenaline coursing through me, a tightness in my gut.

He takes a step toward me.

"I won't tell Jacob if you won't."

CHAPTER
THREE

LOLA

JULY 12, 2022

I awake at 4am, as usual. It is, by all accounts, just like any other day: teeth brushed, body clean and clothed, coffee consumed, oats eaten, and reading complete. I even meet Brandon at the marina, putter out into the water, and collect some data.

It's not until I arrive at the office that I realize something is very, very wrong. I don't know how to describe it, but it activates every sensory alarm in my body. The air around me has changed. It churns my stomach and tightens my chest. But what could it be? I inhale and exhale purposefully to try to regain control, but still, the anxiety makes itself known.

I enter the doors to the Conservancy and see my colleagues huddled together, boisterous but contrived laughter sounding in the lobby. As curious as I am to see what they are so excited about, these situations make me nervous. I don't want to meet new people, even if they are donors. The conversation always feels so forced and it makes me want to wriggle out of my skin.

So, I try to pass through unnoticed, walking lightly and keeping my head down. It's no use though. Dawn, who manages our most affluent donor relationships, turns to scoop her hair out of her face, catching me in her eyesight.

"Lola!" she sings. "I was wondering when you might show up!"

She shifts her weight and reveals what must be an apparition. I can think of no other explanation for the shape I see before me: a tall man with pink skin; long, black, curly hair; and hazel eyes, above which sits an unmistakable scar on his eyebrow. He looks older than I remember as he strokes the slight stubble on his startled face.

I freeze where I am, my body stiff as a board. Dawn tries to tug me toward the huddle around the handsome, haunting figure, and makes me stumble a bit until I am standing right before him.

"Oscar…" I say, the words so inaudible, they are barely a whisper.

"Lola," he replies. His face has gone sheet-white.

Dawn alternates her gaze between me and Oscar, clearly confused by the palpable tension.

"You two know each other?" she asks. "Lola, you never said you knew Oscar Kelly! I have *got* to hear how you met."

Suddenly, I feel unnaturally warm – hot, actually. My skin is on fire and I need to escape.

"Maybe another time, Dawn," I say, slowly stepping away. "I've really got to get back to work."

Dawn cannot hide the disappointment in her face, and neither can Oscar, though I pretend not to notice. I am completely overwhelmed by the flood of emotions I am feeling – so many, in fact, that I cannot even isolate and identify any of them, putting them in neat little categories for me to overanalyze.

I turn to walk away entirely, but I feel a familiar hand hold me back.

"Lola," Oscar says, his voice low and injured. "Please don't leave."

Dawn tries to make our colleagues disperse, giving Oscar and I some much needed privacy. I never thought I would see him again, and if I did, I didn't think it would be here, on public display.

I turn to him and sigh. When I look into the golden rings in his eyes, I see his desperation.

"Can't we talk?" he aches.

Looking at him is difficult. Painful, actually. I look down at my sneakers instead, noting how one knot is dangerously loose.

"Please," he pleads.

I exhale, releasing all of the air in my lungs, all of the rigidness I feel in my body. I suppose there is no escaping this. I cannot avoid Oscar any longer.

"Okay," I say. I notice Dawn pretending not to eavesdrop as she leans against the front desk. Her eyes drift towards us, and if she were a dog, I would almost surely see her ears perk up the second we open our mouths. "Let's go to my office."

The walk up the stairs and down the corridor seems endless, despite having done this nearly every day for the past three years. Navigating my workplace with my ex boyfriend in tow feels surreal, as if I am inviting my past into my present, even though I thought I had left the past behind. I've always felt that the two should be separate, never crossing paths, never overlapping. But here stands Oscar - *my* Oscar - in my office more than a decade after I left him.

I close the door behind him and gesture to the chair in front of my desk. However, he remains standing, blinking at me. I'm waiting for him to speak first, but it appears he is doing the same.

"Oscar, I–"

"What happened, Lola?" he asks. I can hear his voice breaking. "One moment, you were there, and then the next, you were gone."

"What are you doing here?" I say, trying to divert the conversation from the painful truth.

"I asked first," he says.

I sigh and my eyes prick.

"I know what I did was awful," I squeak. "I don't expect you to forgive me, but you have to understand that I had a reason. I just… I'd like to forget it."

I look up at him and meet his gaze. I can see the tattoo ink through his shirt collar and my chest flutters. I want to reach out and touch him, but he isn't mine to touch. Those days have long since passed. I have to accept that the man before me is nothing but a familiar stranger.

"Did I do something wrong?" he says, eyes softening.

"No," I say. "You were perfect."

Oscar shifts his feet uncomfortably. "Then what? Why did you leave without saying a word to me, as if we were nothing?"

Water begins to pool in my eyes.

"Please, don't press this," I whisper.

"Lola, I need to know. I've spent the last ten years wondering what I did to make you go. Now, you're here. You're here and I still don't know. Please."

Blood rushes to my head and the room starts spinning. There's a pain in my gut, right where life used to be before it was evicted. The cramping intensifies, like a phantom limb, and I remember the scraping, scraping, scraping. I still feel the sedation and the guilt, but also the relief. But as Oscar looks at me with his supplicating stare, it's mostly guilt – so intense that an invisible weight falls upon me, collapsing my legs and forcing me to the ground.

Then, a seemingly endless darkness.

When the center of my vision slowly illuminates, it is Oscar's impossibly handsome, hard-angled face that I see looking down at me. His calloused fingertips graze my cheekbones, and when the ringing ceases in my ears, I hear his deep, gentle voice calling to me.

"Lola… Lola…" he speaks softly. "Are you here with me? Breathe."

Slowly, I sit up. Oscar is kneeling beside me as he supports my back in case I collapse once more.

"I'm sorry, I don't know what came over me," I whisper.

Oscar knits his brows together and squeezes my shoulder.

"Listen," he says. "This is clearly more complicated than I assumed. You don't have to tell me what happened today. But someday, I hope you will feel comfortable enough to explain. I just want to know that you're okay."

"I'm okay," I insist, though the word is so vague that I don't know if I actually mean it.

Oscar helps me to my feet, offering his arm to steady myself.

"I know I owe you an explanation. One day, I hope to give that to you. But for now…" My words disappear as soon as they escape my mouth. "Why are you here, Oscar?"

Oscar lets go of me and rubs his thick, sinewy neck.

"It's, uh…" He clears his throat. "I was looking for… something."

I get chills down my spine. Was Oscar looking for *me*?

"Did you know I work here?" I ask plainly.

"No," he says. "I promise. I had no idea. But would it really be so bad if I did?"

Looking at him incredulously, he sees he has struck a nerve. His eyes avoid mine, like a wolf submitting itself to the alpha in the pack.

"I don't know," I admit. "It's just weird. After all this time, why now, Oscar?"

I immediately regret asking the question. Oscar rubs his arms as if he's cold, his eyes wide and haunted.

"Were you ever even going to ask how I've been?" he asks.

For a moment, I even think I see his chin quiver. I sigh. He's right. I was so surprised and threatened by his appearance that I never even thought to ask. I don't know what he's been through all these years. Maybe something terrible happened.

"How have you been?" I say sincerely. I lightly touch his arm, as if it might comfort him, but he flinches. He tries to pretend he didn't, but we both saw it. I guess it's best not to acknowledge it.

"Not great," he says. "I know you're probably thinking 'Oh, poor Oscar, it must be so hard for you to be famous,' but honestly, it is. I feel so stupid complaining about it. I should be grateful, shouldn't I?"

"But you're not," I say.

"No. I'm not." He shoots me a pained stare. "Some desires are better off as distant dreams, rather than enduring disappointment."

Hearing this makes my heart break. This man, who once couldn't stop talking about how much he wanted to be the world's greatest guitarist, is completely and utterly broken. Like an octopus that tortures itself – tearing at its skin, gnawing at its arms – programmed to die. The hopeful becomes the hopeless.

"I don't know what to say," I say. "I'm sorry."

"It's okay. I guess it was bound to fall short of expectations when I imagined it as much as I did. We just finished a tour, you know? Then I came back to Seattle and realized how much everyone was bringing me down. I've surrounded myself with self-serving sycophants. Makes me wonder if I've become just like them."

I blink in disbelief.

"The Oscar I knew would never become someone like that," I offer. "If it's any consolation."

"I hope so," he says, cracking a sad smile. "But I guess that doesn't answer your question about why I am here."

I let out a nervous chuckle.

"No, I guess not."

Oscar sighs heavily. I think I even hear a little moan of

relief. "I want to be better. I want to do better. Jacob suggested I pick a cause I care about, and the first thing that came to mind was whales… because of you."

"You remembered," I exclaim.

"Of course I did." Beneath his black stubble beard, his cheeks redden.

"You really want to help, huh?"

"I really do," he says. I don't think I have ever heard him sound so serious.

"Well, you're in luck. I could use some help tomorrow while my partner is out. Have you ever been on a boat before?" His cheeks grow even more red. "You mean to tell me you've toured the world but you've never been on a boat?"

Oscar shrugs. "Just never came up."

"That changes tomorrow. You can come with me on *one* boat ride, and I will tell you about what we do here."

"Really?" he says. He runs his fingers loosely through his dark curls. "That would be great."

"But you have to get up early – by *my* standards, not yours," I gibe.

"I remember," he laughs.

"I'll see you at Shilshole Bay Marina at five-thirty," I say. "I mean it. Five-thirty."

"Five-thirty," he confirms.

For the first time during this entire conversation, his face lights up. I try to still my heart as it longs to reach for him, but also to push him away.

CHAPTER
FOUR

OSCAR

JULY 13, 2022

It is too early. Lola is a madwoman. But damn it, she has always been right about this being the magic hour. I understand the appeal. However, my body does not.

I sit in my Tesla and watch the water weave and waver, wobbling the boats on the dock. I am earlier than Lola said, by no small amount. If there is one thing to know about her, it's that she is very impatient. She'd call it punctual, but really, it's impatience in a fancy dress and lipstick – or in her case, a North Face jacket. She often said if you aren't fifteen minutes early to an engagement, then you are late. I used to find it so frustrating, but now that I look back on it, it's actually quite endearing. She is so afraid of displeasing people that she is calculated in every action she takes, all to ensure that no one is ever disappointed or uncomfortable – even if it's at her expense. I hate to say her martyrdom is a virtue, but compared to all of the rich people in L.A., it's refreshing to imagine someone so concerned with everyone else. I don't think Lola has ever had an egotistical thought. She will look inward, but always, always outward. God, I miss that.

An old, green Subaru pulls into the lot, parking on the opposite side as me. A short, thin, athletic looking woman with tan skin and caramel hair cascading past her shoulders climbs out of the driver's seat. It's Lola. She still wears the same navy blue North Face jacket that she did in college. Unreal.

As she crosses the lot, I get out of the Tesla. I want her to see that I was here first without having to tell her. I want her to know that I care about this.

"Oscar," she says cordially. "You're on time."

I seethe just a little bit. I want to tell her I was here early, but really, it doesn't matter that she knows that. I can settle with *on time*. Even if it made her smile, I don't want to risk making things more tense than they already are. We aren't close enough to tease each other anymore. Strange how things have changed.

"Yep," I say, lacking my usual confidence. Now that Lola is here, I feel twitchy and faint.

"I'm glad," she says. "Follow me to the boat."

A far cry from yesterday, she is decidedly all business this morning. That's fine, I guess, but I do hope she will soften.

Lola hands me a handful of meticulously wrapped cables to carry, each with a small techy cylinder on one end and a soft hollow ball on the other.

She frowns at me. "Don't drop that."

I am so, so tempted to pretend to drop it, but she is not in the mood to goof around. I have to respect that. She agreed to take me out here. I am in her territory. Instead, I hope I can express my curiosity.

"What is it?" I ask.

"Hydrophones. We use it to listen underwater."

"Cool."

I mean it. It is cool. Her interest in the sounds whales make has always fascinated me. I don't understand what the purpose is, but I am hopeful that today she will tell me.

"This is us," she says, gesturing toward a rusty old boat – much more modest and functional than the others in the marina. On the back, it reads in bold, painted letters: *Don't Krill My Vibe.*

"Nice boat," I say, but it comes out more sarcastically than I would like.

Lola peeks at the boat's rear before continuing to load it up.

"Is it?" A light chuckle. "Dawn's idea. I proposed the name *Humpford and Sonars,* but it was shot down. I'm not good with words like you."

I choke on my laughter. The name conjures the image of a whale playing a banjo.

"I think that is an excellent name," I assure her.

She tries to subtly roll her eyes, but I see it. When it comes to Lola, I have always had a hard time looking away. I love observing her little quirks: how her brows crease when she's worried, how she mimics other people's body language to put them at ease, and how she always needs to be fidgeting with something whether she is anxious or not. Just too much emotion and energy for her small body to contain.

"I actually preferred the runner-up: *Whale, Actually.* Far more true to us scientists. Most people in the office didn't find it as funny as I did," she says.

It appears that she is beginning to lighten up and default to her silly self, but when I try to meet her gaze, she looks away all too quickly.

I still want to hear why she left all those years ago so I can understand why my presence is so painful for her. She said I didn't do anything, but the way she catches herself relaxing before steeling up again makes me think otherwise. I ache to be pierced by her pitch black stare. Why won't she just look at me, for even a second?

"You always did have a great sense of humor," I say. "If I didn't know better, I'd say your talents are being wasted."

I'm nudging her to the past, urging her to reminisce, but she stubbornly dismisses it.

"I wouldn't say that," she says. She starts the boat. "I'd sit down if I were you."

I sit down promptly, obediently – not just because she is the expert, but because seeing her again makes my veins surge and my heart quicken. Truthfully, I would follow her every command, whether it seemed wise or not.

It turns out sitting is a good idea though. She was right about that. As we make our way farther and farther out of the marina, the water is choppy, and even though we aren't going very fast, each wave causes the boat to stutter in the clearing darkness, bouncing me in place.

After a while, the sky ignites into blazing blue and orange, illuminating Lola's face and the entire Puget Sound as she cuts the engine, forcing me to confront the strange, earsplitting silence that exists at sea.

"Now what do we do?" I ask.

"We get to work."

She really has a way of making me beg for information.

"And the work is..." I begin for her, guiding her gently into conversation.

Lola untangles the cables and begins plugging them into other equipment on the boat.

"The hydrophones," she offers. "They collect sounds. We use them to listen to what the whales have to say."

"What are the whales saying?" I prod further.

She smiles.

"That's what I aim to figure out. We think we know why the humpbacks sing, but it's in a language we'll likely never understand. We believe clicks are for navigating the waters to find food or avoid predators, while whistles are purely social."

"They sing? Songs? Like actual songs?"

"Yeah," she beams. "Songs are passed from one whale to another, and occasionally there will be a variation that we can track for thousands of miles. They sing to find their pods, attract a mate, or to determine friend from foe."

God, she is beautiful when she does this, when she removes the veil she wears for others and becomes unapologetically herself. I could listen to her recite a dictionary if her heart was in it. I can't hide my pleasure in this. A wide smile spreads across my face.

"Are you amused?" she teases.

I laugh a little. "Sorry, I'm just imagining whales swimming along, singing something by The Beatles."

This makes her chuckle.

"It does sound a bit like that, doesn't it?" she agrees. "It's actually pretty similar to the evolution of British pop rock. Imagine Beatlemania, but underwater. One pod swims around singing 'Hey Jude' for a breeding season. Then they cross paths with a pod from a different region, and they start singing 'Hey Jude,' too. Or at least parts of it."

The ocean breeze catches her hair. I can't help but stare.

"How do you do that?" I say.

"Do what?"

"Explain things like that. Seriously, you don't need my help. You got this all on your own."

She looks away and scrapes her hand nervously through her hair.

"Yeah, about that," she mumbles. "I do need you, Oscar. Bad, actually."

My stomach lurches like I just dropped from a great height. Those words, *I need you,* are making me feel dizzy and frantic. Those words from her mouth… Entrancing.

However, the words that follow pull me out of my desirous daydream.

"My research is losing funding."

Shit.

I should have known. She wants my money. That's why she agreed to take me out here and tell me about her work.

She was using me, just like everyone else. I can feel my veins pulse and twitch.

"So, that's what you want from me? A check?"

"No!" she apologizes. "No, not that. I'm actually thinking about hosting a fundraising gala. I was hoping you might know some people that could come."

It isn't a simple transaction, but it still feels like she is using my fame. I suppose that is what I wanted though – to use my fame for good. And if it helps me reconnect with Lola, it's definitely a fair exchange. More than fair, actually.

"Okay," I say.

Her brow twists.

"Okay? Just like that?"

"On one condition."

"Name it," she says.

"I get to help you plan the gala."

Her dark brown eyes shine through the glowing sunrise.

"That would be wonderful," she says. "Thanks, Oscar. That means a lot. I wouldn't ask if I wasn't desperate."

"Anything to help," I say, and I mean it. I would move heaven and earth if it would make her happy, even after all these years. Even after she left me.

I am a firm believer that good things should happen to good people, and Lola is the best person I've ever known.

We sit in the stillness of the sea as Lola tosses a hydrophone into the water. It makes a small splash before sending rings of ripples into the briny deep, a ball bobbing on the surface so we can collect it when we are done here.

"That's it?" I say, astounded by the simplicity of the task.

"For now," Lola replies calmly. "We have to wait for it to record the sounds. I will analyze it later at the office."

I don't know what I expected; maybe deep sea diving or listening to whales through headphones together on the boat. Wishful thinking. My thirst for adventure may not be quenched, but my desire to reconnect with Lola is satisfied with each passing second.

"Sorry," she says. "It's kind of boring. Usually, Brandon and I just talk and watch for breaching whales while we are out here."

"Not boring," I say. "Pretty perfect, actually."

Even in the dim light of dawn, I can see Lola's cheeks flush. She brushes her honey brown hair out of her face and turns from me, trying to disguise it. But I know what I saw.

I, however, am bothered by the thought of another man out here with her. He may be just her research partner, but I don't know, something about someone knowing her better than I once did sours my stomach.

Then I remember Madison, how I belong to her and have no right to jealousy. I shouldn't be feeling these things for Lola. Not anymore. She left me without a word, as if I were so easily disposable, so easily forgotten. I clench my jaw tight and then release, letting all of the emotions I feel for my old college love float away, swaying with the tide – or at least, I try.

CHAPTER
FIVE

LOLA

JULY 13, 2022

Knock, knock, knock.

"Coming!" I shout across the apartment, though it is quite small, so it doesn't take much to carry my voice to the front door. I swing it open to find Ruby, my younger sister.

"Your hair is lighter," I say, a little disappointed that it is no longer similar to my own. It is now blonde as butterscotch, which complements her glowing terracotta skin.

"You like it?" she asks playfully. I try to feign a smile, but nothing can fool Ruby. "Whoa, whoa, whoa, Lola. What's up?"

I try to smile again, but the muscles in my mouth won't commit. My chin wobbles, so I turn away.

"Nothing," I say. "Come in."

Ruby shuts the door slowly and slides her brown leather bag off her shoulder and onto the floor.

"Lola..." she says. Her voice is as cautious as her steps across the room, approaching me like I am a wild animal she is trying to capture for examination.

I turn to her, but now, there are tears streaming down my face, dripping off my chin and leaving wet spots all over my graphic hemp t-shirt, which ironically has the words "Good Vibes Only" printed on it.

"Girl," she says pointedly. "Spill the tea. Who do I need to beat up?"

I chuckle at this. Though she is younger than me, she is nearly half a foot taller and so much more confrontational. She is convinced it is her duty to protect me, not the other way around. Ruby is the type of woman that could blind a man with the sharp heels of her stilettos if she wanted to. She wouldn't, but she definitely has that energy.

"I saw Oscar," I whimper.

"*Your* Oscar?" She blinks. "From college?"

I nod.

"Lola, no… Why would you do that to yourself?"

"It's not like I did it on purpose," I sniff. "He literally materialized at work. After ten or so years of silence, he was just… there."

"What did he want?" Ruby asks.

"To support my research – which has been defunded, by the way."

"Shit. I didn't know that." Ruby drops her head. "Well, you have to let him help you, right? Your research is more important than your pride, Lola."

I roll my eyes as hard as I can muster.

"Of course I am going to let him help me. I don't have many other options and I am running out of time."

"Hmm." Ruby presses her crimson red lips together. I tilt my head, gesturing for her to say what she's thinking. "Sorry, I just – I thought you might be more reluctant. Did I miss something? I remember you were pretty adamant about not wanting to see him again."

"I was. But I *did* see him again…" The tears start falling once more. "It just reminded me of everything that happened."

Ruby's eyes quickly dart to my stomach.

"The abortion." She says the word I won't, and it sends me deeper into a fit of crying.

She sits beside me on the couch and pulls me into her chest, hugging me lightly, as if she were handling delicate porcelain.

"We don't have to talk about this," she says.

I cling to her shirt, inhaling intermittent gasping breaths. When I finally steady my breathing, I release her and wipe my eyes with the back of my hands.

"No," I say. "I need to talk about this. It's time."

"What was it like when you saw Oscar?" she politely prods.

"It was weird," I say, not sure how to describe it. "At first, it was really painful. But then, I don't know, suddenly it was fine. It might have even felt good."

"So, you still have feelings for him?" Ruby says.

I need to think about this. I mean, love like that doesn't just go away. He didn't do anything wrong. It was me who couldn't bear to look at him after I aborted the baby he never knew he could have. But I had my life planned out and that just didn't fit inside of it. If he so much as implied that I should keep it, I would have, and then I wouldn't have gone to graduate school, I wouldn't have gotten my degree, and I wouldn't be here right now. Some people may have been strong enough to pull that off, but not me. I know I made the right decision for myself, but what if it wasn't the right decision for *us*?

But, I have to tell myself, sometimes it is okay to put myself first.

"Yes," I say. "I think part of me will always love him."

Every time I turn on the radio and hear his voice, I have to remember what I chose, and regret what I have lost: the love of my life, my soul mate, my alternate future. Whales might not mate for life, but I do.

"Then what is the problem here?" Ruby asks.

"He still doesn't know, Ruby. Eventually, I am going to have to tell him. I promised."

"And you also promised yourself you wouldn't," she points out.

I sigh, my shoulders slumping and my head in my hands.

"I know. If I tell him, he will hate me. If I don't tell him, he will hate me. What should I do?"

Ruby smirks. "You don't know that, Lola. I don't know, maybe he will surprise you. Besides, would you really still love someone that would hate you for that?"

Why does she always need to make so much sense? Oscar isn't a monster. Quite the opposite. He has always been nothing but caring and supportive.

"I guess I never told him because I knew I would have given up everything for him," I say. "But I know my fears were unfounded."

"The Oscar I knew all those years ago would have given everything up for you. Not the other way around," Ruby coos.

It is comforting to hear this, but my irrational mind just cannot accept it.

"What if this is our chance to make things right, Ruby? What if this is our chance and I blow it?"

She smiles. "If you are really meant to be together, Lola, you will be together."

"But – " I protest.

"Listen," she says. "I know you loved Oscar. And Oscar loved you. And if either of you cared for each other as much as I think you did, you'll get through this. You're not going to blow it."

Ruby squeezes my shoulder, and at least for now, I believe her. She has an affirmation for everything, and while I am usually reluctant to attach any importance to them, it feels more convincing when the words are from her mouth and not mine.

"So, I should tell him?" I ask, searching her face for confirmation.

Her midnight eyes, dark as my own, begin to soften.

"Nothing happens by accident," she says. "Least of all love." She hugs me tightly and wipes the last tear from my face with her glazed acrylic nails. "Are you going to be okay?"

"Yeah," I say as I let out a deep exhale.

"Great. So, I need to talk to you about Dad."

"Dad? What is it?"

"Have you noticed that his memory has been getting worse lately? Like, I was over there to visit the other day and I swear he told me the same story three times in a row."

"Kind of," I say, though lately, I haven't been visiting him as often as I should.

Hearing this from Ruby is sobering. Our father, Tino, has always been a little spacey. For a long time, we considered it to be one of his many quirks. But these past few years, he has been forgetting things – sometimes important things. For example, he called to wish me a happy birthday, unaware that it was really Ruby's birthday – and not for another month and a half. Over time, his anecdotes have grown more and more repetitive as he talks in circles, only to forget what the point of the story was to begin with. It's only a matter of time before he leaves the house with the oven on or something equally as dire.

"Well, next time you talk to him, let me know how it goes," Ruby says. "I don't think he should be alone and Eva is pretty useless."

Eva, our stepmother, does little to care for Tino. Everytime he needs something, it has fallen to me and Ruby to help, which is fine, but surely Eva could do *something*.

If I can't continue my research here in Seattle, then I will likely have to move – away from Ruby, and away from Tino – leaving all of the responsibility for caring for our father to Ruby. It's not only unfair, it's dangerous, especially if he is losing his memory.

"What can I do?" I say.

"Nothing for now," Ruby says. "Just... you know, pay close attention." Her voice drops like she is getting choked up, but then she clears her throat. "Well, should we open a bottle of wine and put on some TV?"

"Sure," I say. But I can't help but be rattled by our conversation.

Ruby opens the fridge to retrieve a bottle of rosé while I grab some kitschy mugs from the cabinet. It isn't the classiest vessel for wine, but to be fair, it's not the nicest wine either. And if there is anything I am not, it's classy.

We put on an episode of *Crazy Ex-Girlfriend* that we've already seen dozens of times. It is, after all, our go-to comfort show. We laugh and we sing along, using our wine mugs as microphones. But after a few episodes, it's getting late.

I follow Ruby to the door. She slings her purse over her arm and kisses me on the cheek.

"Good luck with Oscar and everything," she says. "Call me if you need me. And call Dad soon, okay?"

"I will," I say.

Ruby glides down the hallway with her elegant stride, vanishing after she turns the corner for the elevator. I close the door and look vacantly around my apartment. It doesn't usually feel this empty, but when Ruby leaves, I become acutely aware of the small space and how I am alone inside of it.

I feel my phone buzz in my pocket. I assume it's Ruby saying she forgot something, but when I glance at the screen, I am greeted by an unfamiliar number.

The text simply says, *When can I see you again? xx*

I reply, asking *Who is this?*

It takes a moment, watching the bubbles indicating that the sender is typing, but eventually an answer comes through. It's exactly who I had hoped it would be.

Oscar. Is this still Lola's number?

I want to engage, to open myself to his friendship, but until I clear the air, I fear there will be this unspeakable tension between us.

Instead of replying immediately, I dig through a box of photos from under my bed. Inside the box are tons of photos: from vacations, from events, from college…

Finally, I find a photo of me and Oscar during a Halloween party in our second year of university. He is dressed as Slash from Guns n' Roses. His hair is so long that he didn't even need a wig. Beside him, I am sticking my tongue out, holding a solo cup as Bret Michaels.

I snap a picture of it with my phone and send it to him. With it, I send the words, *No, rockstar. It's me, Bret Michaels.*

Quickly, a response.

Yikes! To be fair, you made an incredible Bret.

I smile, *And you made a fantastic Slash.*

After a brief moment of silence, I receive a response. This time, a photo.

It's a selfie. In it, his hair is bedraggled, his stubble long, and his hazel eyes darkened. I catch a small glimpse of chest hair over the tattoos, as it appears he is shirtless.

I press the phone to my heart, pondering the ways his body has changed, picturing his naked torso here beside me. It's almost real enough that I can reach out and touch him. But the bed is empty, and Oscar is far from me, somewhere else in the city.

We'll meet soon, I type. *Next week? At the marina?*

Three words in response: *I'll be there.*

He has always been dependable. But I need to restrain myself, otherwise I'll ruin this – whatever *this* is – before it even begins.

I silence my phone and go to sleep.

CHAPTER
SIX

OSCAR

JULY 18, 2022

The soothing sea rocks the dock I stand on. Small footsteps approach; it's Lola.

"Took you long enough," I tease.

She slaps my arm playfully. "Shut up. I am absolutely on time."

"Nerd," I say. I'd say I'm joking, but she is a nerd – in the best possible way. In fact, there are no bad ways to be a nerd, but she is almost certainly the best.

She hands me some equipment to carry onto the boat, which I do dutifully. I feel like a roadie, but instead of on a band's tour, I am on Lola's science excursion.

She propels the boat forward, guiding us slowly out into the Sound.

I look at her and I can't get the memory of us dressed as rockstars out of my head now that it has resurfaced. That was a wild night. Lola is almost always on her best behavior, but I've seen her let loose, let her stoic mask fall, and that night, she did.

We were at a bar not far from the University of Washington campus. The dirty dive had a karaoke machine set up on a small stage. After being carded, we were met by a gentleman at a table with a sign up sheet. I, of course, signed up, but much to my surprise, so did Lola.

"I'm going to sing 'Nothin' But a Good Time,'" she shouted in my ear to cut through the noise.

I rolled my eyes when she said this, but man, she showed me up.

After I sang Foster the People's hit "Pumped Up Kicks," Lola literally strutted onto that stage with more confidence than I had ever seen. Maybe copious amounts of vodka had lended her some liquid courage, but that girl had swagger.

The music started and as soon as she opened her mouth to sing, the entire bar was captivated. Not only was she dancing around and engaging with the audience, she had also been secretly hiding the most incredible voice. Her rendition of Poison's song was nearly pitch perfect, and I'll confess, it was the only time I found myself attracted to Bret Michaels – especially after she jumped off stage, giddy as can be, and kissed me.

"Where did that come from?" I said, completely flabbergasted.

She shrugged. So nonchalant, like what she did wasn't this big deal. This beautiful, quiet science nerd, for one night, conquered her stage fright and gave the best karaoke performance that, to this day, I have ever witnessed. If she wasn't working her ass off to protect whales, I swear, she could be selling out stadiums – at least when she can find the confidence.

"Penny for your thoughts," she says, bringing me out of my reverie.

"Yeah, sorry," I apologize. But I wonder if she has the same fond memories of us that I do. "Do you remember that Halloween at all?"

"Excuse me?" She tilts her head.

"From the picture."

"More than I would like," she says. "I am still mortified that I got up on that stage."

I laugh, but really, part of my heart breaks to hear this – that she doesn't see herself the way I do: brilliant, sexy, talented.

"You killed it though," I remind her.

She turns away her blushing cheeks.

"Thanks."

"Your voice is incredible. I can't believe you kept that a secret," I muse.

Lola's body becomes stiff and she lifts her trembling hand to her face to scratch nervously at her lip.

"A girl can have her secrets," she whispers in a stifled breath. She turns off the boat engine, making us both acutely aware of how quiet it is out here on the water.

I step toward her, though she remains turned away from me.

"Lola," I say. "I'm ready to hear it if you're ready to tell me."

She closes her eyes tightly, and swiftly turns around to embrace me, collapsing in my arms as she begins to cry.

Rubbing her back gently, I squeeze her into my chest. I'd forgotten what it felt like to hold her in my arms. Now that she's here, I don't want to let go.

"Oscar," she cries, "I'm so sorry."

"Sorry? For what?" I am genuinely confused. I help her to a seat so she can sit down and catch her breath. She is still shaking though, and this makes me very tense. "It's okay. You don't have to do this."

"Yes, I do," she says. "I owe you an explanation."

I sit still beside her, and I realize that I am clasping her hands in my own. Yet, I can't release them – for her sake, and for mine.

She takes a deep breath.

"I had an abortion." She lets the word sit in the silence for a brief second. Suddenly, I feel cold, with a heaviness expanding inside me. "That's why I left. I know I should have told you, but I was afraid you'd talk me out of it. Then, once it was done, I felt so ashamed that I couldn't bear to even look at you."

This revelation makes me dizzy.

"Lola," I say. She visibly braces herself for the impact of my words, but I don't feel anger. I feel hurt. "Why would you think I would stop you?"

Her eyes flash and her voice rises.

"What?"

I shake my head.

"It's your body. Your future. Why would I take that away from you?"

She releases her hands from mine and fidgets with the cord of a hydrophone.

"I don't know," she says. "I should have said something, but I couldn't bear to go through that. If I was going to lose you, I guess I wanted to have control of it."

I inch closer to her – so close that I can feel her honey hair dancing in the sea breeze, lightly lashing my face.

"You wouldn't have lost me," I say.

She looks up at me, her dark eyes rich as soil, grounding me. There is a trace of pain in her gaze. We stare at each other for too long, and I swear she flinches.

"I made a mistake, Oscar," she says. Her voice breaks. "And with it, I lost nearly everything."

"Not everything." It hurts to see her like this. I can't blame her for what she did. If I were in her position, maybe I would have done the same thing. "Look at you now. You became everything that you wanted to be. You did it, Lola."

She allows herself a straight, thin smile, both appreciative and remorseful.

Truthfully, seeing her now makes me so proud. All those nights studying, all that passion for what she believes in. It paid off. I guess we both turned out okay, all things considered.

"I guess you're right," she says. "But it doesn't matter. I am about to lose funding anyway."

She unravels the cord of the hydrophone and rises to her feet. She is steady despite the swaying of the boat. I rise to follow, but my stance is not as stable. I topple backwards toward the side of the boat, and for a second, I realize I am going overboard. I think of the headline: The Unadored's frontman Oscar Kelly drowns in the Puget Sound.

They say that in moments like these, your life flashes before your eyes. I find that to be absolutely true. Every family holiday, every date, every kiss I shared with Lola – all of it floods my brain at once and I can't think. I can only fall backwards into the water.

My head and shoulders make contact first. Then, I am completely submerged. I try to exhale, pushing the water from my nose and mouth, but too much has already entered. The more I try to exhale, the more water I swallow into my lungs. My eyes are wide open and I can see the golden hue of the sunrise glistening, rippling in the waves. This is where I need to go.

I wave my arms and legs furiously in the water, clawing for the surface, when I feel a firm, round thing floating at the top. I grasp it, testing its buoyancy, before pulling myself up onto it, my face finally free of the enveloping sea.

At first, everything is muffled and I can't make out a single sound except my own heartbeat. Then, the water clears from my ears and I can hear Lola shouting my name. I expel some of the salt water in my lungs and it burns like hot lava.

Lola tugs a rope tied to the lifebuoy I cling to, pulling me toward the back of the boat.

"Can you climb up onto the stern?" Lola yells.

I don't answer. I can't.

Lola clambers down on the platform on the back of the boat and grabs me by the arms. She tries to pull me onto the platform with her, but my wriggling doesn't help as much as I want it to. She topples forward, nearly falling into the water herself, but my legs finally catch on the lip of the platform and, as Lola keeps hold of me, I propel myself out of the water only to tackle her. My soaking body is pressed against hers, salty sea water dripping from my curls onto her cheek.

I blink open and her wide eyes soften as she realizes that I am okay. I want to thank her for saving me. I want to cup her beautiful face in my hands and kiss her for the first time in ten years. But I do none of these things. I simply stare into her coffee-colored eyes and lose all sense of time and space. All that matters to me in this moment is the feeling of her curves against mine, her eyes looking up at me – not with regret, but with something familiar and tender.

"You scared me," she whispers.

I smile. "Oh yeah? You still care about me?"

Her face blooms bright red, but she keeps her eyes locked with mine.

I feel my face getting closer to hers, like opposite ends of a magnet, our lips inevitably lured together. Her eyelids flutter shut and her lips part slightly to invite my own, but just as they are about to touch, I stop myself.

Madison.

I pull back and clamber to my feet. I may not be perfect, but I am *not* the guy who cheats.

"Sorry," I say. I can't meet her gaze anymore. Too tempting. "I can't. I... I have a girlfriend."

Even without looking at Lola, I can sense her anger. It's like feeling the heat when you stand too close to a fire.

She doesn't say anything. She simply hops back onto the boat deck and starts the engine, no mind to the fact that we collected no data today.

I can't help feeling a swelling nausea and a tingle in my chest. It is unsettling. I may not have kissed Lola, but I wanted to, and that seems just as bad as cheating because now I know what my heart really wants, and it's not Madison. Not anymore.

As we putter back into the marina, there is a weight in the pit of my stomach, begging me to fix this before I lose someone important. Something must be done, because when all is said and done, I know that my heart has always, and will always, belong to Lola.

CHAPTER
SEVEN

LOLA

"He almost *kissed* you?"

"Yes!" I say. "I swear, our lips were basically touching. And then he just backed off."

Ruby gently rubs her temples.

"What – and I don't say this lightly – the actual fuck?" she says.

"I know!" I pace the floor of my apartment. "Just when I thought I had made things right, he said he has a girlfriend."

Ruby puts her pink kitty-socked feet up on the couch, sitting up tall.

"Why didn't he bring that up *before* almost kissing you?" she says.

"I didn't exactly ask him," I say. "For all he knows, I am seeing someone, too."

Ruby laughs at this, almost too much for my liking.

"Yeah, right. When was the last time you even went on a date?"

I put my hand on my hips. I want to refute this, but I honestly can't remember the last date I went on.

"Fine," I sigh. "You win. I don't date. It's just not the best use of my time."

"Right," Ruby says sarcastically. "Because studying sea creatures is so much better than kissing hot guys."

"It is!" I protest. "Have you ever looked into the eye of a humpback whale?"

"Can't be better than an orgasm, Lola."

I gasp at the very mention of it.

"Ruby!"

"What? It's true," she says. "I may have never locked eyes with a whale, but I am telling you, an orgasm is better. No competition. Why are you even arguing with me about this?"

"Because. Science comes first."

"When really you should be coming first," Ruby smirks. "Come on, Lola. You mean to tell me you would rather do science than kiss Oscar?"

I blush. In a perfect world, I would be able to do both.

"I do not want to kiss Oscar," I say. "Or any guys for that matter. Not if it is going to distract me from my work."

"Sure," Ruby says. "Whatever you need to tell yourself. I'm not buying it. I think you're just afraid of getting hurt again."

I cross the room to pour another glass of white wine. Rich, golden liquid swirls in my glass. I take a sip and it's slick and buttery on my tongue.

"This is good wine," I say.

"We are not done talking about your love life, Lola. What are you going to do about Oscar?"

"I don't know," I say. I'd say I haven't given it much thought, but truthfully, it's all I can think about. And yet, I still have no answers. "We still need to be able to work together on this gala, and he needs to learn enough about my work to sell it in a speech. Whether I like it or not, we're kinda stuck together."

"You can't just pretend that he didn't almost kiss you. That's so awkward," Ruby says.

"Only if I make it awkward," I say.

"Can you make him jealous?" Ruby dances a little in her seat. "You know? Like flaunt yourself in front of him, show him what he's missing."

"Make him jealous, how? It's just me and him out there."

Ruby takes a minute to think about this.

"Does it have to be? Just you and him? What about your coworker? The tall, blonde surfer-looking dude?"

"Brandon!?"

"Yeah, Brandon. Why hasn't anything ever happened with him?" Ruby plops a piece of popcorn in her mouth.

"Because," I say. "We work together. That seems like a really bad idea."

I sit down from my pacing and Ruby clasps me by the shoulders, shaking me lightly.

"Come on, Lo. All of these guys and you won't do anything with a single one of them?"

"The keyword being *single*," I say.

"Okay, so Oscar's not – for now. But Brandon is cute! And you both love the same things. Either it works out or it doesn't." Ruby sips her wine. "You can't live your whole life in fear."

She's right. I have been too cautious when it comes to love my entire life, always running away and hurting someone else before they have a chance to hurt me. And the irony is that I end up hurting myself in the process.

When it comes to love, the hurt, it seems, is inevitable.

"Fine," I sigh. "So what should I do?"

"Text him," Ruby says bluntly.

"Text who?"

"Does it matter? If you text any guy at all, I will be satisfied."

I retrieve my phone from my pocket. But when I open my text messages, Oscar is at the very top. One new message, unread.

Sorry again about yesterday. When can I see you next?

I don't know why, but the text makes my body tense, my heart pound, and my skin sweat. Why is he so certain that I want to see him again? So soon after rebuffing me like that?

I grind my teeth as I draft a new text.

Hey, you up?

"Oh no, what are you doing, Lola?" Ruby tries to grab my phone, but I hold it high above my head.

"I'm doing what you said! I'm texting Brandon!" I yell.

Ruby sets her wine glass down on the coffee table and lunges at me.

"Give me the phone! I want to see what you wrote!"

She digs her hands under my arms and tickles me, causing me to drop my phone (nearly on her head) and curl up into a helpless ball.

Ruby grabs the phone and reads the text.

"*You up?* The best you can do for a booty call text is *You up*? Come on, Lola! Have you ever flirted before? Wait – wait – he's typing back!"

We both huddle together to see what he says.

The dots that indicate he is typing pulse for too long, as if even he doesn't know what to make of it. Then, finally, a response.

Yeah, what's up? Is everything okay?

"You have put out so few feelers that he assumes you're in trouble if you text him? What the hell, Lola?" Ruby says. "Okay, I am taking over."

She wrestles me out of the way so she can respond for me.

Feeling nauti? She types, adding a winking face emoji.

"Ruby!" I scream. "What the fuck!? I work with this guy. He is probably going to report me to HR!"

"No, he won't," Ruby says. "Just wait."

I bite at my nails. Often – too often – I am met with confusion or rejection when I attempt to flirt with men. All I know how to do is share everything I know, as if that will impress them, always leaving emotions (and my libido) out of the equation. Like I could tell them the story of the 52-hertz whale that communicates at a different frequency that other whales don't understand, making it the world's loneliest whale – as if that will move a man enough to invite me out for dinner instead of straight to his bed.

My phone vibrates in Ruby's hand.

"What does it say?" I squeal. I hide my eyes with my hands, bracing for impact.

Wow. Really? Maybe a bit. ;) Want me to come over?

"Excuse me?" I blink in disbelief. "He wants to come over?"

"Quick. Let's get you dressed into something sexy," Ruby says, launching herself from the couch. She heads straight for my closet, rips it open, and begins rifling through my wardrobe. "Too bad Patagonia doesn't make lingerie. Seriously, Lola. What is this?"

I swallow. "It's not that bad, is it? Besides, you don't really expect him to come over here, do you?"

"You're the one that initiated the booty call," Ruby laughs.

I feel my chest tighten. My breathing is rushed. "Oh god, Ruby. What am I supposed to do?"

"It sounds like you want to sleep with him," she says. "The text said it, not me."

"But I don't! You sent the text!" I am hyperventilating as Ruby removes a red tank top from the closet.

"No one is forcing you to sleep with Brandon, Lola. But it might be good for you to at least try to connect with this guy."

Brandon and I were fast friends. We have always got along and I have always recognized the fact that by all standards, he is very handsome. But never have I ever viewed him… sexually. No particular reason why. He's just… Brandon.

"Ruby! Why are we doing this?" I groan.

"The best way to get over someone is to get under someone else," she says.

"Can't I just eat ice cream and watch a chick flick?"

Ruby tosses me the red tank and a pair of short black shorts.

"Here," she says. "Change into this."

I do as she says and pose in front of the floor length mirror in the corner. It needs to be cleaned, but even through the spots and the dust, I can tell I look very exposed.

Ruby snaps a photo of me.

"And sent!" she says.

"Oh god, what now?" I say. This is spiraling out of control way faster than I would like.

"Just showing him a little of what he is missing," she says. "Oh, and I *might* have sent him your address, so I better get going." She grabs her purse and slips on her shoes by the door.

"Ruby! Wait!" I chase after her, holding my phone helplessly in my hand. "I don't know what to do. I'm kinda freaking out over here."

She hugs me tightly and kisses my cheek. "You can do this, Lo. Just be yourself. Text me in the morning, okay?"

"Okay," I stammer.

She closes the door behind her, leaving me with my phone and an incoming romantic rendezvous with my research partner. I am clueless what to do next.

Quickly, I tidy up, putting dishes in the dishwasher and fluffing pillows, as if the first thing Brandon will notice the first time in my apartment is the volume of the pillows.

I stare in the mirror one last time, pushing my shoulders back and perking up my chest. I feel so clownish, like I am impersonating a sexy woman in a fragrance ad, when really, I am just the nerdy whale girl. I like listening to ocean sounds and reading books. I am not the exciting woman that guys like Brandon dream about. He is charismatic, charming, and confident – all things that I absolutely am not.

I am interrupted by a loud, incessant buzz beside my door.

He's here. He's here and he's ringing my buzzer.

I smooth the wrinkles from my clothes and ring him in. After a minute passes, which feels like an eternity, there is a gentle rap at my door. Quickly, I check my breath and open the door.

Brandon is leaning casually against the doorframe, a slight grin on his blushing face.

"Hey," he says.

"Hi," I say, unable to break free from his icy blue, frozen stare.

I step aside, and Brandon strides forward. But before he even fully enters my apartment, before he even looks around, he catches me by the waist and pulls me toward him.

His smooth, minty mouth is on mine, tongues colliding, as he slams the door shut behind him and presses me against it. As I tangle my hands in his soft, blonde hair, I can feel warmth gathering between my legs.

The friendship that Brandon and I had built is broken now, and all that remains between us is intense longing. I ache to connect, and his body is begging to be banded with mine.

His lips brush down my neck before he bites my collarbone.

"This is crazy," Brandon pants. "I never thought you wanted this."

I can't speak. All I want is to feel him rocking into me, pushing Oscar from my mind.

Brandon pulls my shirt over my head and tosses it across the room, urging me clumsily toward the couch. Before I even understand what is happening, my bare breasts are pressed against his sturdy chest and my shorts are wrapped around my ankles.

Gently, he lays me down on the couch and gets on top of me.

"Is this okay?" he asks.

I nod, breathing heavily, and pull him into me.

CHAPTER EIGHT

OSCAR

JULY 20, 2022

I press my fingers deeper into the wire strings – plucking and strumming with greater and greater ferocity.

"Careful," Jacob says. "You're either gonna cut your fingers or break a string. Either way, don't. We have work to do."

This just makes me play even harder. The wire won't cut my fingertips; the skin is too thick and calloused. But the strings are taking a beating. Just as Jacob warned me, I strum hard once more and snap the high E string.

"Told ya," Jacob sighs. "It's been way too long since you changed those."

I am tempted to drop the guitar on the ground, but this guitar is special. It's not the nicest one I own, but it is the oldest. This acoustic beast has been with me since I was a teenager. The sound isn't perfect, but it's familiar: the frets are worn and the neck bows outward. But I like to keep it because if I can make music that sounds good on this, I know it will sound even better with a newer guitar and better gear. That, and it reminds me of simpler, happier times.

Jacob opens the pocket in his bass case and removes a restringing tool for winding, cutting, and pulling the strings out. I can feel the sting of his stare on me as he hands it to me.

"Thanks," I say.

"Wish you'd tell me what's going on," he says. "You look like shit."

"It's hard to explain," I say. I don't want to get into this. I'd rather finish writing this song so we can go out for drinks.

"I seriously doubt that. Your problems are not as deep as you think, Oscar."

I grunt as I loosen the strings.

"I did something bad," I say.

Jacob perks up, looking up from his bass guitar. "Oh? How bad are we talking?"

"This doesn't leave this room, got it?" I say. "Promise me, not a word to anyone."

Jacob mimes zipping his lips. He even throws away the key. Nice touch.

"The other day, I almost kissed Lola," I admit.

"Almost?" He looks back down at his instrument and begins quietly dancing his fingers along the thick strings. "That doesn't sound so bad. You really had me for a second. I already have to worry about Tyler. I don't want to have to worry about you, too."

"Dude, have you forgotten about Madison?"

"Oh, yeah," he shrugs. "Shit."

It's no secret that Jacob has never liked Madison. I'd fault him for forgetting about her, but he spends so much time pretending she doesn't exist that it only makes sense that, in his mind, she is never there.

"What am I supposed to do?" I cup my head in my hands.

"Well." Jacob looks up at my scowling face. "Do you still love Lola? Actually, don't answer that. Of course you do." He's probably right, but does he have to presume to know me more than I know myself? He seems to clock my displeasure. "Look, Oscar. You aren't as opaque as you imagine yourself to be. Seriously. How long have we known each other?"

"Since elementary," I mumble.

"Yes!" Jacob says. "I have you figured out, dude. We grew up together, and I have never seen you love anything as much as you loved Lola – except maybe that Frankenstein guitar of yours."

"But I love Madison now," I counter.

"Do you though?"

"Yes." My voice cracks, just a little higher than usual. "Yes, Jacob. Hate to break it to you, but I do love Madison."

Jacob tips his head back and looks skyward.

"Tell me, Oscar. How are you so sure?"

I pause. I don't mean to pause.

Shit.

"She, uhh…" I try to fill the silence. "She's beautiful, okay? And she has a good heart. She means well, it just doesn't always translate."

"She has a good heart? Listen to yourself." Jacob's tone sours. "When you talk about Madison, you are noticeably disappointed. Seriously. You hunch, you sigh, I swear to god, I have even seen you cringe. Don't try to tell me you love her because she has a good heart. First of all, we both know that she absolutely does not. And secondly…"

Jacob stops himself.

"What? Go ahead. Finish that thought," I say.

He rises to his feet. "Forget I said anything."

"Say it, Jacob. Don't just get up and leave."

"Oscar," he rubs his eyes. "You already know. You have to already know."

"Know what?" My voice is getting louder, my fist clenched.

Jacob sits down heavily on the couch.

"Tyler," he says. "She's been sleeping with Tyler."

Suddenly, I feel cold, like there is a sack of rocks in my stomach.

"She's what?"

"I'm sorry," Jacob hangs his head. "I really thought you knew."

I reach for the stringing tool once again and snip the wires. They bounce and wave, so light now that they are freed from the tension.

"We can talk about this if you want," he says.

I grimace, continuing to remove the strings from the guitar, pulling at the pins.

"What's there to talk about?" I say wryly. "My girlfriend of two years has been cheating on me with our drummer. I feel so fucking stupid."

"Maybe it will help put things in perspective though," Jacob offers. "Like almost kissing your ex-girlfriend isn't such a big deal after all."

And now, knowing this, I would do it all again. If I hadn't been so blind, I wouldn't have pushed Lola away. I would have held her closer. I would have stared into her eyes a little longer. I would have kissed her.

I *should* have kissed her.

I drop the tool to the floor and release my guitar, allowing it to fall clumsily against the sofa and then to the ground, a wooden crashing sound from its hollow interior. None of it prepares me for the strange grief that comes over me, layering like heavy snow. It's not grief for my relationship with Madison. It's grief for losing Lola for the second time.

"What do I do now?" I groan.

"I mean, break up with Madison, for starters," says Jacob. "But don't say I told you. I'm not a snitch."

"You've been telling me to break up with her before we even started dating." I let out a light laugh. "Man, you must be pleased as punch right now."

Jacob's face tightens, like every muscle is tensed, casting severe shadows under his blue eyes and sharp jawline.

"Why would you say that?" he says. "You're my best

friend, Oscar. It doesn't make me happy to see you like this – even if I was fucking right from the beginning."

I laugh a little louder. "Okay, fine. You were right. But what do I do about Madison?"

"Don't you actually want to know what to do about Lola?"

I shrug.

"Once you're free of Madison," Jacob says, "you're free to get your girl back."

"It's not that simple," I say.

"Why not? There is no future with Madison. When there's no future with someone, you break things off. That is an unspoken rule of dating, bud."

"She's vindictive," I say. "I'm afraid of how she will react. She could ruin me."

"Ruin you how?" Jacob's eyebrows twist together.

It's surprising to me that Jacob is aware of her and Tyler, but not everything that they do together. The drinking, the drugs – it all stems from them. But I cannot expose them. It's not my place to do so. As they say, *let he who is without sin cast the first stone.* I'll keep my stones close.

"She is young. She is an up-and-coming actress. From an outside perspective, don't you think it looks like I was using her?" I say.

"What do you have to gain from that?" Jacob says. I raise my eyebrow at him. "Okay, fair point. Sex. But compare that to her blatantly using you to advance her career. Seems to me like you used each other."

"Some people might not see it that way," I say.

Jacob scratches his eyebrow, looking pensively at the floor.

"Then how can we handle this delicately?" he asks, more to himself than to me. "How do we get *her* to break up with *you*?"

"Amicably," I say. "Upsetting her would just create the same problem."

"Amicably," Jacob agrees.

We sit in silence for a moment, brainstorming the possibilities.

Finally, Jacob chimes in.

"I've got it. Give her space – like *a lot* of space. Maybe she will feel things naturally end and break things off?"

"Not if she wants something from me," I say.

"Then get mean. Blame her for things, talk about your exes, be fucking cold."

I sigh. "Look, you might not have any respect for her, but I am not like that. I'm not about to gaslight this poor girl to avoid taking any responsibility here. Maybe I should just talk to her, let her down gently."

"Whatever you need to do," Jacob says. "Just do it."

My relationship with Madison is more complicated than Jacob understands. Sure, we might be a bit volatile and possibly even codependent, but in the end, I always try to do what is right by her. She has been by my side for two years, and during those two years, we have been *through* it.

From long, lonely stretches of touring to the general lack of privacy – Madison was always there: to console me, to distract me, and take the parts of fame I hate most and turn them on herself. I realize that was self-serving to a point, but I really don't believe the entire relationship was a farce. The things she did were for herself first, but for love second. I'm okay being the second one on that scale.

The fact that she could go and be with Tyler, but hasn't, tells me she cares at least a little bit, that I still have value in her life of schemes. Maybe she is afraid of hurting me, or maybe she is afraid of the optics.

"I'll do it," I say. "I just need to find the right time."

"And what about Tyler?" Jacob asks. "What are you going to say to him?"

It's a good question, and one that I haven't even considered.

Tyler and I aren't as close as me and Jacob. While Jacob and I go way back, Tyler and I didn't meet until after college, after Jacob and I had already started our band, started writing songs, and started to get noticed. It was when we were signed to a label that they insisted we have a real live drummer, not just recorded beats from percussive amateurs like us.

The label was right; it added a lot of complexity to our sound that wasn't there before, but it also added a lot of complexity to our lives, and only one of those things was for the better. Between Tyler's drug use and rockstar attitude, he has always been a lot to manage – and I'm afraid I have only enabled him.

"Do we need to find a new drummer?" Jacob asks.

"No," I say. "I'll talk to him."

I say talk, but deep down, I know what it will devolve to: more harbored resentment, more drama, more secrecy.

"You don't suppose you could talk to him about his drug problem, too, while you're at it? He's been driving me insane lately. I can only put up with so much, you know what I mean?" Jacob says.

He goes back to plucking at his bass strings. The sound reverberates in my bones, rattling me to my core. There is so much that Jacob doesn't know, and I don't want to be the one that tells him – not with everything else going on.

"Yeah," I rub the back of my neck and clear my throat. "Maybe."

CHAPTER NINE

LOLA

JULY 22, 2022

"You're late," I say loudly. "Again."

Brandon walks towards me as I stand on the dock at the marina, his gait both bouncy and self-assured, until he picks me up by my waist and swings me around.

I giggle a little. I can't help it.

He sets me down and kisses my cheek.

"Sorry, Miss Early Bird," he says "It won't happen again."

But I know it will.

"Come on," I say, forcing a laugh as I climb onto the boat.

He follows a little too closely, and after unloading the gear, he hovers behind me, too, holding my waist as I start the engine and guide the boat into the open water. It is still mostly dark, with only the light from the masthead and the faint glow on the horizon to guide us out to sea. The water is calm though, and we make it out into the Puget Sound with very little turbulence.

"It's lovely out here," I think aloud. I don't necessarily expect, nor want, a response, but Brandon is eager to engage.

"Not as lovely as you," he growls in my ear.

He pulls me tightly against his sturdy chest. I reach for the keys to turn off the engine, barely able to touch the cold metal with my fingertips.

The engine sputters as it shuts down.

"Brandon," I begin. I want to talk. I want to discuss what is happening, how his energy is just a bit too strong for what we are, which in my mind, is nothing.

He spins me around so we are face to face, the vapor from his mouth curling around my nostrils.

"I love when you say my name," he says. "Have I ever told you that?"

"Brandon," I repeat sternly. "This isn't –"

I am silenced by his mouth covering mine. His tongue parts my lips. I reluctantly invite him in.

His hands are tangled in my hair, which is already in damp knots from the sea breeze. Politely, I guide him toward a seat, urging him to sit down. He does as my body commands, but tries to pull me onto him.

As if saved by some divine miracle, a humpback whale breaks the surface of the water just a dozen or so feet from the boat. Its massive body launches upward before crashing down. The enormity of its weight is felt from the sound alone, a crashing so fierce that it startles both of us. Then, the aftermath: a splash so big that it nearly topples the boat. While we remain afloat, Brandon and I are soaked.

"Oh my god!" I shriek – partly from awe, and partly from cold shock – and scurry over to the edge of the boat, searching for where the whale must have gone. "Did you see that?"

Ocean water drips from the tips of his messy blonde hair.

"Didn't need to," he says. His face is slack and slightly pale.

I can't hide my excitement. "We should start recording. Quick, grab one of the hydrophones."

Brandon stands, his erection now gone, and retrieves the equipment, handing it to me solemnly.

I am so determined to get the hydrophone in the water

that I don't even register the chattering of my teeth, the tremors in my hands.

"Lola, stop," Brandon says.

I don't listen. Instead, I plop the gear in the water and stand proudly, leaning over the edge of the boat to watch it float.

"Lola," he says again. "You're shivering."

I look down at my drenched clothes, vibrating in an attempt to conjure warmth.

"We only have one blanket," he mutters. "You should take it."

He says this, but he is shaking, too.

"No. We can share," I say, swallowing the lump in my throat. "But we need to get out of these wet clothes first."

I hate to say it, but Brandon smirks – just like I knew he would.

Without breaking eye contact, he peels off his wet shirt that clings to his abdomen. I try to look away, to offer him as much privacy as one can give on a boat, but then he removes his pants, as well. I blush as I eye him up and down, with him standing there in wet boxer briefs that reveal the deep "V" cut from his hips to his pelvis.

My teeth rattle, reminding me that the warmth I feel from admiring his form is not enough to still my shivers. So, I unzip my jacket, sodden with absorbed water. Then, my soggy shirt and leggings. I am hesitant to remove the rest, but I know it would be wise to get warm faster. Slowly, I strip my sports bra and my underwear, until I am standing on the deck of our research vessel completely naked.

Brandon follows suit, tearing off his soaked briefs. It makes a wet slapping sound as it lands upon the boat deck. As I gaze upon him, the golden light of the sunrise reflects off the droplets on his bare skin, casting a surreal glow.

This, I think. *This might be okay.* There is something carnal that clicked between Brandon and I since that night, and while I have tried my best to deny it, it's actually quite thrilling.

I grab the scratchy wool blanket from the compartment under one of the seats and wrap myself in half of it.

"Come on," I say. "It's alright."

Brandon smiles as he comes closer, ducking inside the blanket wing that I have raised, urging him beside me.

"Is this okay?" he asks.

I appreciate the question. Not all men are that considerate.

"Yes," I say honestly.

His arm wraps around me, his hand grabbing my waist. My skin tingles and each little hair rises as I am flush with goosebumps. I rest my head gently against his.

He doesn't try anything – just holds me tight as our shivering bodies grow more and more still.

Every so often, a whale will breach or spyhop and we stare in awe. I should feel comforted by the proximity of Brandon's beautiful body, but it is still unfamiliar, which sets me slightly on edge. My hands mimic the things they used to do on late nights when I was wrapped up with Oscar; caressing, grazing, circling skin, searching for recognizable textures that aren't there, because this skin is different. It belongs to someone else. This cruel reminder sends an intense twinge of pain throughout my body.

Brandon notices, but doesn't say anything. He squeezes me tighter.

I want to bury this feeling, to lose myself in something – someone – new. So, I lift my chin and gaze at him. Brandon lowers his head and his blue eyes meet mine. There is an instant spark, a connection that is hard to place.

"Kiss me," I whisper.

Brandon's mouth curls into a seductive, wanting grin before meeting my own. I close my eyes and feel his thumb tracing my jaw, while his other hand runs up my thigh, even as it still clutches to a corner of the wool blanket. The blanket is itchy against my skin, but his hands feel smooth and foreign. They aren't rough and calloused like Oscar's. Even so, they glide between my legs with zero resistance.

The sun has completely risen by the time we emerge from under the blanket. We catch our breath, clinging to one another in one last desperate plea for warmth.

"I can't tell you how many times I've wanted to do that," Brandon says. "Each time we were alone out here, I've wanted to know what it would be like if we…"

His words trail off, but I know what he means. I, personally, had never felt the urge to touch him like this. But he knows exactly where to touch me, and when, with a level of expertise I've only felt once at the hands of a musician. It's just a shame he's such a bad kisser.

I simply respond by lightly kissing his cheek. While my feelings might not match his, our bodies are very much in sync. If I cannot placate him with words, perhaps I can with contact.

"I just never thought you'd want to," Brandon continues. "Seriously, I think I am still in shock from the other night. I've loved you for so long and – " He stops himself. The word – that word – has accidentally slipped out, and my body immediately becomes rigid. "I'm sorry. I didn't mean it like… I just…"

"It's okay," I lie. I try to honey my tone like bitter tea to disguise my discomfort.

"Is it?" He sits up and hides his face.

I do not love him, but I cannot tell him this. I want him to come back to me so I can feel that closeness again. But I do not love him.

"Yes," I say, stroking his arm. "Sorry, this is all just so new. I don't really know what to say."

Brandon casts a desperate glance my way as a plea for reciprocity.

"I want this. I want you," I say. "I don't want this to stop."

He seems to sense my truth because he relaxes and kisses my forehead.

"I don't want this to stop either," he says. "I want you to be mine."

I prickle at the phrase. I don't want to belong to anyone.

"You cannot own a person, Brandon," I say. "You can only be *with* someone."

"Then will you be with me?" he asks plainly.

I've never seen him want like this, like a man dying of thirst, but I am merely a mirage in the desert.

I try to focus on what it feels like to touch him, but Oscar occupies my mind. I can't shake that moment when he hovered over me, the intensity of his stare as he leaned in to kiss me, and the way my heart sank when he pulled away. It's a new memory that I am forced to replay over and over in my brain, wondering what I did wrong. But I remember, it was Oscar that was wrong. It was Oscar that was promised to another woman. And it was Oscar that nearly broke that promise.

I can make promises of my own.

"Or I can be yours, if you like," Brandon prompts, waiting eagerly for my answer.

"No," I say. "I'll be with you."

He smiles wide and hugs me hard, as if somehow I had answered his prayers. He holds me for too long, and when he finally pulls away, this feeling of vengeance is gone. It's a hollow box and it's been replaced by something akin to regret. I smile anyway, and I do feel tenderness toward him. After all, before all of this, Brandon was a close friend. Now, I'm afraid that has irreparably changed.

"Let's get dressed," I say, rising to my feet.

There are other boats on the water now, but they seem distant enough to not see our naked bodies.

I scramble toward our crumpled clothes, but Brandon holds me steady.

"Hey," he says. "There's no rush. We don't have to rush things."

"Seems a little late for that," I say. My eyes not-so-discreetly drift toward his groin.

He laughs. "Maybe. But we can slow down. Whatever you want."

I wrap my arms around his neck and pull him close.

"I told you," I say. "I want *you*."

At least, I think I do. It would be easier if I did.

Our clothes have had a moment to warm a bit in the morning light, though they are still impossibly wet. We put them on regardless, wincing at the unpleasantness that is such a large contrast from the immense pleasure we felt coiled together on the deck.

Warm inside, and cold outside, this moment feels bittersweet.

CHAPTER
TEN

OSCAR

JULY 22, 2022

I roll over onto my side and pick up my phone from the bedside table to see the time. *3:30am.* I've only been asleep for an hour or so, but during that time, Madison has crawled into bed, too. Predictably, she is out cold.

I set my phone back down and slide across the sheets until I feel her body against mine. Even though she is asleep, she squirms away, trying to evade my touch. Perhaps she got enough of that from Tyler earlier. Who knows anymore?

I pull her back toward me and she groans before fluttering her eyes open. Her fake eyelashes reflect the light coming through the window, making them look impossibly heavy.

"What, Oscar?" she prickles.

"I missed you," I lie, but I want to see how far she'll bend the truth, too. "Where have you been?"

The silence that follows is too long for comfort. I can see the gears turning in her head as she attempts to manufacture an alibi.

"I was out with the girls," she says. "I'm really tired."

"I bet," I say, biting back the bitterness in my tone. "How is Amy?"

Amy is probably the only friend of hers that I know, and as far as I know, they haven't seen each other in months. Little does Madison know that I follow Amy on Instagram and it appears that she is in the Maldives based on recent pictures.

"Amy is great," Madison turns over onto her other side, facing away from me. "Please, can we talk tomorrow?"

"I can't sleep," I say, which is the truest thing I have said to her in quite a while. "I don't know, I just feel like you are drifting away." The truth can be addicting.

She turns back over and I can see the fear in her eyes, overly bright in the darkness of the room, staring at me but not seeing me.

"What are you saying?" she says. Her voice is more awake now: more clear, less gravelly.

"Do you still love me?" I ask plainly.

"Oscar, stop it. You're being stupid."

"I'm being stupid?" I remain calm, but it's hard not to get riled up. I know that is what she is trying to do. She wants to push my buttons so that I start a fight. It's practically a ritual between us.

"Yes, you're being stupid. Seriously, where is this coming from? I hate when you get all insecure," she says. Her words are venom dripping from her teeth.

"Amy isn't in Seattle," I say. Even though it is too dark to see well, I know her face has flushed. Her shame in being caught in a lie glows brighter than the waning crescent moon.

"So what?" Madison barks. "I never said I was with Amy."

I roll my eyes. "You said she was doing great."

"I'm sure she is." She sounds hoarse, like her mouth is dry, but her voice does not waver. She may be annoyed, but she is stubborn as hell.

I sigh, perhaps too audibly because Madison sits up and tears off the sheets. She is trying to leave.

"Where are you going?" I ask. I launch myself from the bed and stand. "Why can't you ever give me a straight answer about where you go, what you do?"

Madison hastily puts on some pants and begins stomping toward the door.

"Because it's none of your fucking business!"

"You're my girlfriend!" I shout. "Of course it's my business!"

"You don't own me," she spits. She tries to take a step toward the door, but I block it with my body.

"I never thought I did," I lower my voice so it is slow and mild. "I just want to know what is happening."

"Who said anything is happening?" She tries to match my demeanor, but I can tell she is boiling inside, like a tea kettle that is just about to scream. "Where is this coming from? I have been nothing but devoted to you, Oscar, and to doubt that is a slap in the face."

I want to back down, to let her pass so she can go lie with Tyler in the room down the hall. I want to give up because fighting like this only makes the situation worse. My pride isn't worth this.

"I know about Tyler," I say, defeated.

Her eyes widen briefly before narrowing once more, aiming for the kill shot.

"We all have secrets, Oscar," she bites. "Tell me. Does Jacob know about yours?"

And there it is. The thing I feared most, coming true.

All I can muster is one single word. "Don't."

Madison laughs. "Try me."

Part of me always knew that Madison was cold-blooded, that she would do anything to get what she wants, but I never thought she could be this cruel.

I step toward her. She steps toward me.

"If you even think about telling *anyone*..."

I'm visibly simmering now. She knows that she has gotten under my skin. She knows that she has won.

She takes another step to me and wraps her hand tightly around my throat.

"You'll what?" she snarls, squeezing my neck tighter in her firm grasp.

My body betrays me, and as she presses up against me, I can feel my manhood stiffen. Madison notices this, too, and runs her other hand slowly down my abdomen, teasing me, coaxing me into submission.

I close my eyes. Her fingers dip under the band of my briefs and stroke the skin therein. I try to turn my face away from her so she can't see me fighting back the pleasure, but her grip on my throat releases and moves to my jaw instead, jerking my head back toward her. She wants to see how much I struggle.

This is the game. I am foolish for thinking it would end any differently. I was foolish for thinking it would end at all.

As I look straight into Madison's icy eyes, I am overcome: with love, with hate, with desire. Forcefully, I grab her by the back of her head and pull her in. Her mouth on mine is rigid and riotous, but she releases my jaw, moving instead to scratch and grab at my bare skin.

We stumble toward the bed and she falls upon me, clawing ravenously to release the tension. The moment that I feel her, all of her, I realize my mistake. But it is too late to turn back. We are trapped in this web, and with my secret in her hands, as delicate as glass and fragile as the human ego, I cannot escape.

Hours pass and Madison is once again asleep beside me. A thin sheet covers our naked bodies. The sweat has since dried and we have caught our breaths.

Quietly, I open the drawer of the bedside table and withdraw a small bag of powder. On nights like this, I like to arrange a thin line on the glass and inhale it sharply through my nostril. Madison typically initiates the ceremony, but tonight, I don't want to involve her. Not this time.

I snort the bitter white powder. Immediately, a rush of pleasure flows through me and at least for now, I am able to relax and ignore the situation. Still, Jacob can never know, and especially not Lola. If word spread about this, I could lose my best friend, my band, everything.

For now, I am warm and relaxed. Today's problems do not exist at this moment, and I forget that they will be waiting for me when I sober up. I lie back on the bed with Madison, quietly snoring beside me, but my thoughts instantly drift to Lola. It's like I can still feel my wet body dampen her clothes as I hover over her on the boat. She saved me – more than once. I need her to save me one more time.

I open my phone and begin texting her, but the words in my head are cloudy and I don't know what it is that I want to say, what I *should* say.

It was me who almost kissed her, and it is me who carries the shame of being the man that was going to hurt not one, but two women within a few seconds of wanting. She needs to know how sorry I am, but I'm fearful that I can't apologize without betraying Madison and the fucked up relationship in which I find myself trapped.

It's hard, wanting to be a better man but being cursed with this much desire. My gut instinct is to be reckless and selfish, to hurt people to get what I want. But it's just that: a gut instinct, and it is at war with the principles I hold in my heart.

I begin typing. Not just a short apology, but an entire wall of text that I will probably regret when the sun comes up:

I know it's early, but knowing you, you're probably already awake.

I am so sorry about the other day. I should have been open about my relationship from the beginning. Seeing you again has been a shock to say the least, and I promise I had no ulterior motives for this project.

I didn't. I do now.

The last text surprises me, but I don't unsend it. I need to say what I feel. My stomach flutters and my typing fingers twitch and quiver.

I know I don't deserve it, but I would kick myself if I didn't beg for another chance to kiss you. Please, Lola. Let me be yours.

I hover over the send button for a long time before I take a deep breath, wincing as I tap it.

I know she is awake, and has been for at least an hour or two. Euphoria from the heroin shifts into an uncomfortable anxiety. My breathing is sharp and shallow, and my hands have yet to cease shaking. Looking at my phone again and again, impatient as I wait for a response, is only making it worse.

I read what I sent, just to imagine how I am perceived, and even I can see that I have crossed a line. In my stupor, I have sent an apology that basically ends with, "I'd do it again."

And if I am being honest, I would do it again if she let me, but she can't know that.

Hastily, I tap the last text bubble to try to unsend it, but just as I am about to, the word "Seen" appears at the bottom of the conversation.

Fuck.

Lola saw it. The whole thing. And all I've done is dig my grave deeper, reinforcing what an asshole I really am. I am such a fucking idiot.

I wait and wait to see if she types back. Nothing. And who can blame her? If I received an unhinged text like that from my ex, I'd leave them on read, too.

Eventually, I lose hope of a response. I lie back on the bed with my phone pressed to my chest and take long, deep breaths as I try to calm down.

As I look over at Madison, I feel hot and tense. I clench my jaw so hard it hurts. It shouldn't be her next to me right now. God, how I wish it wasn't her lying next to me right now.

Unfortunately, I am stuck.

I haven't forgotten Madison's threat to blackmail me, but the drugs – although they are the root of the problem – help me set it aside, at least for a little while. Jacob can't know, and if he finds out, it needs to be from me.

The question is: how much worse do things have to get before I tell him? How much am I willing to lose?

CHAPTER
ELEVEN

LOLA

JULY 27, 2022

"There he is!" Dawn shouts across the café.

Brandon's mouth twitches as the server leads Oscar to our table. It's not like Oscar to be late, but I suppose it saves him the awkwardness of having to wait for anyone else. Still, it drives me crazy, and after that text he sent the other night, I would have liked to clear the air. I wanted to type my reply so many times, but what do I say? What *can* I say when my coworker is sleeping beside me?

I owe him nothing.

And yet, I can't seem to get him out of my mind. Oscar Kelly is my new hyperfixation.

"Hi, everyone," Oscar says, taking his seat and scooting the chair closer to the table.

"Hi, Oscar," Dawn coos. She is looking up at him dreamily through her lashes. She may be twice our age, but she is the biggest flirt I have ever encountered. And she is completely enamored with Oscar. After all, who wouldn't be?

Although, he looks tired. Very tired. His eyelids hang and he has dark circles under his eyes that look all the darker contrasted with his pale skin. I'm trying to catch his attention, but he won't even look in my direction. Should I be worried?

"Dawn," Oscar says. He kisses her hand lightly. "How are you, darling?"

Dawn practically melts in her chair. She may be able to dish it out, but she can barely take it when someone flirts back. Especially someone like Oscar. I know it's all part of the rockstar persona, but I am surprised to feel a twinge of jealousy.

Please. Just look at me.

"Hi, Oscar," I say. It comes out more monotone than I would like, but I don't want to send the wrong message. Not until I know that he no longer has a girlfriend.

Oscar casts a sharp, brief look in my direction before immediately darting away. He clenches his jaw and I think I see pink blooming on his cheeks.

"Morning, everyone," he says, addressing no one in particular. "Let's plan this thing, shall we?"

The server comes by to take our orders, but he orders nothing but black coffee. He never even looks at the menu, just simply hands it back to the server before delicately weaving his fingers together and placing his pretzeled palms on the table.

"So," I clear my throat. "Where are we thinking for the venue?"

Oscar still won't look at me, at least not until I feel Brandon's arm on the back of my chair. That seems to grab his attention.

"I was thinking maybe the Emerald," Dawn chimes in, stealing his worried eyes from me. "It seats up to six hundred, and it's very modern. Nice rooftop, too."

"Six hundred?" I gasp. "Do you really think that many people will reserve a plate?"

Oscar laughs.

"I know some people," he says gruffly before taking a sip of his plain, hot coffee.

I lean away from Brandon's arm on my chair. "I'm confused. I thought we were going for an exclusive event."

"If you want funding – a lot of funding – you need to cast a wide net," Oscar says, swallowing and audibly tasting the coffee on his tongue.

"I realize that," I say sharply. "But don't rich people want to feel… special? Doesn't scarcity generate demand?"

Oscar rolls his eyes. He opens his mouth to speak, but Dawn chimes in before a sound can escape his lips.

"Lola," she says, steepling her fingers. "I've been managing donors for more than twenty years. All people, rich or not, give because they feel connected to the mission. Well, for tax write-offs, too. But you just need to focus on connecting the guests to our work. Let me worry about the rest."

I realize my tapping foot is shaking the table and I can hear the clinking of ice in the water glasses on the surface. I am only stilled by the feeling of Brandon's hand pressing on my shoulder.

"Babe, think about if even half of the guests made a donation. This could be great for us," he says.

It's not just my eyes that widen, but Dawn and Oscar's, too.

"Did he just call you 'babe'?" Oscar asks. He chokes a little on his coffee, and though it seems as if he tries to set the cup down lightly, it clatters loudly as it makes contact with the table.

"I –" I begin, but Dawn interjects.

"Well, isn't this lovely!" she says. "See Brandon? I told you she'd come around. I'm so happy for you two! Oh, love – is there anything sweeter?"

Oscar clenches his fists.

"Oscar," I whisper. I'm staring right into his eyes, begging for him to listen. I want to reach for his hand, but then his next words jolt me back to our cold reality.

"Madison and I offer our congratulations," he says. He lifts his cup of coffee in salutation, but Dawn gently urges him to set it back down.

"Oh, no, no, no. We've got to order a round of mimosas if we are going to celebrate properly," Dawn clicks her tongue.

Madison.

"Oh, you two are still together?" I ask politely, but beneath the surface, I am seething.

Oscar can see this plainly, and he smirks, as if he just won a hand in poker, taking possession of all my chips.

"Yep," he says. "Two years now. We're *very* happy."

He utters the words, but I don't believe him. People in happy relationships don't almost kiss their exes, and they certainly don't send texts like the ones he did. Still, hearing him say it like that, to deliberately hurt me – I feel a piercing in my chest, as if he plunged a dagger directly into my heart and twisted the blade to watch me squirm.

The server returns, carrying a tray of mimosas in crystal champagne flutes. I take mine directly from their hand.

"Incredible," I say. "Cheers."

I swallow the entirety of my mimosa in a matter of seconds before politely gesturing to the glass before the server leaves.

"Another one, please, when you get a minute," I say.

The server nods and chuckles as they walk away.

I can feel everyone eyeing me in horror. I don't care. I flick my eyes up at Oscar, just long enough to show him that he hurt me. His cocky smirk disappears and there is so much tension between us that it feels like it might snap like a rubber band. I look away before one of us gets the chance to make even more of a scene. Or maybe I want to make a scene.

I turn towards Brandon and set my hand on his knee. He clasps my hand and grips it tight, but he still looks concerned.

"So," Brandon coughs. "The Emerald, then?"

"Yes," I say. "That sounds great, *babe.*"

I place way too much emphasis on the word and it comes off more sarcastic than cute. It must be very clear to everyone here that I am playing a game, but what else can I do when Oscar insists on toying with me like this? Instead of owning his mistake, or breaking things off with his girlfriend, he doubles down with that text. And then *he* has the nerve to be mad at *me*?

Dawn lets out a nervous laugh.

"I'm glad that's settled. Now when would you like to have the gala?" she asks.

Everyone is stepping on eggshells now.

"How quickly can we get things ready?" Brandon says. He understands the urgency as well as I do.

Dawn ponders this a moment.

"End of September, maybe? It's hard to say. This is the first time we've organized a donor event of this scale, but if Oscar is able to help, autumn seems possible."

"Always happy to help," Oscar agrees. "But I'll still need more context around Lola's work, just so I understand things fully."

"Of course," Dawn says. "That shouldn't be a problem, should it, Lola?"

My face is hot, and suddenly I feel a little dizzy – possibly from the mimosa that I downed too quickly.

"Not at all." I fake a smile.

"We have a good time out on the water," Oscar says. He's got me trapped and he knows it. I hate that he knows it. "I'm looking forward to it."

The server returns with another mimosa. I snatch it up as soon as they leave it on the table.

"To the whales!" I say, lifting my glass.

Everyone else reluctantly does the same. We drink in unison, although they sip theirs while I appear to be trying to douse a flame burning within me.

I set my glass down, moving my hand from Brandon's leg

up to his face, brushing his sharp jawline with my fingers – the way I used to with Oscar.

Brandon's eyes flutter closed, losing himself in the soft sensation of my skin on his. I smile, though it is weighed down by guilt.

Dawn looks away, but I can feel the burn of Oscar's stare as I trace circles on Brandon's neck. Brandon finally looks down at me, beaming. His skin feels hot to the touch, and his cheeks are a little pink, too. I recognize that I am blatantly teasing him, in public, to make my ex-boyfriend jealous. But if Brandon is enjoying it and Oscar is fuming, then I won't lie, I am feeling a little drunk on power – or maybe I'm just drunk.

"So," Oscar says. "When did this start?"

He gestures flippantly at me and Brandon. It comes off more curious than rude, but I know his true meaning.

Brandon wraps his arm around me and squeezes.

"Oh, what would you say, Lola? About a week ago?" he says.

I nod.

I can see Oscar doing the math, how just over a week ago his wet body was on top of mine, his mouth lingering near my lips. Even thinking about it gives me goosebumps. Involuntarily, I shudder. What will Oscar think when he figures out how quickly I went from being under his body to Brandon's?

"Adorable," Dawn says. "Brandon, I know I said I wouldn't say anything but Lola simply has to know."

"Know what?" I ask.

"How long I've wanted to be with you," Brandon says.

He plants a kiss on the top of my head while Oscar rolls his eyes. If he thinks he is being discreet, he's doing a terrible job.

"Oh," I laugh. However, the laugh is forced and sticks in my throat.

"Ever since he got the job, he's been telling me that one day you were going to be his girl," Dawn says.

Brandon blushes.

"Dawn, stop –"

Dawn continues.

"I still remember that Christmas party. You walked in, and his jaw was practically on the floor. He turned to me and said, 'I'm gonna marry her someday,'" she says.

Brandon's face is violently red now. Whether from embarrassment or anger, I can't tell.

Not like me. I can feel the color drain from my face.

It is now clear that this thing with Brandon is not the casual hookup I thought it was. Not only was I not aware that he has been in love with me for years, but he wants to *marry* me. One week, we're having fun. Now, this.

"Excuse me," Oscar says hurriedly. He gets up from the table, but he leaves nothing behind. He walks toward the exit instead of the bathrooms, and I get this sick feeling in my stomach that he isn't coming back.

"Where do you think he's going?" Dawn asks, blind to the situation.

Brandon rubs my back gently.

"We ought to get going, too, don't you think?" he says.

"Sure," I say.

But in my mind, I am chasing after Oscar to undo the damage that has been done. Even later, as Brandon drives me back to my apartment – and even later after that, when Brandon's naked form is pressing into mine, all I can think about is Oscar.

CHAPTER
TWELVE

OSCAR

JULY 28, 2022

"Play that last little melody again," Jacob says.

I strum the chord progression on my acoustic guitar for him and Tyler to hear. The sound swells and fills the penthouse.

"Okay, okay. Let me try something." Jacob plucks at his bass guitar, slowly layering notes until he creates a short groove.

Tyler wipes at his nose as he returns from the bathroom and falls heavily upon the couch. I clench my hand. I'm not mad at Tyler. I'm not even mad at Madison. All of the contempt in my body is directed at one person and one person only: *Brandon.*

At first I was angry with Lola, too. But that isn't fair. I royally fucked things up with her and drove her into the arms of another man. I made a move before either of us was ready and now, I must suffer the consequences.

I just worry that I will never get the chance to fix things. How am I supposed to have an honest conversation with her when Brandon is around? He'd probably punch me square in the jaw, and I would deserve it, but that doesn't mean it isn't worth trying.

"What do you think?" Jacob says, his face beaming with pride for his bassline.

"I like it," I say. "Tyler?"

Tyler grunts his approval, to which Jacob immediately rolls his eyes.

"Cool! Well, I had this idea for the words," Jacob says. "Unless you had something else in mind. I don't want to step on any toes."

"Actually…" I say. My fingers run along the rugged edge of my guitar neck, taking notice of every bump, every chip in the wood. "There is something on my mind. I just can't find the right words for it. Maybe you can help me."

Jacob's face softens. "What's going on, dude?"

I want to tread lightly. Tyler is in the room, and I realize that anything I say to him could easily make its way back to Madison. There's no need to give her more leverage.

"Jealousy," I say. "Seriously, what could a man say to the woman he loves when she's fucking someone else?"

I unintentionally lock eyes with Tyler as he listens from the couch, and all of the color in his face disappears. Jacob sees this ghostly transformation and chuckles lightly to himself.

"I'll have to think about that one," he says.

"Yeah," Tyler stammers. "Me too."

I don't want to play with Tyler when I am so unbothered by his betrayal at this point, but I would be lying if I said watching him squirm didn't make me feel better.

I play the chords again and again, until the picture comes to me. I mumble improvised lyrics in sync with Jacob's bassline.

"I found lust in me,
Ooh, but now I'm starving.
Now I can't find the starvation within you,
Starving and new.
I've tried pleading before,

Starvation without you."

A long silent pause follows, during which even Tyler seems to find reverence. Hunger is what I feel: an intense longing – not for someone I want, but someone I need to survive. This jealousy I feel isn't a tantrum or machismo bull-shit. I ache for Lola, and each moment without her brings shooting pain throughout my body, so long as it isn't pressed against hers.

"Damn," Jacob says. "I would hate to be you."

"Shut up, your life sucks, too," I laugh.

"Yeah, maybe, but not as much as yours."

Tyler tries to rise to his feet quietly, but the leather of the couch squeaks against his hands.

"Sorry, I need to use the restroom," he says. "Carry on."

I am tempted to follow him, whether to punch him in the dick or bum off a hit is unclear. Truthfully, I have the urge to do both, even if my anger is misdirected.

"Wouldn't be practice if you didn't miss ninety percent of it," Jacob calls to Tyler as he rounds the corner to the hallway. But he probably didn't hear it, even though we wish he would. "Okay, Oscar. You're freaking me out. What the *fuck* is going on?"

I sigh. "Long story."

"I take it you're still with Madison," he says. "But those lyrics aren't about her, are they?"

"No," I admit.

"Then who? Lola?" Jacob slaps his forehead. "Oh my god, it is Lola. Dude, you are digging your own grave."

"Why do you say that?" I swallow the lump in my throat and cross my legs.

"You're never going to get the girl when you're still with someone else," he says. "Seriously, get rid of Madison."

"I'm trying," I say, "But it's not that simple. Besides, Lola has a boyfriend now. I missed my chance."

Jacob groans. He is visibly fed up with my drama.

"Dude, you keep saying that leaving Madison isn't an option. But why not? What could she possibly have on you? Is it really worth all of this?"

I fall backwards onto the floor and moan.

"No, it's really not."

"Then I'm telling you, end it. You have it within your power to change your circumstances. I'm sick of seeing you act all helpless when really, you're just being stubborn," he says.

The weight of this guilt and shame is unbearable. Jacob is going to find out soon, and I will lose everything: not just Madison, not just the band, but Lola, too. I could lose the first two, but I can't stomach losing Lola again when the universe placed her in my path, maybe for the last time.

The thought makes my stomach churn, but I can't do anything about it. My skin itches and my pulse quickens. I can't sit beside Jacob and lie to him over and over again.

"I need to go for a walk," I say. "To sort this shit out."

"Want me to come with you?" Jacob asks. He's already setting down his bass.

"No, I need to be alone," I sigh.

Jacob nods. He and I understand each other. In fact, we might know each other too well, and I wonder how much of this he can see right through. Maybe he already knows everything and is waiting for me to come clean.

Is it pride or fear that keeps me from telling the truth?

Fear. Definitely fear.

So, I walk away, but my footsteps bring me in a beeline toward the restroom where Tyler is hunching over the counter, catching his breath.

"There's still some there if you want it," he says, nodding toward a line of powder next to the sink.

I stare at it. It seems my starvation is not limited to Lola. Our lunch replays in my head like a broken record, with Brandon's arm around her, Lola's hand on his thigh. Yet, here in this bathroom lies the only relief I can find, the only thing that takes away the ache in my chest. I step forward, lean down, and inhale with one finger pressed against my nostril.

"Fuck!" I whisper. It's bitter. So, so bitter.

Tyler turns his head away from me.

"Oscar, I'm sorry," he says. "You must think I am such an asshole."

"For what?" I say, trying to compose myself. Admittedly, it is hard to focus.

"For everything: the drugs, the attitude, but especially Madison."

I'm cold and dizzy. After fuming for days, imagining this conversation, I am suddenly at a loss for words.

"At first, it was an accident – something that just happened when we were high one time. But then, I don't know, I just kept doing it. I knew I was doing something bad, but it felt good and I've never exactly been good at restraint. Madison's just using me for the drugs though. And I keep letting her. There's nothing emotional. Not like between you two," Tyler watches himself in the mirror while he says this, like maybe it's easier to confront himself than it is to confess it to me.

"There's nothing emotional between us either," I say. "Not anymore. Not anything that's healthy."

"I completely understand if you want to kick my ass. I deserve it," he says.

I do briefly consider it, but the rage isn't there, at least not for Tyler. Besides, kicking anyone's ass won't solve any of my problems.

"No. No, it's fine," I say. "I mean, it's really not. That is a shitty thing to do. But it's already done."

"What happens now?" Tyler asks.

It's a good question, one for which I wish I had the answer. I'm just riding this out with no plan, hoping that things resolve themselves, but I know if I do that, things probably won't resolve in my favor. The more I ignore this, the more people I will hurt, and I will still lose everything.

"I don't know," I say. "Are you going to stop?"

Tyler doesn't say anything.

After a long pause, I scratch my head.

"It's fine. I don't care. None of this matters anyway."

"What do you mean?" Tyler asks. "Of course it does."

I lean against the countertop, cold marble cooling my sweaty palms.

"This band is being held together by a thread, Tyler. It's only a matter of time before Jacob finds out I'm using, too. Madison will tell him and we'll all go our separate ways."

"It wouldn't be the worst thing," Tyler says. "I know you two are close, but I don't know. Isn't it better to burn out than to fade away? Maybe The Unadored has run its course, you know?"

I wince. Tyler is just confirming my worst fears.

"I don't want this to end," I say. "What else am I supposed to do if I'm not writing music with my best friend? You may prefer burning out, but I'd rather fade away if it means I get to keep doing what I love."

He claps me on the back.

"No one is stopping you, Oscar," Tyler says. "Whatever happens, you'll always have music."

"And what about Jacob?" I sigh.

"You have been friends for a long time. If he is that quick to turn on you, then maybe you're better off. Don't be so quick to make assumptions. Things will work out, even if I've fucked it all up."

I want to believe him. If it were Jacob in my position, I would stand by him. But it's not. I'm the one on drugs, and I can't seem to detach myself. My fear is that Jacob hates me as much as I hate myself. And even if he were forgiving, there's no way Lola would see me as anything other than an addict.

How do you come clean when there is no empathy for your mistakes?

"You'll figure it out," Tyler says. "And don't worry about me. I'll be fine. You worry about yourself. I'm gonna go lie down."

Tyler leaves me propped up against the counter. I wipe the residual heroin into the sink and lower myself to the ground.

Suddenly, I feel nauseated and my skin itches like hell.

I can't keep doing this. I want to stop, but it's too late and the drugs are already in my body. And though I wish I could undo everything – the drugs, the almost kiss, the text message to Lola – it's already done.

I am imprisoned by my own poor judgment. You'd think I would learn, but I just keep fucking up. So, what is the point? Where do I go from here?

CHAPTER
THIRTEEN

LOLA

JULY 29, 2022

My thermos is warm in my hand, but I nearly drop it when I feel my phone vibrate.

I'm here. Come outside. :)

It's still early in the morning, but Brandon is twenty minutes later than he said he would be to pick me up, which means Oscar is probably waiting impatiently for us at the marina. This is the reason I hate carpooling.

For the most part, I actually don't mind the delay since our uncomfortable lunch the other day. But I would hate to upset Oscar more than I already have. At first, it was satisfying to try to make him jealous, but the way he left was so abrupt, I knew I had taken it too far – or rather, Brandon did.

I know the smart thing would be to break things off with Brandon now, before things get more serious than they already have. But besides Ruby, he might be my only friend, and the fact that we are research partners makes things doubly complicated. I'd also be lying if I said being with him didn't make me feel a little bit better about the situation with Oscar. If he is sleeping with someone else, why shouldn't I?

I climb up into the passenger seat of Brandon's SUV. He greets me with a kiss; not just a peck, but a slow, wanting one with open mouths and wandering tongues. It's more messy than sensual, and all I seem to be able to fixate on is the passing of time – another reason we are late.

I pull away.

"Hey, is everything okay?" Brandon asks.

Now would be a good opportunity to talk, to say everything that I've been thinking this past week, but he is looking at me with such tenderness that I can't bring myself to break his heart.

"Yeah," I lie. "Let's just get going."

Brandon reluctantly puts the car in drive and peels out from the curb. I keep trying to speak up during the drive to the marina, but the music is too loud for me to compose my thoughts and I'd rather not shout over it while he unironically sings along to Sisqo's "Thong Song".

Just as expected, Oscar is already on the dock when we arrive. I glance at the clock on my phone. Thirty minutes late. Unbelievable. Imagining Oscar sitting here by himself, waiting, makes my skin itch. It's not just a lack of respect for others' time. It's a lack of thoughtfulness and preparation.

"Hey, Oscar! Sorry, we just –" I say, but he waves his hand and cuts me off.

"It's fine, Lola. I get it."

Ouch. This is not how I wanted to start this day. I wanted to clear the tension between all of us, but instead it appears that Brandon and I have just poured gasoline all over the situation and lit a match.

Brandon takes the duffel bag I'm carrying and slings it over his shoulder.

"I'll load these onto the boat," he smiles. "Don't worry. It's chill. Talk to him."

He leaves me on the dock with Oscar, who is pacing pensively along the squeaky wood. His shoulders are slumped and his hands are in his pockets.

"Oscar," I say.

He stops pacing and looks up at me. I am immediately gutted by the pain in his eyes. He looks haggard and miserable, like he hardly slept. Maybe even like he has been crying.

I open my mouth, but the words come out as a whisper.

"I'm sorry."

"Sorry for what?" He shifts his weight onto the other leg.

"I did not intend for any of this to happen," I say, my voice wobbling. "But I don't know what to do when you keep making advances while you're with another woman. I know I am being unfair, but you're being unfair, too."

"I want to make it right," he says. "I'm *trying* to make it right."

Oscar takes a step toward me, but instinctively, without thinking, I step away.

"Are you still with her?" I ask.

"Lola. I –"

"Answer the question."

He hangs his head in defeat, and while I want to comfort him, I am furious.

"Oscar, I can't keep playing this game with you. It's exhausting. You come back into my life unexpectedly, and for what? Revenge?" My voice gets louder with each word, cutting through the silence and the water gently sloshing against the wooden dock.

"Do you really think that little of me? That I would do something that cruel?" he says.

I shrug.

"Lola, I am here purely by accident. I wanted to change my life for the better, to find a greater purpose. I don't know what I expected, but instead I found you." He rubs his stubbled face and diverts his eyes, kicking his shoes on a loose plank. "I don't think that is a coincidence. If anything, I think it is a clear sign that you were, are, and will forever be the greatest purpose."

There's a tightness in my chest, and suddenly, my body turns ice cold.

"Then why are you still with her?" I plead.

Before he can answer, Brandon interrupts, appearing at my side with his arm wrapped around my waist.

"We're all set. Are you two ready?"

Oscar and I lock eyes, pained and desperate. But I can't keep entertaining his affections, not while he belongs to someone else.

"Yeah," I say. "We're ready."

The waves are choppy the farther we get out into the Sound. We won't be able to stay for long which, for me and Oscar, is preferable.

The boat is eerily quiet, making the force of the waves all the more terrifying. With nothing to distract us while the hydrophones record the songs under the surface, the violent beating of my heart betrays the song beneath mine.

"Just a while longer," I force a laugh, but it's tight in my throat.

Oscar grunts.

"You know, I nearly cried when I was analyzing one of the last recordings," I continue. "The data shows that these whales feel immense love as well as emotional suffering. And I swear, in this file, I could hear the suffering."

"There's also the spindle cell," Brandon adds.

"And what is that?" Oscar asks, though he is rolling his eyes while doing so.

"It's what allows us to feel love," Brandon says. "Well, not just us. Apes and primates, too. And whales, obviously."

"Fascinating," Oscar says. His tone is sharp and mocking.

I am so fed up with this: the macho, jealous bullshit.

"You know, Oscar, if you're still serious about this, it wouldn't hurt to learn this stuff," I say. "We're only trying to be helpful."

Oscar rubs his face, dragging the bags under his eyes downward, casting a ghoulish expression.

"I know," he groans. "I know. I'm sorry. I just… I just have a lot going on."

A chill runs up my spine. We all have a lot going on, but something in the way he said it… I am actually starting to worry about him.

"Go ahead, tell me more," he says, but I shoot him a look flooded with concern. "It's fine. I'm fine. Go ahead."

Reluctantly, I continue.

"The spindle cell is one of the pillars of our work. It provides scientific evidence that whales are more complex than we ever imagined, not just because of their unique language and social structures, but because they are capable of feeling empathy," I say. "Humpbacks are known to be altruistic in the wild, going as far as to protect seals from orcas. In fact, a pod of belugas once adopted a lone narwhal simply because it would never survive on its own. This behavior is very common. This is why they need more protection."

Oscar appears to genuinely ponder this.

"Just because we cannot understand something," he says finally, "doesn't mean it does not feel."

I am stunned into silence, not just because of how quickly he understands what we are telling him, but because I know that he isn't just referring to the whales. I think, perhaps, he is referring to himself.

"That is the gist, yeah," I say. I want to stop there, to leave it at that, but I can't help but lean into his subtext. "It's not fair of us to use whales to serve our impulses and needs, especially when alternative resources are available."

Oscar blinks at this.

Brandon seems oblivious to the conversation we are actually having, hearing only the words spoken in our common language and not the layers within it, which is good. It's best that he doesn't know how much friction there is between each word, each syllable, each letter uttered between us.

"And what about other cultures that rely on whaling?" he says. "What if they have no choice?"

"What are you getting at, Oscar?" I say, rubbing my temples.

Oscar fidgets with a strap on one of the duffle bags.

"I'm just saying it's all more nuanced than you might think."

He's right. And I hate that he's right. Not just because it pokes holes in my own stance, but because now I feel guilty.

The waves are getting larger and the sky, which has been illuminated by the rising sun, is gray and cloudy.

"We should probably head back," Brandon says. "Storm's coming in."

"Yeah," I say, shivering. "Of course."

Steadily, I walk over to the starboard side of the boat to retrieve the hydrophones, but as I lean over the edge, Brandon's hand finds its way to my lower back, and then it lowers and lowers more, until he is smoothing his palm over the curve of my ass.

I try to ignore it, but when I turn around, Oscar's face is pale and green as phytoplankton – and he is staring right at us. He leans forward, groaning, as he puts his head between his knees.

"Sea sick?" Brandon asks teasingly. He does, however, offer him a water bottle. "Here. Drink this. Might make you feel better."

Oscar lifts his head, but declines the water, clocking the hand that holds it.

"Bro, seriously, fuck off," Oscar says.

"Oscar!" I shout. "Stop it."

Brandon doesn't seem all that perturbed. He simply tosses the bottle onto one of the empty seats on the boat.

"It's fine, Lola," he says. "Can't help a drowning man if he doesn't even try to swim."

Hastily, Oscar rises from his seat. His fist rips back before thrusting forward, catching Brandon square in the eye.

I scream.

"Oscar! God damn it!"

Brandon shoves him so hard that he falls back into his seat.

"Dude, what the fuck is your problem?"

"You!" Oscar shouts, pointing his finger at Brandon like a brandished knife. "You're my problem!"

A wave of frothy ocean water splashes over the edge of the boat, causing it to rock even harder than before, forcing all of us to hold on to something to stabilize ourselves.

"Whatever. I'm getting us out of here," Brandon says, turning toward the helm. He gently touches his eye, immediately red and swollen, but flinches at his own touch.

The start of the motor rattles through me, though I might just be shaking with rage. I don't speak a word to Oscar. In fact, the entire way back to the marina, we are drenched with a tense silence, all of us clearly harboring secret anger. Oscar sits there pouting like a child.

Brandon expertly navigates the rough water, keeping us steady until at last, he gently maneuvers the boat to the dock.

Before the boat is even secured, Oscar launches from his seat and clumsily jumps to the dock. I dare not do the same, not until I get the rope around the cleat.

"Brandon, can you tie this? I should –"

"Go," he says. "I got it. Figure out whatever his damage is."

I kiss him on the cheek, and climb down onto the dock.

My legs reach a full sprint, the wooden planks below my feet knocking and creaking with each long leap.

Rain drops begin to fall, and though they streak my vision, I can see Oscar opening his car door. I run faster.

Oscar cannot leave. Not before I've had a chance to give him a piece of my mind.

CHAPTER
FOURTEEN

OSCAR

JULY 29, 2022

Lola's unmistakable voice shouts through the gathering fog as I open my car door.

"What the hell, Oscar?"

I freeze. What should I do? It seems as though everything I say and do is the wrong thing, and unfortunately, once I've committed those transgressions, they cannot be undone.

Lola slams the car door shut and shoves me backwards. She blocks the driver's side of the vehicle with her body, challenging me to try to leave.

"Please," I beg. "Get out of the way. Let me go."

"No," she says. "Not until you explain why you're being such an asshole."

Her jaw clenches and she steadies herself as if she is bracing for a fight.

"We've already talked about this. There's nothing left to say," I say.

Her eyes narrow.

"Try."

I sigh. I am tired, I hurt, and I want to go back to the penthouse. Despite this, I can never say no to Lola. Even when she is angry like this, I want to reach out and hold her.

"I can't be around both of you. Together." I say. Raindrops

begin to trickle from the sky, leaving teardrop stains on Lola's beautiful face. "It's bad enough knowing that you're together when I am not around. I wish I weren't such a jealous man, but I can't do it, Lola."

"Well, somehow you've managed all these years," she says. "Why should now be any different?"

"Because you left me, Lola!" I shout. "You left me without so much as a word. How am I supposed to get over that?"

How could she bring that up, knowing what she did? Hearing this sends a sharp pain through my chest, as if the separation had been easy for her. God knows it wasn't for me.

Her pupils dilate as she's stunned into silence.

"I told you why. Maybe not then, but I told you," she says.

"After what? A decade? And that is supposed to erase all those years where I blamed myself, when –"

"When you could have been blaming me instead? Is that it?" Her voice sours. "Don't act like you were the only one who was hurting, Oscar. I hurt, too."

I don't believe it. Not for a second. I am here, begging her for another chance – and I know things aren't neat and tidy and perfect, but fuck. I need her like the air I breathe: rain-soaked and crisp, invigorating to inhale.

"Prove it," I say.

She stumbles backwards against the door.

"Excuse me?"

I take a step toward her, pinning her to the car.

"Prove that it hurts."

Prove that you love me, Lola.

She is staring at me, the intensity between our held gaze so electrifying that I swear I see sparks. Gears turn behind her deep, dark eyes, and I feel a fire burning inside me. Before I know what I am doing, I am slowly leaning in toward her face. My lips graze hers. At first, soft and inviting, then suddenly, they go rigid.

Instantly, I feel a heavy sting on my cheek. My eyes open

to see Lola's open hand swinging and I know that once again, I have made a huge mistake.

"What the actual fuck is wrong with you, Oscar?" she yells. "Jesus Christ!"

I don't know what to say. I'm crazy about her. Literally crazy. I don't know how to read her anymore, how to be around her. It makes me do stupid things.

"I'm still in love with you," I whisper. "I'm sorry, I don't know what to do with that."

She lets out a long, heaving sigh.

"Sort your shit out. I don't know what is going on with you, but you need to stop involving me. You can't just walk around punching and kissing people." She groans, pulling at her hair in frustration. "I did love you once, Oscar. But not this. I don't want whatever this is."

Ouch. She goes for the jugular: *I did love you… once.*

The sad thing is, I can't really blame her. I have been awful, and there's no way I can explain without making things worse. I am a monster.

Yet, I cannot move. Lola is still pinned between me and the car, and her lip – it's trembling.

"Please," she whispers. "This has to stop."

I remove my arms from her periphery and step back.

"Okay."

"Okay?"

"Yeah," I say. "I quit."

Fresh eyes flicker, tear drained and splenetic. They crease and quiver with an unknowing anger before Lola pushes me against the car parked next to mine. The alarm starts screaming, but that doesn't stop her. She just screams louder.

"What do you mean, 'I quit'!? You think you can just drop in and drop out like that? This isn't a fucking biology course, Oscar! This is my life, and you are making it so much fucking worse!"

Her face is soaked, whether from the rain or from tears, I can't tell.

"What do you want me to say, Lola? Apparently, that's what I do," I say. "I am not the guy you knew; I'm a bad person."

Her fists clench around the collar of my shirt, twisting and wringing it like a dirty dish rag.

"No!" she yells, the car alarm still blaring. "You don't get to do that! You don't get to play the victim!" Now it's her mouth that twists, contorted by the discomfort of this thing between us. I feel it, too, and it's written plainly on my face. "God, Oscar! Why do you think this is okay? To come here, to find me, and pretend like you care? You don't care – not about anything but yourself. I am an idiot for believing you. And I am an even bigger idiot for entertaining this…" She gestures between us, hands emphatic with forcible fingers, pointing and waving with both distinction and ambiguity. "This! And what is this?"

"I don't know," I stammer. "I only know what I – what *you* – want it to be."

Her eyes narrow.

"Wanting is a fantasy, Oscar. I can't hitch my hope to a fantasy."

I don't say a word. For once, I am out of words. But I cannot remove my steely gaze.

"So, what? You're done then?" she bristles. Still, I stare. She releases my shirt and sways back cautiously. "Great. That's just great."

I swipe my soggy curls from my face, eyes glued to the torrential downpour splashing upon the pavement. I can't look at Lola any longer. The shame is too severe.

"I guess I should let you go," she says. I can barely hear it through the noise, but the pain is unmistakable. She speaks as though she is stitching up a wound with no anesthetic.

I look up and she winces as she reaches for my hand.

"Lola…" I choke.

She bites the inside of her cheek, a little indentation where the teeth suck and scrape at the flesh.

"Oscar," she says. "I am truly sorry about our past. I am. But I cannot be your future if you won't let me. I don't want to be a footnote or a tabloid headline. And I can't keep waiting. If you were certain about this, you –" Her words begin to shake. "You would have chosen me."

The appropriate thing – the smart thing – to do in this moment would be to touch her; to pull her into me and swear that it's her, that it's always been her, and always will be; to set down my fears about Jacob discovering my secret and sever ties with Madison; to put aside all of the guilt and all of the resentment and for once in my life, take responsibility, so that Lola and I can be together, the way we were destined to be.

But no.

Instead, like a fool, I do nothing. I stand with arms dangling at my sides, wide-eyed and frozen. And then Lola's entire frame starts shuddering, convulsing as she comes to terms with the fact that I cannot conjure the bravery to be the person she needs me to be. The car alarm finally ceases as she stifles her sobs, and I step back.

"You don't need me, Lola," I whisper. "You're better off with him."

I nod toward the dock where Brandon is tying up the boat.

Lola swallows: perhaps her pride, or perhaps her pain.

"That could never be true," she says, twisting the slick fabric of her sleeve. She won't look directly at me, and I can't look at her either. "But if this is what you want, Oscar, I won't stand in your way."

None of this is what I want. But all of this is what both of us need. No more being together without *being* together – with this invisible, yet tangible distance between us, where wanting hands wander and cease and spasm before they register the touch – it's too much for either of us to bear. And I could fix this; I know I could fix this, but it would cost me everything else.

So, I kiss her dripping cheek. She closes her eyes which betray the reticence she wants to exude, stepping away from the car door. As she moves farther and farther away, my body yearns to pull her back. But right now, in this moment, with the Seattle rain pounding on the pavement, drenching us in our many regrets, it seems best to let her go.

She was rid of me for ten years, and her life seems better because of it. She got the degree she needed for the job she wanted to live out her passion. And she did it. She made it. Now, she is on the cusp of becoming one of the most influential whale scientists in the country. Maybe even the world.

She is better. Why should now be any different?

I open the car door and crawl inside, defeated and alone. I can see her through the drops on my windshield and the fog that forms on the inside of the glass. Even through this misty barrier, I can see her shrunken silhouette. It's not until I see the shape of Brandon's broad shoulders behind her that I can muster the strength to turn on the vehicle and drive away from the best thing I have ever known.

When I get to the penthouse, I immediately storm Tyler's room, rifling through each and every drawer until I find what I'm looking for: release. It's white as angel wings and bitter as a dirty dime, and right now, it's the only thing that will take away the sting of not just losing Lola, but giving her up entirely.

"Hey, man." I hear Tyler's baritone voice behind me. It's tight and fearful, which is appropriate: I went through his things and am stealing his drugs. "What are you doing?"

I shoot him a dark and desperate look, charged and feral,

as if I were a predator protecting its fresh kill, and Tyler were my next potential meal. He clocks this immediately, a sheen of horror and understanding in his stare. I am no longer a man; I really am a monster, and I'm ravenous for blood.

"Close the door, Tyler," I say. "Today, I want to forget everything."

Tyler does as he is told, and for the next several hours, we float above this fucked-up world of our own making – finding bliss by consigning to oblivion.

CHAPTER
FIFTEEN

LOLA

AUGUST 4, 2022

"What do you mean he just left?" Ruby sneers.

She hands me another tissue, retrieving the soiled one from my hand. As she crosses the room to place the tissue in the trash can, her shoes click upon the concrete floor; she didn't have the opportunity to remove them before I started crying. I'm always reminded of the raptors in *Jurassic Park* when her stilettos snap like that, like it's a hunter's warning.

I look up at her standing by the rain-splattered window. Even in the relative warmth of my studio apartment, I can't help but be chilled by the rain, by the memory of it when Oscar told me he quit – after he pinned me to a car door. The thought of his body pressed against mine and his eyes daring me to touch him is enough to make my heart stutter.

"Lola, focus!" Ruby says. "How am I supposed to kick this guy's ass if you don't give me all of the details? Like maybe his home address? Credit card number? You have got to give me *something*."

I sniff.

"I don't want revenge, Ruby. I just –" The shuddering cries come boiling up my throat once more. "Oh, god! What should I do? Everything I've done up to this point has just made things worse."

"No," Ruby scowls. "You stood your ground when he pulled you into his celebrity drama. Revenge is sounding pretty reasonable, if you ask me."

I hate when she makes sense. Still, exacting revenge isn't exactly on my list of priorities. All that matters now is that we figure out how to move forward with the gala without Oscar's connections. But that doesn't make it any easier to silence my screaming heart that, even now, beats only for him.

"No revenge – I mean it," I say. Clumsily, I lean forward to snatch up the open wine bottle. I screw off the top, and pour a long, hungry stream of cheap rosé into my chipped mug.

Ruby steals the bottle from my hand.

"I think that's enough," she says. It doesn't stop her from swigging straight from the bottle herself, all without the slightest smear of her crimson lipstick. "Look. If we aren't kicking someone's ass, why am I even here?"

"To support me? Nonviolently?" I plead, looking up at her, eyes glossy with an innocent sheen.

She clicks her tongue.

"Fine. Seems inefficient though."

"I just need to move on," I say. I take in a large mouthful of air and force it down past my lungs and into my gut, as if that might stifle the sourness I feel from even thinking of leaving Oscar in my past. "Just move on and get the funding for my research. And who knows? Maybe there's something in Brandon that I am just not seeing. Things will work out. They have to, right?"

"That's right," Ruby says. "Brandon is a good guy. I wish I knew how to bag one of those for myself. You don't even know how lucky you are."

And there it is: that familiar guilt, the kind that stings every time I remember how much Brandon adores me while I've been pining for my stupid ex-turned-rockstar who would only entertain a relationship with me if it were part of some sordid affair. My logical brain tells me that I am lucky, that things with Brandon are perfect – and they should be, at least on paper. But my irrational, erratic brain – the one that loves Oscar – craves chaos, crumpling up any amount of self respect I might have, just to get the smallest morsel of passion.

"Yeah, really lucky," I sigh, taking a sip from my wine mug.

"Well, god, Lola. Don't sound too appreciative," Ruby scoffs. "Besides, I already told Dad about your new boy toy."

I set my mug down on the coffee table.

"You did what?"

"Dad bets he is handsome," Ruby cackles.

"Ruby! Tino is already confused without your help. Now I'm going to have to do damage control when he asks about my supposedly handsome boyfriend."

"I mean, he is handsome," Ruby points out. "That is, if you're into the whole Paul Walker aesthetic. And besides, you're welcome to tell him whatever you want, but it's not like you ever call or visit."

The temperature in the room seems to shift, as if I am surrounded by the heat of flames and I am choking on smoke.

I mean to call. I mean to visit. I really do. It's just that seeing our dad's mental state getting worse is a reality I'm not ready to face. I love our dad so much that my heart splinters at every fault in his memory. And if he forgets who I am... The thought twists my gut into knots. I can't do it. I can't see him. Not yet.

"I – I've been really busy with this gala," I say.

"More like *busy* with Oscar. Don't try to tell me I'm wrong," she says. "You tell me too much as it is."

My stomach feels as if it's been dropped from the height of the Space Needle.

"Maybe I should tell you less," I say. I cannot meet her gaze. A silence follows that sits like poison, and it's enough to get me to start vomiting words. "Look, I will call Dad. I know I have been a shitty daughter lately, and you need me to step in and take care of him sometimes. Oscar is out of the picture now. I can help."

At least, I hope I can.

Ruby smiles, which clears away the toxicity in the room.

"Lola, it's okay. I wasn't trying to guilt you. You've got a lot going on. I know you'll be there when things calm down. Take a deep breath."

I inhale slowly, filling every crevice of my lungs with air dampened from the rain.

"Okay," I say.

"You're okay?" Ruby tilts her head to examine me closer. "You're sure?"

"Yes," I say, pushing Oscar from my mind. "Everything will be okay."

She claps her hands in quick succession, urging me to rise from the couch.

"Then put that wine down and let's go dancing!"

To be clear, I never feel like dancing, even though I will do it occasionally out of my love for Ruby. But right now, in this moment, while I am on the verge of tears and a panic attack that seems to be building toward a climax, it is the last thing I want to do.

"Ruby, I really don't think –"

"Fine," she acquiesces. "We'll watch a sappy rom com, but don't think for a second that you are off the hook. You *owe* me."

I laugh, but it has a nervous edge. The guilt I feel over damn near everything is seeping into everything else, reminding me that there is so much more that I can, and should, feel guilty about. It's not just my forced feelings for Brandon, or the neglect of my family. It's every decision I have made since Oscar reappeared in my life.

So, maybe with him gone, I can begin to repair my relationships. Except the only one I seem to want to repair is with him. I guess I can always appreciate irony.

Ruby switches the TV to HBO. Neither of us speak another word until she finally decides on a movie. The opening scene begins with a father and daughter talking on the phone, and I swear, I audibly choke on my breath.

Ruby's eyes nearly jump out of her skull as she scrambles for the remote.

"Lola, I promise you, I had no idea –"

"It's fine," I say, trying to steady my breathing. But the breathing is getting shallow and ragged, and my peripheral vision begins to darken.

Ruby clasps my hand in hers.

"Are you sure? You look really pale," she says calmly, but even in this state of panic, I know that she is as fearful as I am.

I don't respond. I can't. I can only inhale sharply and place my free hand on my chest as it rises and falls with each breath. Remembering that breathing techniques can stabilize my nervous system, I count each inhale, each exhale, to four seconds – then deeper, to six, to eight, and then, gradually, it stops. But I know what I must do.

"I have to call Dad," I whisper.

There's no argument from Ruby. She gathers her things and kisses me on the cheek.

"He'll be happy to hear from you," she says. "I love you, Lo. See you again soon."

Ruby closes the door behind her after exiting the apartment. Hastily, I lock it and pull out my phone, my finger hovering over the dial button. Finally, I get the nerve to call.

"Hello?" a woman's voice answers, even though I dialed my dad's cell phone directly.

"Eva," I say. I'd recognize her smoky voice anywhere. "Is Tino there?"

She pauses, I imagine to take a drag of a cigarette.

"He's busy. Can I take a message?"

"I really need to speak to him," I protest. "Whatever he's doing, can you interrupt? It's urgent."

Another pause, then her deep voice crackles into the receiver.

"Urgent? Since when, Lola? Seriously. We haven't heard from you in weeks."

That familiar pang of guilt strikes me once again – a typical feeling during any exchange with my stepmother.

"Eva, I'm sorry I haven't been there. Work has been… challenging," I say, knowing full well that there is no excuse that either of us would accept.

Suddenly, I hear Tino's voice in the background, saying my name as if it were a question in his usual high volume.

"Let me talk to her!" he shouts, then there is a loud shuffling noise, as if he is wrenching the phone from Eva's hand. At last, I hear him close and clear. "Lola?"

"Dad!" I say. I am excited to hear his voice. He sounds well, but I worry about him alone with Eva. She doesn't have a nurturing bone in her body, and if there's one thing he needs right now, it's that. "It's me. It's Lola. How are you? How do you feel?"

"I'm good, Dot. Today is a good day," he says.

"Oh yeah? Why is that?" I ask. It's not often that I hear he's having a good day, not since he started declining so quickly.

"Because I get to hear from my daughter."

That splinter of shame twists inside me. It seems everyone is aware of how distant I have been lately, and the reminder just makes me resent not only myself, but Oscar, as well.

"I'm sorry, Dad. Work's been a mess. My life has been a mess. It's no excuse. I'll visit soon, I promise. Are Eva and Ruby taking good care of you?"

"Don't worry about me. I'm a fighter, same as you. But I am very tired – very, very tired all of the time."

"Ruby mentioned that," I say. "Have you said anything to the doctor?"

"Ruby…" I can hear his brain shifting, as if silent gears were stalling in his head, coming to a full stop before changing direction. "Ruby, is that you?"

My eyes prick and I hold back a sob. Slowly, my own father is forgetting me.

"No, Dad, it's me. It's Lola," I squeak out the words. "Are you okay? Talk to me."

"Ah, Lola," he says, completely unphased. "Today is a good day."

Tears stream down my cheek now, and I press a clenched fist to my mouth to stifle a sob.

"And why's that?" I manage.

"Because I get to hear from my daughter."

I break. Hearing him struggle to carry a conversation without talking in circles is heartbreaking. It's part of the reason I distance myself. I know it's selfish, but this – this cyclical guilt – is excruciating.

I hear Eva take the phone from Tino's hand.

"Maybe it's best you don't call," she says. "He's quite distressed."

"Eva, please," I say. "I need to talk to him."

"Our door is always open, if you can find the time." Her tone sours. "I've got to get him back to bed."

Eva hangs up, and I am left holding my phone in my shaking hand, blubbering as I sink to the floor.

I wish Ruby was still here. She always knows what to say. My second thought is to call Oscar, as if opening Pandora's box would make me feel any better, but I stop myself. If there is one person I should let into my life right now, it's my boyfriend.

God, that feels strange. *Boyfriend.*

Still, I suppose if he is going to play that part, then he

should be here. Who knows? Maybe he'll actually make me feel better.

Through my tears, I type out a text:

I need you.

I send it to Brandon, but in my heart, I know I'm sending it to the wrong man.

CHAPTER
SIXTEEN

OSCAR

AUGUST 6, 2022

"Can you stop being a dick for just one second?" Jacob scoffs.

My blank stare must give me away. I'm coming down from a high – so is Tyler – but I don't want to let Jacob know that. Not yet anyway.

The thing is, I don't want to be a dick. But lately, it seems like no matter what I do, I upset someone. This whole lovesick situation has really gotten under my skin, but I am not exactly great at apologizing, even when I know I am wrong. Call it pride, but I believe it's rooted in deep insecurity instead.

"I don't know. Maybe Oscar has a point," Tyler says.

Jacob rubs his forehead as if his head is aching from dealing with not one, but two drugged-up assholes.

It's grim that I feel closer to Tyler right now than I do to my own best friend. But only Tyler knows the full situation. In a way, that is freeing, at least until I remember that it should be Jacob on my team instead. But I suppose things wouldn't have gotten this bad if I placed my trust in him in the first place and not the drug-powdered hands of Madison and our annoying drummer.

"Tyler, for once, will you please stay out of it," he spits. "It's bad enough that I have to deal with your bullshit all the time, but it seems like now Oscar has stolen your lead role as *the* pain in my ass. Congratulations."

"Jacob, come on," I say, straightening my focus. The euphoria I felt before has quickly morphed into agitation.

Jacob's head snaps toward me.

"Don't," he says, pointing his finger in my face. His face is red and the veins in his neck look like they are about to burst. "I don't know what is going on with you, man, but I know it's not that this guy's been fucking your girl while you pine after someone else."

Tyler sucks in his lips and squirms in his seat on the black leather couch. Fortunately, this is not news to anyone here, but my lack of reaction raises Jacob's suspicion.

"Fuck this," I say, slinging my guitar strap off of my shoulder. I step toward the door but Jacob gets even closer, shoving me backward. I can feel the anger radiating off his body.

"Come on, you stubborn shit," he says. "You want me to be your enemy? You got it."

I don't want to escalate the situation with my fists, but I can't ignore my clenching hand at my side. Jacob and I have fought just two times since we were kids, and both times, he knocked me out. The man knows how to throw a punch, and each time, it puts me in my place. I see no reason why right now would be any different.

In an effort to restrain myself, I try to step around him, but he blocks my exit with his arm.

"We're not done here. Not until you apologize," he seethes.

He knows how difficult that is for me. I want to comply, but there is a mental block in my brain that prevents the words from escaping my mouth.

It's funny because I am actually sorry. I regretted calling his song shit the second I said it. It wasn't even bad. It just reminded me of Lola, whom I am trying – and failing – to forget.

"Jacob," I warn.

He does not want to stray down this path. Neither do I. I'd prefer not to throw a punch just to get my lights knocked out. This is not a fight I can win, especially in my current state.

Tyler gets up from the sofa, trying to wedge himself between me and Jacob. But we are too close, too in each other's faces, to make space for peace.

"Come on, man," Tyler groans. He sets his hand on Jacob's shoulder. "It's not worth —"

Jacob's fist interrupts him, crashing into the side of his face and knocking him to the ground. Immediately, Jacob turns to me, not even taking a second to observe Tyler writhing on the floor beside us.

"Jacob! What the fuck?" I shout.

Don't get me wrong, I have thought about punching Tyler in the face more times than I can count. But even when I found out that he was sleeping with Madison, I couldn't bring myself to do it. And it brings me no joy to see this.

I have to choose my next words carefully; I know I'm next.

Jacob winds his fist back, preparing to strike me. But rather than knuckle up, I simply flinch, curling my arms around my face in hopes that it will stop the blow.

But the blow never comes.

When I peek through my arms, I see Jacob's fuming face, wide-eyed and gritting his teeth as he exercises more restraint than he had with Tyler.

He lowers his fist.

"You aren't worth it," he whispers.

Is it too much to beg my best friend to punch me? At least it would clear the air. This is so much worse. Now, all I can do is beg for forgiveness instead. If only I could bring the words forward.

Jacob spits at my feet as he steps toward the hallway.

My heart races and I feel like I am choking on the sharp shards of a broken friendship. Just as he is about to leave, I splutter an apology like the blood coming from Tyler's mouth.

"I'm sorry," I say.

The words are surprisingly clear, despite my shaking. I've already lost Lola because I didn't want to lose Jacob. Turns out that I could lose Jacob anyway. I fully expect him to keep walking, leaving us behind. Instead, he freezes.

Slowly, he turns around and stares me dead in the face.

"Say it again," he says. The rumble of his voice is severe, demanding compliance.

I may be stubborn, but not enough to ignore Jacob's authority. The man is like my big brother – the closest thing to family that I have, besides Lola. But I guess that's not true anymore.

I fill my lungs with cool air, trying to steady myself. And then, surprising even myself, the words slip out again.

"I'm sorry, Jacob," I say. I cannot meet his gaze.

He nods his head and walks out the door.

I know that he is too upset to fully accept my apology, but a nod is probably more than I deserve. It's a small gesture, one which I understand too well. We'll be okay once he has time to cool off.

Tyler groans. He wipes the blood from his lip with the back of his hand, trying to push himself back to his feet. I rush to his side and offer my hand, which he accepts gladly.

"Thanks for trying, Tyler," I say. "Sorry you got caught up in that."

Sorry? To Tyler? It appears that the floodgates are open. Now, I suppose I can't stop dishing out apologies. Maybe it was the immediate relief I felt when Jacob's stature relaxed, or maybe it was because saying sorry soothed the shame I feel for keeping so many secrets. Whatever the case, I can't ignore the weight of this burden and the way that a simple apology allowed me to set it down, at least for a moment.

And there's no one that deserves my sorrys more than Lola Marin.

I've been so fixated on trying not to lose her again, that I have pushed her away entirely. And there is a simple solution here – to leave Madison and tell Jacob the truth – but I'm not there yet. I feel myself getting closer though.

Regardless, Lola doesn't deserve the vicious vitriol that I've been casting at her since Brandon entered the picture. When I look past the jealousy, he actually seems like a nice guy. If accepting him as Lola's boyfriend means that she is still part of my life, I can do that. At least, I *should* do that. No more fighting. No more fists.

I walk out onto the penthouse balcony, phone in hand, and look out at the Seattle skyline glimmering in the deep darkness that follows dusk. The cloud cover is too thick to see stars, a promise of more rain. And when I listen carefully, the soft sound of water cuts through the din of traffic. It reminds me of Lola.

Before I know it, I have my phone pressed to my ear, waiting for Lola to answer, praying that she doesn't dismiss it. If I were her, I'd ignore my calls, too.

Then, there is a click. The dialing stops and I am met with cold silence.

"Oscar?" Lola answers.

Hearing her breathy voice makes my stomach flip. If I could reach through phone lines to press my lips to hers, desperate and feverish, I would. But I can't do that anymore. I have to use my head. I have to respect her relationship with Brandon and accept that this thing between us is over. But that's okay if it makes room for something new.

"Lola," I whisper. Then, my hand begins to tremble, realizing that this may be my last chance to make things right. "Please don't hang up. I just want to talk."

"I'm done talking, Oscar," she says. "It's always the same conversation. I'm tired."

She's right, but I am determined to prove her wrong, to show her I have changed.

"Then why did you answer my call?" I say. She doesn't respond, but I can hear her exasperated exhale. "I know you don't want to talk to me. I've been a real asshole. But I wanted to let you know I am sorry. If you can forgive me, I'd like to keep helping with the gala."

"And what if I don't forgive you? What then?"

"Then I'd like to help anyway. I was serious when I approached the conservancy. This means a lot to me. It means more knowing that I'll be helping you, too, even if you hate me," I say. And the thing is, I am completely serious. I would dive headfirst into a whale's wide open maw if it meant she got to continue her research. No strings attached.

Lola pauses, then, with a shaky breath she says my name.

"Oscar…"

"Lola, please. You don't have to forgive me," I say. "Just listen to my apology."

"Okay," she says. "I'm listening."

This is unexpected. I'm surprised she hasn't hung up on me yet. My heart is racing and my hands are still trembling as they try to delicately navigate this conversation.

"I am sorry for being a jealous prick. I have no right to be. Brandon is a good guy. I'll stop trying to make us happen and give you the space you need, whatever I have to do to see this through," I say.

"Keep going," she says. Her voice tilts as if she is smirking, and the thought makes my heart swell.

The apologies keep rolling out like ocean tides. "I'm sorry for kissing you. I'm sorry for pressuring you, for guilting you, for being a complete and utter piece of shit. You deserve better. Let me be better. Please…"

"Okay," she says.

I am taken aback. Lola is not one to forgive easily. I have seen her hold a grudge for something as trivial as eating the most heavily loaded chip from a plate of nachos. We were sharing, and I swore that I only took it because it was easier to grab, but she insisted she was saving it to better distribute the toppings onto smaller, barer chips. She has a method for everything and I was oblivious. She gave me shit for it for the rest of the semester.

To hear her forgive me now is actually kind of shocking.

"Really?" I say.

She chuckles. "I didn't say I forgive you, Oscar. But I'll give you another chance."

There it is. No forgiveness after all. That's more like her.

I start pacing on the balcony, overcome by this intense longing to start over and be the good guy for once. It's a lightness in my brain – a far cry from the heaviness I so often feel.

"I won't fuck this up," I say, unable to contain the excitement in my voice. It cracks with delight, but I hope she doesn't notice. "Just tell me what to do and I will do it."

"Fine." Lola lets out a dramatic sigh. "The day after tomorrow, meet me at the marina."

CHAPTER
SEVENTEEN

LOLA

AUGUST 8, 2022

He came.

He actually came.

Oscar saunters toward the dock, wearing his usual leather jacket and weathered white t-shirt. Though the rain has ceased for now, his clothes cling to his torso tight enough that I can make out the grooves in his abdomen. Warmth spreads through me, settling in my core. I try to shake it off, but there's no denying that Oscar Kelly is an absolute vision – even if he *was* an asshole.

Stop it, Lola. He isn't available. You've already been over this.

The skies are clear enough to see the stars, but the sun will rise soon. Before it does, I want to be on the water so I can see the whales breach. They are most active before sunrise and after sunset. Most other boats know this, but don't dare cruise out into the harbor this early in the morning. But I've done it a million times. I know there are things that are much scarier than a dark ocean. It's not the creatures beneath the surface we should fear, but their absence. A still ocean is a dead one.

"Sorry, I'm a little early," Oscar says, approaching the boat.

I gesture for him to board. To me, being early is never a problem. In fact, it's preferable. I haven't actually made it out onto the boat before dawn in a long while. I suppose I have Brandon to thank for that.

"No apology needed," I say. "At least for that."

Oscar balks as if I have stuck him with a knife.

"I deserve that," he agrees. "But I'm going to make it up to you. I promise. Need a hand with the ropes?"

I shake my head.

"No. Thanks though."

It's sweet that he would even offer, but he doesn't know what he's doing. I don't need him getting tangled and falling into the water, just for me to have to save him once again. Call it a control issue, but it's best that he leaves all of the marine and biology stuff to the marine biologist. *Watch and learn.*

I hold the boat steady while Oscar climbs aboard. I follow, letting the ropes loose and starting up the motor. Oscar keeps a respectable distance while we putter out into the harbor, though I kind of wish he were closer. There is a chill against my skin – not just the ocean breeze, but rather a palpable reminder of his distance. I know he is trying to be better, to respect boundaries, but what if the lines I drew in the sand are at war with my heart? I may have scorned him for making advances, but if I am being honest, I actually kind of enjoyed the connection. And therein lies the problem.

We're supposed to be scouting for spouts on the water's surface, expelled from whales' blowholes. So, I maneuver the boat slowly, killing the motor every so often so we can drift in the sea's silence.

"I can't hear anything," Oscar says. "Can you use the underwater mic thing?"

I shake my head as I try to conceal a smirk. He's cute when he's wrong.

"It wouldn't do any good," I say. "Those audios are meant for analysis anyway, to figure out what they are saying and why. Not necessarily *where*. Just listen for the spouts."

A hushed calm sweeps over the water. I can see Oscar

getting antsy. But to his credit, this work requires a lot of patience, and that has never been a strength of his.

"Why do they sing?" he says, finally reaching his limit.

"They're calling to their pods, their loved ones. Mainly to hunt, mate, and evade predators. But I believe they just don't want to be alone. A lone whale cannot survive," I say, though I realize my error. "Well, that's not really true. There is one humpback whale that lives alone, and as far as we know, it's been alone for about one hundred and fifty years."

Oscar's eyes shift from the open water to the laces of his shoes.

"That's a long time to be alone," he says.

I step away from the helm and pace the dock where he sits.

"It's called the 52-hertz whale. The loneliest whale. Doomed to swim the ocean, always calling out for someone, but never reaching them because its songs are in a frequency that the other whales don't understand."

He smooths his calloused hands over the stubble on his jaw.

"That's so sad," he manages. "But I guess now I know what to say when I speak at the gala."

"If you can get through the story without crying like a baby," I tease. I finally stop pacing and take a seat beside him.

Oscar gives me a playful nudge.

"Oh, and like you could, huh?" He looks at me for just a beat too long before tearing his head away. "Yeah, okay. You could. You're stronger than me anyway."

Hands wringing, I can't look away from him. His form and my gaze are caught up in this magnetic pull, one which I am powerless to stop.

"What do you mean?" I say softly.

His eyes snap back to mine with an intensity that melts the thick ice that surrounds my heart. And only now do I feel my thawing, dripping heart free itself from animosity. I can't stay mad at Oscar. I never can.

Then, suddenly, his stare is ripped away and he chuckles.

"You're able to exercise restraint," he says. "Not exactly the kind of person to let your emotions get the better of you."

My breath catches in my throat. If he only knew how much effort it takes to suppress those emotions. I feel like every problem we've ever had together is directly because what I think is in direct opposition to what I feel. My logic can't always come out the victor.

I want him to look at me, and I know he feels my eyes on him, urging him to just shift his eyes from the water and meet me here, in this moment.

I can smell him, like garden soil after a rainstorm, and it unlocks hidden memories I thought I had lost long ago: college days when we would lie in bed for hours after classes, holding and kissing and touching each other, just because even the duration of one class was too long to keep our hands to ourselves. I miss those days. I'd do anything to get them back.

Before my brain is able to listen to reason, I lift my hand and slowly inch it towards Oscar's thigh. But just as I am about to make contact, a low groan followed by the spray of water sounds across the sea's surface. Oscar bolts from his seat and races to the opposite side of the boat.

"Did you see that spout!?" he shouts.

I didn't see it, couldn't, because my attention was fixed solely on him.

"Pretty cool, huh?" I say, rising to my feet. "Just wait. Stay alert."

Golden light spills upon the rippling waves, shimmering flecks reflecting off the water to illuminate Oscar's grinning face. I can see the excitement, the frantic searching of his eyes in hopes that he might catch another glimpse of the whale that's swimming somewhere below.

Then, there's a soft splash of water. We both look in the direction of the noise, toward the horizon, only to see a whale's fluke – fringed in light like a holy halo – slip back into the ocean.

Oscar gasps, turning to me to make sure I saw the same thing he did.

"Wait for it," I whisper.

I steady myself on the bobbing boat, bracing for the breach. The silence that envelops us is eerie, perhaps even painful, as anticipation so often is. There's a pressure building in my chest, and only now do I realize that I am holding my breath.

Just as the anticipation becomes completely unbearable, I can see tell-tale bubbles twenty feet in front of us. Within milliseconds, the bumpy, barnacled nose of a humpback whale bursts from the water, following its behemoth body which slaps upon the surface with a thunderous crack. As quickly as it appeared, its shape darkens and diffuses as it swims far down into the ocean's depths.

I release the air in my lungs. Oscar, however, is frozen.

I rush to his side, stumbling a bit as the boat rocks from the whale's disturbance.

"Hey," I say calmly. "You okay?"

His dark, wet curls are trembling. I can see the water shake from each soaked strand. He doesn't speak – just turns to face me slowly, eyes wide with either awe or horror.

Without thinking, I grip his arm with a light touch, smoothing the leather from his jacket across the tip of my thumb. He looks down at my hand, his brows knotted and twisted in confusion. I feel his stare sweep up my body before meeting my eyes.

There's so much I want to say to him, to *do* to him, that I simply stand there, stunned into paralysis.

And then, there it is: the darting glance toward my mouth. It's quick and subtle, but unmistakable in its intent.

I run my hand up his chest, his pulse quickening under my touch.

"Lola," he whispers, a shaky breath catching on his lips.

Hearing my name on his mouth is enough to make my knees buckle, but I hold myself upright by wrapping my hand around the back of his neck and pulling his face into mine. I kiss him with heated fervor, which he greets without reluctance, his fingers threading themselves in my sea-sprayed hair.

His tongue slips past my lips, smoothing against my own. It tastes like icy peppermint, and I can feel its cool tingle as our breaths collide. He releases a deep moan, the vibration of which radiates down my throat and into my heaving chest. Teeth bite down on my bottom lip, lightly scraping as they pull away.

Oscar slides his smooth lips across my cheek, along my jaw, down my neck. I can't help but gasp.

"Oscar," I pant. His name passes through me like an intoxicating word in a foreign language that I once knew, but have since forgotten. Only now am I familiarizing myself with the language again.

He grips my ass and lifts me off the deck. Flooded with desire and luxuriating in the firm touch of his hands, I wrap my legs around his waist. I want to consume him, to make him mine – until I realize that he isn't.

I think he realizes it at the same time, because his body stiffens while his hold on me relaxes, until he releases me entirely. Though our mouths have stopped trying to devour each other, there's a lingering hunger in our stare. It warns of our intentions, as if one more touch would be enough to light the match that causes our desire to ignite.

But we know we can't go there.

"I can't," he whispers.

His arms drop from my sides, his gorgeous golden-green eyes dropping with them.

"I know," I say.

I reach for his hand, weaving my fingers in his. There's no romance in the gesture. Only disappointed comfort as we navigate these treacherous waters – the ones I swore never to swim with Oscar.

What about his girlfriend? Fuck. And what about Brandon!? I feel like a terrible person, hypocritical to the most extreme degree. How could I forgive myself for admonishing Oscar for kissing me when he's taken, and then doing the same damn thing while I'm taken, too?

"Maybe we should head back," he says.

I note his solemn tone, as if his very voice is weighed down by our guilty consciences.

"Yeah," I agree. "We should."

And just like that, I release his hand and return to the helm, starting the motor and steering us back toward the marina.

I should feel gross: for leading on Brandon, for kissing Oscar, for *enjoying* it.

But I don't.

I only feel the heat between us, static and charged, as if a simple glance would be enough to cast our principles into the open ocean and let them sink to the bottom.

I want him, but I know I shouldn't.

CHAPTER
EIGHTEEN

OSCAR

AUGUST 8, 2022

I am floating. Whether it is from the drugs or the lingering high from Lola's kiss, I can't say. It may have been two days since the incident on the boat, but I cannot get her yearning touch and sweet taste out of my head. I am brimming with both extreme guilt and ecstasy. The battle between them is enough to make my head hurt.

The television flashes bright colors before me and the volume is so high that I can feel the sound radiating from the ground, up my legs, and into my frantically beating heart. Madison scoots closer to me on the sofa, lifting my arm and curling up under it, as if she were an innocent baby bird seeking cover under my wing – except she is anything but innocent. I can't say I am innocent either.

Madison relaxes into me, a soft moan escaping her lips as she settles in. It's suspicious how close she is willing to get, and her docile demeanor betrays her true nature – the one that lashes out, cheats, and blackmails.

"What are you doing?" I ask.

She looks up at me, but her eyelids are so heavy, I doubt she can see me at all.

"Mmm," she coos, wrapping her arm around my waist. "This is nice."

I want to rip her arm from me and cauterize every inch of skin she has ever touched. This is not how anyone should feel about their girlfriend.

The time has come. Somehow, I have to break up with Madison.

"This isn't like you," I say. "What's going on? Why are you being… nice?"

I wonder if she can feel how rigid I am beneath her touch as she traces circles on my stomach with her fingers.

Her voice is a strained whisper, as if she is struggling to stay awake. "I'm always nice."

Lies have a way of sobering me up, and this particular lie is egregious.

"No, you're not, Madison."

She doesn't answer. Instead, her hands speak for her, drifting down my abdomen until they reach the top of my jeans. When her fingers start running against my groin, I inhale sharply.

"What do you mean?" Her lips curl into a devilish grin, but only if that devil was strung out and half asleep.

Though I want to stand up and flee this situation entirely, my body is aroused and immobile. But every touch with Madison feels like a betrayal to Lola. *God, this situation is so messed up.*

I groan in protest, but Madison must mistake it for pleasure, especially when there's a growing bulge in my pants. In some cases, it's mind over matter and I can resist her seductions, but when we are like this – after we have snorted far too much heroin – my mind is weak and everything around me feels so much better. It's like my body forgets whose hands are on me.

Her bitter breath brushes against my ear. "You like that?"

I begin to protest and shake my head, but her hand dips below the denim, making me hiss instead.

Despite how badly I do not want this, my dick is hard in

her hands, encouraging her to free it from my pants and begin pumping.

"Madison," I say. I'm trying to sound stern, but it feels too good for me to be convincing. Her grip tightens and strokes quicken until I feel close to bursting. "Madison, stop, stop, stop…"

Surprisingly, she listens, releasing me from her hands and straightening up beside me. Her eyes flicker slightly, but she still looks doped to hell and back.

"Is something wrong?" she asks.

Oh my, where do I even begin? There is so much wrong between us that it hardly needs to be spelled out.

"Yes, there is." I move myself a few inches away from her. I don't trust that I will be able to say what I want to say if she's touching me. "Of course something is wrong, Madison. *We* are wrong."

"But I love you," she pouts. "Don't you love me?"

Her words are slurring and I am realizing that this isn't going to be as easy as I had hoped. How do you break up with someone when you are both high as a fucking kite?

"Not anymore," I admit.

I brace myself for her wrath, but instead, her eyes close and she reclines back on the sofa. In fact, I'm not even sure if she heard me. So, I repeat myself.

"I don't love you anymore, Madison."

She starts squirming, only able to repeat the same word over and over.

"No… no… no…"

Shit. I should have known this was not the time to do this, inevitable though it may be. I thought maybe she would be more agreeable about breaking up after snorting a line, and perhaps a line of my own would give me courage. While both of those things happened, she is much too high to have this conversation. When she sobers up, I doubt she will even remember.

I rise to my feet and sigh. I can't be around this woman anymore. It's for the best since she is seconds away from falling asleep. So, I drape a blanket over her and call Tyler's name. He's somewhere in the penthouse. If he wants her, he can have her. I don't want this responsibility anymore.

I hope that I will find the courage to revisit this conversation after we both rest and recover, but I know that it means I'll have to reveal my truth to Jacob. Whether I am ready or not, the time has come to let him know.

I am ready to risk everything for Lola. I just hope that Jacob will still accept me.

I can't tell Lola though, not when I am finally earning her trust. But I can't lie to her either. I'll try to be better. I have to be better.

CHAPTER
NINETEEN

LOLA

AUGUST 9, 2022

Dawn flips open a silver compact and smiles at her reflection. There's a piece of arugula stuck in between her front teeth, which she removes with the edge of her fingernail and a horrible high-pitched sucking sound that makes my blood boil. I prefer not to have these meetings over lunch, but she always insists.

"So, you and Oscar went out on the boat yesterday?" she asks, sucking her teeth once again.

I shudder.

"Yes," I say plainly. "He's back to help, so we should –"

As always, Dawn interrupts with the intention of getting far more personal than I would like. "And Brandon? Did he join you?"

Oh god. Does she know?

"No." I swallow. "It was just Oscar."

She smirks. "Popular girl. Does Brandon know?"

"It's not like that," I protest.

"Tell that to Brandon's black eye," she says. "I know how they both look at you. If you aren't careful, you're going to have a big mess on your hands, hun."

Bless Dawn. Sometimes she is an absolute angel, but most of the time, her nose is somewhere it shouldn't be, sniffing for secrets that she can swap for other secrets. It's her social currency.

"I'll be fine," I say with a slight edge. "Oscar is just here to help. He finally thinks he knows what he's going to say during his speech at the gala. I told him about the 52-hertz whale."

"Gets them every time, doesn't it?" she cackles. "I'm still waiting on him to provide the guest list. I know it's a lot to ask, but this is serious, Lola. If this gala fails, the conservancy can't sponsor your research anymore. And then you and Brandon will find yourselves in competition for the same jobs, which as you know, are already too scarce."

"I know, I know," I say. "I'll talk to Oscar. Everything will be fine."

I say everything is fine, but really, it isn't. I leave out the fact that fundraising is her job, not mine, though I am happy to help, especially when it's my career, my future on the line. Without this job, I'll have to open myself to jobs outside of Washington, and then I would be too far from Tino and Ruby – too far to be of any use as the dementia worsens.

"I sure hope so," Dawn says. "I know you think I am being snoopy when I ask about your personal relationships, but please know that I am just looking out for you. I can see the tension between all of you, and it's difficult to watch, waiting for everyone to snap."

"We'll be fine, Dawn. Really," I say.

She gives me a knowing look.

"If you say so. Think about how you're going to juggle their jealousy though," she smiles. "I'd hate for you to get caught up in their drama."

The mere fact that Dawn would say such a thing feels like a veiled threat, even if she doesn't know it. While I would never confess to her what happened yesterday on the boat between me and Oscar, she suspects something and I don't believe for a second that she will keep that information to herself, especially when she is so close with Brandon.

So, I slap on a fake smile and raise my voice an octave, the way friendly people do.

"Thanks, Dawn. I'll take that into consideration."

She breaks her stare and nods, as if she is pleased with her work for the day – even if it was just meddling with my personal affairs. Emphasis on the affair part.

Shit, what am I going to do? I didn't mean to kiss Oscar. I was actually vehemently against it. But something about him changed. He seemed determined to be better, all while appearing completely disinterested in me, which hurt. It's not easy to watch the love of your life drift away, not once, but twice. I guess I was afraid that this was it. If I didn't kiss him right then on the boat, then I would lose him forever. Despite everything, I don't want that.

I regret the next words that spill out of my mouth.

"I'm going to break up with Brandon," I say. Monotone. Emotionless. *God, Lola. You could at least pretend to be choked up about it.*

Dawn's head snaps back to me.

"No," she gasps. "Wait! Is this because –"

I stop her right there. "No, Dawn. Brandon and I just don't work."

"But that boy adores you!" she says. She's clearly more upset about this than I am. Possibly more than Brandon will be when I (eventually) give him the news.

"I know, but –" I draw a blank of all the reasons that we don't work, besides the obvious. Brandon is kind, handsome, and smarter than he lets on. And while he isn't a great kisser, he surprisingly knows his way around my body. Useless when there's no emotion though. Still, I should be holding onto him for dear life, but unfortunately, it's just not enough. "He's just too much, Dawn. I'm suffocating. I want things to go back to the way they were. I want my research partner back."

Dawn clicks her tongue.

"Think about this, Lola. Think really hard. Is this what you want?"

"Yes," I say sternly.

She sighs. "Can it wait until after the gala?"

I know what she is really asking: *Is this going to be a problem for her?* And the answer is that I don't know. Honestly, it probably will, but I cannot be in this relationship with Brandon any longer, not when I can't keep my hands – and my mouth – to myself. As long as Oscar is around, both of us dancing around the notion of getting back together, exercising restraint is an unusual form of torture. It's not fair to me, and it certainly isn't fair to Brandon.

"No," I say.

"Alright," she relents. "Then I hope you're ready for the fallout. This gala is about to get interesting."

CHAPTER
TWENTY

OSCAR

AUGUST 15, 2022

By the time Jacob returns to the penthouse, my entire body has gone cold. I had texted him while he was out getting lunch, sending just four words: *We need to talk.*

He didn't respond right away. Why would he? But it only amplified the fear I feel telling him about the drugs. Based on how much he resents Tyler, it's not a conversation that I am eager to have. Madison blackmailed me though, and if there is one thing I have learned about her these past two years, it's that while promises can be broken, she always makes good on a threat.

While I was waiting, I restrained myself from getting high to quiet the discomfort. I can't tell him this if I am in an altered state; I have to be sober. So, I waited.

After what seemed like a lifetime, Jacob texted me back.

On my way.

No ETA. Just enough words to fuel my anxiety about the imminent demise of our friendship. Now that he is standing in front of me, I don't know if I can do it.

"Hey, what's up?" he asks. But I don't answer. I can't even look at him, even though I know he can sense the tension in the room. "Oscar? You're scaring me."

Jacob's stare burns into me. I have spent so much time

worrying about this conversation that I never considered that when I finally worked up the courage, it would feel so much worse.

"Hey, man," I say. That's all I can manage.

Jacob stalks towards me, both curious and cautious.

"Everything alright?" he says.

He's being gentle about it, but he doesn't need to be. This would be a lot easier if his fist was hovering in front of my face like it was last week. Not that Madison's blackmail isn't enough. It is. That's why I'm here.

"I need to talk to you about something," I say. "Something kind of serious."

Hastily, Jacob takes a seat on the black leather sofa opposite of me.

"Oh, shit," he whispers. "Is it canc–"

"No."

"Is it –"

"No, Jacob. Please. This is hard. Let me talk," I say sternly. Jacob swallows, his stare now practically setting me entirely aflame. "About a month or so ago, I, uh… I started doing heroin… Like, frequently. *Very* frequently." The confession comes out in a choking squeak, but it's all I can do to admit to it at all.

Jacob hangs his head.

"Fuck," he whispers. We sit in silence for a minute, the only sound in the penthouse being the whirring of appliances and the slow drip of the kitchen faucet. Eventually, Jacob reacts the way I had expected. "What the fuck, man? Why?"

"I know," I say solemnly. "It was the night of our last show, on the rooftop. I went to find Madison, and when I found her…"

"She was with Tyler," he says. It isn't a question. He must have known, too, feigning ignorance to protect me. And while he could protect me from the affair, he couldn't protect me from everything.

"She was with Tyler," I agree. "Snorting lines in the bathroom."

"Why did you do it? Why didn't you just leave?"

I sigh. "Because I am a fucking coward, Jacob. They told me to close the door, and before I even knew what I was doing, I was closing the door with me inside, sniffing powder off the folded bill in Madison's hand."

Jacob rubs his face as if he is willing away a migraine.

"And you didn't stop?" he asks.

Shame floods every corner of my body and it feels like drowning.

"No."

He rises from his seat and paces the floor. I can see him trying to follow my logic but it's useless. There is no logic, and that is the problem. I have always been guided by emotion, and I always will be.

"You've got to stop," he says. "This isn't you. You can't be like them. You have to stop, Oscar."

I'm surprised by his calmness. Maybe it really would have been easier if he just punched me.

"I know," I admit.

"And for the love of god, please break up with Madison, man. You're never going to get clean with her around."

I laugh. "Believe me, I've been trying. But I'm breaking things off today. We're done." Jacob smiles. It's only slightly, but it catches me off guard. I didn't expect smiles. "So, we're still a band?"

"For now," Jacob says. "I'll deal with Tyler another time. But you're my brother, and I've always got your back. Blood doesn't determine that."

My chin wobbles, so I suppress what I'm feeling: relief, guilt, and gratitude. All of that can go to hell. Instead, I stand up and slap Jacob on the back.

"Thanks, man," is all I can muster.

Jacob chuckles and pulls me into a big bear hug. "It's all

good. I know that was hard for you. But we'll work through this."

I want to sob on his shoulder. *This guy. What a fucking legend.*

Playfully, he pushes me away, grabs my old, beat up acoustic guitar off the stand next to the couch, and swings it into my hand. "Come on, let's jam before Tyler gets back."

"Alright," I say.

I twist the tuning keys on the guitar, plucking the strings until they sound right.

For once, band practice is as it should be. Just me and my best friend, playing our songs, with no secrets between us.

I want to be better. I am going to be better. Not just for Jacob, but for Lola, too. All I need to do is get Madison out of my life for good.

It's getting late and Madison still hasn't returned to the penthouse. I'm almost worried until I remember - I may not know exactly where she is, but I have a decent guess who she is with.

Tyler.

I wonder what Jacob will say to Tyler, and when. Will we fight like we usually do, or will he kick Tyler out of the band once and for all? For my sake, I hope it's the latter.

As I begin drafting a text to Madison, I hear keys clumsily clang against the lock until I see the door handle twist. I expect a sneakier entrance, but the door swings wide open, putting Tyler and Madison on full display. They're making out and he's carrying her with his hands tightly gripping her backside with her legs wrapped around his waist. They don't even notice I am here.

I want to clear my throat, but I doubt my presence would stop them. At this point, they both know I'm aware of their affair. It doesn't bother them, and by now, it doesn't bother me either. But the longer I sit here, watching them stumble inside, clambering at each other's bodies, I feel like a voyeur. I'm about to cough when Tyler slams Madison against the wall and ravages her neck. Her eyes are closed, but as they start to lift in their dreamy state, they lock onto mine.

"Tyler, stop," she says, tapping him repeatedly on the shoulder.

He doesn't.

"There's no stopping this, baby," he growls.

He bites her neck, making her squeal. But she taps again, exhaling deeply before sobering her tone.

"Tyler, I'm serious. Look."

He turns to see me sitting on the couch, idle and a little brooding. Startled, he gasps and takes a step toward the door as if he is trying to leave.

"Tyler, can Madison and I talk alone?" I say.

His eyes narrow like he is trying to read me, but there's nothing to read. I don't feel anything about this. After a moment of brief hesitation, he staggers down the hallway to his room, leaving me and Madison in the dim light.

She approaches slowly, wiping the corners of her lips with her fingertips.

"Oscar…" she says. Her voice is soft and weak – lacking her usual bite. Must be the drugs, or maybe she actually feels remorse. It's hard to tell when the lamp only lights one side of her face, as if it's illuminating her duplicity.

"Have a seat," I say.

She eyes me with caution, beads of sweat forming along her hairline, making little hairs stick to her skin.

"What is this? Are you ambushing me now?" she asks. I know she means for it to sound snarky, but her nervousness is palpable, as if she already knows what I am going to say.

"It's over, Madison."

I plant the words like I am staking a sovereign flag in the space between us.

A wave of relief washes over her. And then, she's laughing. It's loud and mocking, but every so often, I can hear it crack.

"God, Oscar. Really?" she snips. "I thought we've been over this. Are you ready for Jacob to find out your dirty little secret?"

She expects me to stiffen, but I remain calm and collected.

"I already told him," I say.

Her pupils shrink even more. She's caught in her own trap, unable to grasp for leverage.

"It's not like I need you anyway," she scoffs. "I have Tyler."

I smile, knowing full well that Tyler's days in the band are numbered. It isn't the threat she thinks it is.

"Enjoy it while it lasts," I say. "I'm done here. And so are you."

She stands up straight and stomps a stiletto on the ground.

"What did you do, Oscar? What did you say to Jacob?"

My smile slackens. "The truth."

She huffs. I can't believe it, but she actually huffs.

"Is this because of that girl you've been seeing? That charity bitch?" she sours.

I rise to my feet and stalk toward her with my finger pointed.

"Do *not* call her that," I seethe. "She's not just some girl."

Madison rolls her eyes. "Sure, whatever you need to tell yourself. I wish her luck trying to measure up to this."

Her hand reaches for my groin, slowly rubbing up and down the length of my zipper. I grip her wrist and tear it away.

"That shit isn't going to work. You've got nothing on her," I say. Her hand retreats like she just touched a burning stove.

"I don't care if you stay here with Tyler, but don't even think about coming to my bed when you're bored with him. Like I said, we're done here."

"Fucking asshole," she spits. "I hope she's worth losing everything. If you think I won't talk to the press, you –"

"The press doesn't even know who you are," I say.

Despite the low light, I can see her face flush to a violent crimson. Her mouth tightens into a thin line, gears turning behind glazed eyes.

"They will," she says with finality. Then, she stomps off to Tyler's bedroom.

It feels good to be free of her hold on me. It's a gift that Lola doesn't even know that she has given me, and the weightlessness of it is intoxicating. This should have happened a long time ago, but I was so afraid of being alone – and so was Madison – that it kept feeding the toxic cycle.

Things are different with Lola. She sees me. She isn't interested in fame or optics. Her selflessness permeates into everything she does. All she wants is to save the world, the one thing that gives her anxious mind peace, and I want to help her.

I only wish I were Poseidon himself. Then I could control the tide – protect her precious work. But I know she doesn't need me for that. If her research is funded, she could save the world all on her own.

She can be the goddess of the seas, and I will bow before her, eager to serve in any way I can.

CHAPTER
TWENTY-ONE

LOLA

AUGUST 16, 2022

"He's coming!" Dawn shouts excitedly, tearing her head from the front window of the conservancy. But I think I am more excited to see Oscar than she is.

Or is it dread?

Eight days. It has been eight days since I kissed him, disregarding the fact that both he and I are in relationships – and not with each other. And while I still intend on breaking things off with Brandon, there's little point in rushing it. Oscar has someone, and for one reason or another, he refuses to give her up. I knew that, but I went for the kiss anyway.

Stupid, stupid, stupid.

Dawn scrambles from the window, as if Oscar couldn't see her big green eyes and witchy nose pressed against the glass just seconds ago.

The door swings open, chiming a little bell. Nervously, I flatten the fabric of my impossibly soft, striped shirt and shift my feet around to find a more natural-looking position. But it's no use. I'm awkward as they come, and my posture won't make this conversation any less uncomfortable.

"Hi, Dawn," Oscar teases.

He twinkles his fingers at her, causing her cheeks to pinken. It's brief, like the flicker of a flashing tilefish, but I see it. I'm pretty sure Oscar does, too. He knows the power he yields.

"Oscar," I say. It's far too formal, but it creates some distance between us, halting him mid-step.

"Good to see you, Lola," he smiles sheepishly.

He tousles his gorgeous, thick locks and it's enough to make my knees buckle just the tiniest bit. When his eyes finally meet mine, I have to grip the front desk for support.

Without another word, I lead him to my office on the second floor. Brandon is at a conference in Cape Cod, so while I have the lab to myself, I really hope Oscar doesn't try anything. I don't think my conscience can take anymore deception.

Oscar steps inside the lab and closes the door behind him. As he stalks toward me, my heart sinks to the pit of my stomach. There is a primal intensity in his stare that has me feeling too weak to resist. But just when I think he is going to grab me by the neck and kiss me, he pauses and reaches for my hand.

Reality presses in, and I pull away.

"Oscar, the thing on the boat was – "

"Don't," he says. "That kiss wasn't a mistake. Don't turn me into something you regret."

He reaches for my hand again, but this time, I keep my hand still. My fingers wrap around his, dancing and twisting under his touch. Normally, I would wring my own hands, but anxiously twining them with his is more comforting.

"We can't keep doing this – sneaking around, hiding what we feel. It's not only making me insane, it's compromising everything I believe," I say. "I don't want you to be the guy that makes me forget who I am."

He flinches at my wounding words. Yet, he won't release my hand. He keeps caressing my fingers with his.

"Do you believe in love, Lola?" he says. His voice is low and hushed, and for a moment, I wish I could feel its rumble against my ear. I open my mouth to answer, but no sound escapes except for the littlest squeak. "This thing between us is love. Not the lost love of our youth, but the real thing. I know you, Lola – the real you. I won't ever let you lose that."

"You think I'm the kind of girl that breaks others' trust?" I say.

The corners of his mouth droop and his skin pales.

"No," he says. "I don't think that at all."

"Then why are you trying to make me that girl? Why are you being that guy?" I ask. I retrieve my hand from his, stunned by the insinuation. I cannot in good conscience continue to crumple under his hand.

"I'm not like that, and you know it," he says sternly. "If I was that guy, I wouldn't have *stopped* kissing you – not once, but twice." My mouth snaps shut. "If I was that guy, Lola, I wouldn't have been able to stop myself. I would have taken you right there on the boat."

I swallow. Instantly, I am overcome with images of him ravaging my body and I must confess, it takes every ounce of effort not to let him do it right now in the middle of this lab. In fact, I kind of wish he would. Saying things like that softens my resolve.

But he makes a good point. He has always been the one to resist, even if he did initiate that almost-kiss when I pulled him from the water.

I am shocked into silence.

"I am still in love with you. I always have been and always will. Please, Lola. Stop pretending you don't feel this, too."

My eyes burn, and before I know it, water swells between my lashes, producing a single tear that falls down my cheek.

"How can you say that to me when you are with someone else?" I choke.

Oscar reaches his hand across the chasm I've created between us, his thumb gently brushing the wet streak from my skin. He holds my face between his two colossal, calloused hands and stares directly into my warring heart.

"I'm not with anyone," he says. "Not anymore. The only person I want to be with – that I ever want to be with – is you."

My breathing comes to a halt. I don't think I could release the air in my lungs if it was forced from me.

"What?" I whisper. "When did this happen?"

"Last night," he says.

I can't believe he actually did it. After all this time, whatever was keeping him from me relinquished its hold, and now... now I'm the one that can't seem to break free.

"Why now?" I ask. "What changed?"

"I was being blackmailed," he says plainly. "It doesn't matter anymore. None of that matters if I can be with you. I'd risk it all, over and over, just to be yours again."

He cups my face, eyes burrowing beneath my goose-bumped skin. But even now, he doesn't kiss me. Why won't he kiss me? And why, despite everything I've said about fidelity, am I wishing he would?

"Oscar..." I whisper. My eyes drop to the floor. I can feel my bottom lip trembling until suddenly, it's met with the pad of his thumb brushing against it. "I can't. I can't do this."

Oscar's thumb drifts from my lip to my hairline, brushing honey-brown strands behind my ear.

"Because of Brandon," he says knowingly. It's followed by a sigh, though I can't tell if it was Oscar's or my own.

I nod, solemn in my stature as I remove Oscar's gentle hand from my hair.

"Yes. Because of Brandon."

CHAPTER
TWENTY-TWO

OSCAR

AUGUST 18, 2022

The roads are wet on the way to the marina. The lights from the other cars, though there are few of them, cast a kaleidoscopic glow upon the slick asphalt. With the lack of sleep conspiring to blind me, I have to blink them away and focus on the task at hand.

Lola is waiting for me at the marina, but I don't know how much she wants to see me. The last time we spoke, I held her in the laboratory while she retreated more and more into herself. She feels guilty, as any normal person would. But I'm not normal, and I could care less about Brandon. Still, I don't want to taint this thing between us with more lies before it even begins. She needs to break things off with him, and soon.

There is a lingering fear that, in the end, she will choose him over me and it's enough to send me spiraling. I'm here though, and I am going to prove how dedicated I really am – to her and her work. He may be a marine biologist, too, but I challenge him to love this girl more than I do. He'll fall short every time.

I roll into an empty space and slip the car into park. But I notice that someone is in the beat-up station wagon next to me, sobbing over the steering wheel.

It's Lola.

I whip open the door, leaving it ajar without giving a second thought to the rain beating down on my leather seats. All that matters right now is Lola. I run to her driver-side window and gently tap on the glass. She lifts her head from the wheel, revealing a hollow, scarlet face dripping with tears. Her body doesn't stop shaking.

Jesus Christ. The pain of seeing her this broken is immeasurable. I only hope that it isn't because of me. I'm not sure I would be able to live with myself.

"Lola," I say calmly. "Will you please unlock the door?"

I point at the lock in case she doesn't hear me over the rain pounding on the steel body of the rusted vehicle. The door clicks. I swing it open and wrap my arms around her like a cocoon. She's trembling so hard that I can feel her bones rattling beneath her skin.

"Hey," I whisper, pressing my cheek to her soft, gilded hair. "What's wrong?"

She opens her mouth to speak, but only a tremorous sound escapes before she is wailing again. Her hand reaches for my arm and grips it, beckoning me to hold her tighter. So I do, urging her to stillness.

"Let it out, baby. It's okay. I'm here. Just let it out."

My words just make her cry harder. I pet her head and rock her lightly side to side, the way I would when she got overwhelmed in college all those years ago. I'd find her curled up in a corner of the library, stifling a cry with her hand over her mouth, and I would sit beside her and hold her until the episode passed. I never knew exactly what caused it or how it must have felt, but no one should have to face that alone, especially the woman I love.

After a moment, with my back soaked from the rain, she catches her breath.

"Oscar," she says softly. "I – I don't know what to do."

Though she is speaking now, the tremors won't stop, so I hold her closer and kiss the top of her head.

"Talk to me, sweetheart," I say. "I'm here. Breathe. I'm listening."

She inhales sharply, and then exhales slowly. The air catches in her throat, releasing tapping breaths like morse code. Then she breathes again and again until slowly, the shaking stops. She looks up at me with glassy eyes, dark and sleek like a wet river stone.

"Why do you have to be so wonderful?" she manages.

It feels nice to hear, but it's not why I do it. I need to make sure she is okay.

"If I could fight the things that plague you, I would," I say.

She cracks a smile, sending a flood of warmth throughout my body – enough to abate the cold of the rain.

"Can you fight guilt?" she says. Then her smile disappears. "Oh god, I don't know if I can do this."

"Do what?"

She looks away, her eyes pinned to the lights lining the dock. Her lip quivers. "He's not a bad guy, you know? I don't know if I can break him like that."

My fingers drift to her chin. I tip her face upward to meet mine.

"Do you love him?" I ask.

The silence that follows goes on far longer than I would like. I brace for impact.

"No," she says finally. "The only person I've ever loved is you."

She actually said it. She said *love*, and I know how hard that is for her – not just because of Brandon, but because I know how carefully she chooses her words. She would never say she loved someone if she didn't mean it. And when she does love someone, she says it sparingly.

Not like me.

I will tell her I love her a million times a day if that's what it takes to make her understand that, to me, she is everything.

"You love me?" I smirk.

She gives a small giggle and punches me in the arm. "I'm not going to say it again, Oscar. You know what you heard."

I press my lips together to conceal a cocksure grin. I do know what I heard, but you can't blame me for wanting to hear it again after nearly a decade without it. It is a cool glass of water, and I am a man dying of thirst.

"Alright, fair enough," I concede. "You know I love you, too, right?"

She practically cackles. "Yeah, that's what you keep saying."

I grimace and dip my chin. It's embarrassing how much I love this girl, and she knows it. Hell, the world knows it, or at least they will soon enough.

I peer into her eyes, still misty with tears.

"Are you going to be okay?"

Tears are pooling around her lashes again, but she doesn't look away.

"I don't know," she says frankly. "I've never broken up with anyone before. I've only..." She doesn't finish that thought, but we both know what went unsaid. She's only ghosted someone, and that someone was me. "I'm not good at this, Oscar. I don't know what to say when he gets back to Seattle without completely blindsiding him."

Hearing that makes my skin crawl, remembering all the ways that he has probably touched her, and all the ways that she has let him. She doesn't belong to me – I know this. No one belongs to anyone. But it doesn't stop the pang of jealousy when I am imagining Lola passively pretending to love someone else. I'd do anything for that kind of affection from her, even if it wasn't true.

But the thing is, it is true. She does love me, and that makes me unbelievably lucky.

"Tell him the truth," I say. "That's all you can do. No more lies."

"No more lies," she agrees. "But then he'll know I've been keeping secrets. It's hard for me to admit that."

A familiar pain emerges in the back of my throat. I know exactly what she means. It's why it took me so long to come clean to Jacob, and why I'm still hiding things from Lola. Now would be a good time to tell her everything, but I can't. I just can't. Not when only one minute ago, she told me she loves me. And not when she is about to leave Brandon to be with me. Admitting my addiction risks losing her again, and I can't let that happen.

"Belated honesty is better than none at all," I offer, but the words feel treacherous pouring from my lips.

Her forehead wrinkles as she considers this.

"Yeah, I guess you're right."

She looks down at her wringing hands, which I hold in my own. Searching her face for meaning, I ask, "Do you want me to be there when you tell him?"

She ponders this, too. But when her eyes drift up toward my face, I can tell she's undecided.

"I don't know," she says. "His flight back is in two days. I can't do it until then."

Two fucking days? I have half the nerve to fly to Massachusetts and break things off with them myself. That's two days of limbo, and while it seems painful to go that long without kissing Lola again, I respect it. I've waited ten years for her. I can wait another two days.

"Can I still see you?" I say, hoping to god that she allows it. I can exercise restraint. But I can't let her disappear, not now that a future with her is within reach.

My forehead is pressed against hers, and I can feel the sudden heat as her face flushes.

She swallows.

"Yes, please."

I trace my fingers along the side of her face, remembering every curve with a simple touch. Gliding my thumb over her cheekbones, my gaze softens.

"We'll get through this together. I'm not going anywhere," I say.

She smiles, eyes quickly flicking toward mouth and back up again. It's brief, but time slows just enough for me to catch it. I lick my lips. I want to kiss her – no, I *need* to kiss her. I may not be the most honorable man, but I want to be better. That starts now by resisting every way I want to touch her. I won't do anything she doesn't explicitly ask for.

So, I remove my hands from her hands and face and step back into the rain. The storm was small, and drops of water fall slower now, just small specks that mist the air around us.

I offer her my hand to help her out of the car. She accepts after wiping the final tears from her face with her sleeve.

"You sure it's safe out there?" I ask, nodding toward the dock.

"No," she says. "But it will be soon."

She doesn't let go of my hand, nor do I let go of hers. We hold onto each other as we walk toward the boat.

I'm already breaking my own rules.

CHAPTER
TWENTY-THREE

LOLA

AUGUST 20, 2022

"I can't believe you just went out on the water with him after that!" Ruby's voice chirps. Her voice seems higher when it's blasted through tinny phone speakers. Or maybe she really is that excited. "Just give that dreamy surfer boyfriend of yours my number when you discard him, okay?"

"I will do no such thing," I say. "He *is* back later tonight, you know. Can't you just break up with him for me?"

"Absolutely not. You got into this mess, you can get yourself out."

I sigh. I was joking anyway, but part of me wishes she would actually do it. There's no scenario in which things end well between me and Brandon, especially when he finds out I'm leaving him for Oscar. Oscar's feelings for me are not a secret – he's made that abundantly clear. But my feelings for Oscar? Not as transparent.

My phone buzzes.

Shit. For a second I nearly drop my phone, the vibrations slipping it from my tremulous fingers. Fully expecting to see Brandon's name on the screen, my heart pounds faster when I see Oscar instead. My brain short-circuits. We haven't spoken for two days, not since I told him I still love him. The silence was becoming unbearable, if I am being honest.

I stand immobile and frazzled, gripping my phone tightly in my hand.

"Lola? Everything okay over there?" Ruby asks. "Do I need to come over?"

"It's… It's Oscar," I stammer.

Ruby shrieks so loudly, I almost throw my phone against the kitchen wall.

"Oh my god! What does it say?" she gasps. Her words are bubbly, as if soaked in champagne.

I open my messages, hovering my finger over the unread conversation. I squeeze my eyes shut and tap the thread, flinching as I flick my finger. When I look down at the screen, I am met with a single line of text.

Today's the day. Want to meet for drinks? xo

"Well?" Ruby asks.

"He wants to meet for drinks," I say. "I'm still waiting for Brandon though. I'm not sure it's such a good idea."

"Who cares? Stop wasting your Saturday night talking to me – although I am a goddamn delight – and go have fun. You'll go crazy if you sit here waiting on Brandon all night."

I start responding to his text, though not without hesitation.

"Okay, okay. I'll go, Ruby. Talk to you tomorrow?"

I can hear her try to stifle a laugh. She knows she's right about everything and she revels in it. "You better. Good luck, you little slut. Love you to bits."

I groan and hang up. Sometimes I think she intentionally pushes me into drama for her own entertainment. If I am a slut, then it's because she encouraged it. Can't say I don't kind of love it though. Up until recently, my life has been extraordinarily boring.

Hastily, I type my reply to Oscar.

Just tell me when and where. I'll be there.

I'm first to arrive at the bar. It makes sense though. Oscar would probably be mobbed by fans if he was the one sitting here, alone in public. I'm also chronically early to everything. Hell is a real place on Earth and it involves waiting. I'm sure of it.

Twirling a coaster between my fingers, I look around, hoping to see his face somewhere in the crowd. It's dark inside, with ebony walls and warm, dimmed lights along the perimeter. The music is loud, too, but not so loud that I can't make out the chatter, like the group of men to my left, for example.

One of them, a cheesy looking guy with slicked hair and a paisley button-up, claps another one on the back who's wearing a bucket hat.

"She's hot. Go on, dude!"

I can feel their eyes on me, and then suddenly, Bucket Hat is moving towards me with so much forced swagger that it's actually a little embarrassing.

"Hey, beautiful," he says, leaning on my table.

"Hi," I say in a tone so icy, I'm surprised frost doesn't escape my mouth.

His brow knots slightly before holding up a glass of pink wine. "I got you a drink. Can I sit down?"

"No," I say. "Thanks though."

He pulls out a chair anyway and takes a seat, scooting it mere inches away from me. He leans in toward my face, tilting at my neck and mumbling in my ear. "Come on, sexy. Have a drink with me."

His breath is horrid, reeking of cigarettes and sour beer.

I try to wriggle away. "I really don't want –"

"She said no," a voice booms behind me. The man's face goes sheet white, and his mouth falls wide open. Then, I feel a gentle hand touch the small of my back. It's Oscar.

"You're – you're Oscar Kelly!" the man exclaims. He's too starstruck to move.

Oscar's other arm wraps around me and picks up the wine glass, bringing it to his nose. After a series of deep sniffs, he hands the glass to the man in the bucket hat.

"Drink," he says.

"What?" the man stammers.

"Go on, drink the wine."

Oscar's broad stance is scary, even to me. It's enough that the man starts babbling, unable to get a word out. I bet he wasn't expecting to be confronted by a celebrity while trying to pick up girls at the bar.

"I can't, I uhh… I don't really like wine that much and –"

"Oh, yeah? She doesn't like drinking roofies either," Oscar spits. It's enough to make the man choke. "Drink the fucking wine or I'll knock your teeth out."

The man tries to leave, but Oscar grabs him by the collar. Trapped, Bucket Hat grabs the drink and sips at it.

"All of it," Oscar says. His eyes are bright and wild in the dim light of the bar. He's not bluffing.

The man then chugs the entirety of the wine glass, and slams it on the table so hard that it cracks.

"I did it, man. Can I go?" he pleads.

"Ask them," Oscar says, nodding at security, who is bee-lining through the crowd towards our table. "Now, get the fuck out of here."

He gives him a hard shove, causing him to stumble. Gathering his feet and composure, Bucket Hat makes a run for it, but security grabs him by the wrist and drags him toward the exit. The other men, including the one in the hideous paisley shirt, are also removed from the premises.

"Oscar," I say breathlessly. "How did you know?"

"I saw them spike the drink when I was looking for you," he says. "When I saw that you were the intended target, I thought I was going to have to kill a man."

I am frozen, unable to move past the fact that I almost got drugged. But every time I need help, every time I am in danger, Oscar is there to save me – the lead singer of The Unadored himself.

"Thank you," I say, air catching in my throat.

Oscar smooths the hair out of my face and leans my head against his chest. It's warm and inviting, and he smells like rain and wet earth. I want to melt into him. In fact, I start to fall deeper into his hold until my phone illuminates on the table. I see a flash of Brandon's name and for a second, I think I might vomit.

He's back.

Oscar sees the screen, too, before picking the phone up off the table and placing it in my hand.

"You can do this, Lola. I'm right here, and I'm not going anywhere."

His smile is gentle, a balm to my electric nerves as I tap to answer the call.

"Brandon," I say, trying to conceal my surprise.

"Hey, Lo. My plane arrived early, and I was thinking – what's all that noise? Are you at a *club*?"

Oscar looks at me, the corners of his eyes wrinkled in concern. Then, he takes in a large mouthful of whiskey from his glass. Wiping his mouth, he glances at me once more, but this time his hazel gaze is urging.

"No – well, yeah, kind of?" I say, not turning my eyes from Oscar. "Brandon? Can we, umm… I need to talk to you about something."

I can hear the sharp intake of breath through the phone, even with the music surrounding me and the din of dozens of conversations.

"I don't know how to say this, Brandon. I just…" I sigh so hard that I think I lose at least a few inches of height when my body sags. I rub my forehead to alleviate the ache in my brain. "I think we should just go back to being friends."

I squeeze my eyes shut and time slows. I know the

answer: he'll say no, and just like that, my best friend will be gone.

"Did I do something wrong?" Brandon murmurs. His voice cracks with pain, and it's enough to make me want to call the whole thing off.

I can't bear hurting him like this, but an encouraging caress up my spine gives me strength.

"No, of course not," I say. My words are spilling out faster now. "You and I make a great team, as friends. My heart isn't in this, Brandon, and it isn't fair to keep giving you hope. You have to understand that I can't keep lying to you. I'm sorry."

"Lying?" Brandon asks, his tone soured. "Lying to me about what?"

Shit. I didn't mean to say that part. He would have figured it out sooner or later, but I thought I could spare him the details. Now, I have exposed myself, and the only way out is through honesty.

"I kissed Oscar," I wince. "I... I still love him."

Silence. Deafening silence.

Then, as Oscar sets his empty glass on the table and squeezes my shoulders, I realize that there is no easy way out of this. Brandon and I will never be friends. Not anymore.

"Okay," he says.

"Okay?"

"Yeah," Brandon sighs. "I suspected something was off, but I didn't think... I didn't think you would..."

My eyes prick. I can feel tears start welling in my eyes.

"I'm so sorry, Brandon. You deserve better than this." Oscar looks at me and then rolls his eyes doubtingly. "I'm so, so sorry. This is for the best though. You'll find someone –"

He cuts me off. "It's fine, Lola. I will always have feelings for you, and I don't wish you anything but happiness. Just don't let him hurt you, okay?"

"Okay," I whisper.

"Take care of yourself, Lo. I'll see you on Monday."

Promptly, Brandon hangs up. Our friendship is over, and I'm the one that ruined it.

And yet, it's weird that after all of the ups and downs of the last month or so, Oscar and I are finally free to be with each other. And though I am sad about hurting Brandon, I still feel a gathering lightness. I know in my heart that now, moving forward, things might be okay. That's what happens when you liberate yourself with the truth.

Oscar rubs my back.

"I know that wasn't easy," he says. "Thank you."

I sniff.

"For what?"

"For choosing me."

As if I had a choice. Oscar is part of me. Even after ten years apart, he still holds my heart, and I'm not sure if I can ever get it back.

"Oscar, I would choose you a million times over."

He chuckles, brushing a strand of my hair behind my ear.

"What do you say? I grab us a few more drinks?" he asks.

"Yeah," I say, drying my eyes. "I'd like that."

He kisses my cheek and walks to the bar. And I... I am in way over my head.

Just don't let him hurt you...

Don't worry. I won't.

CHAPTER
TWENTY-FOUR

OSCAR

AUGUST 22, 2022

When my eyelids lift to see the glow of diffused morning light behind drawn curtains, I can feel that things are different now. For once, the day seems full of possibility, and the temptation to numb myself is minimal.

It's only been a day or so since Lola broke things off with Brandon. She seems apprehensive about everything now, as if she deserves to be miserable, but I want to show her that it's happiness she deserves instead. I need to transform the knots in her stomach into butterflies, the frantic pounding of her heart into steady beats, and the pang of guilt into waves of pleasure. She is owed nothing short of bliss.

I rip the blankets from my body and swing my legs out, stretching as I place my feet on the cool floor. The sensation is kind of exhilarating, or maybe my excitement stems from the fact that today, I will surprise Lola at the conservancy.

Brandon will be there, no doubt, but he is fully aware of the situation. In the end, nothing could keep Lola and I away from each other. We are two bodies of water that always meet, my rivers coursing into her ocean – an inevitable pairing that neither Brandon nor Madison could keep apart.

After a hot shower and spending way more time picking

out a shirt than I would care to admit, I am grabbing my keys and heading out the door.

My future – our future – together starts now.

———

"Wow, we really can't keep you away, can we?" Dawn jokes, greeting me in the lobby.

I laugh. "Not a chance."

Dawn eyes me up and down before sucking her teeth.

"You're looking for Lola, I'll take it."

Out of the corner of my eye, I can see Brandon's form pausing in a doorway. It feels like he is taking aim, and I am stuck in the crosshairs.

I am used to being stared at; it comes with the fame. But the way that Dawn and Brandon look at me is far more intense. My intentions are as plain as day, and their disapproval is palpable.

In my discomfort, all I can do is look away and nod.

"She's in the lab," Brandon says. While it sounds friendly on the surface, knowing what I know, the words are laced with an unfathomable animosity. And when I look him in the eye, I can see hellfire in his stare.

"Thanks, man," I say cordially.

But he knows better. For Lola's sake, we seem to have agreed on a truce. However, I can't help but feel like I am one misstep from inviting his fury.

Still, he doesn't scare me.

Without breaking his gaze, I step around the front desk and toward the stairs to the lab. I won't be intimidated by him. Nothing, and I mean nothing, will keep me from Lola. Not even meatheads like him.

I ascend the stairs to the second level, cross the hall, and gently knock on the closed door to the lab. It has a small window, through which I can see Lola spellbound by data on her laptop. But she looks up, and the way she lights up, I swear it's like seeing the sunrise with her for the first time.

She skips to the door, swings it open, and wraps her arms around my neck. I hold her tightly, afraid that if I relax for even a moment, she will slip through my fingers once again.

"Oscar!" she squeals in delight. "What are you doing here? I wasn't expecting you today." She steps back to look me over. "Nice shirt, by the way. Green suits you, with fleur-de-lis, no less. What's the occasion?"

I smile. *Smart girl.* That's one of the things that I appreciate about her – she notices everything. She can detect even the most seemingly insignificant details. That's probably why she is so good at her job.

"I actually wanted to ask you something," I say.

Her smile drops and she eyes me with suspicion.

"Oscar…" she warns.

Playfully, I get down on one knee and hold her impossibly soft hand, gazing up at her. It takes every morsel of self control I have to not burst out laughing.

"Lola Marin," I say. "Will you –"

"Stop. This is insane. Please don't –"

"Go on a date with me tonight?"

She lets out a huge breath and crouches to the ground. "Jesus Christ, Oscar. You scared the shit out of me."

I laugh. It was a mean joke, but I couldn't resist. We used to joke around like this all the time in college. I guess I wanted her to remember how we were back then, to let her know that even though a decade has passed, I'm still that goofy guy with the guitar.

"Get up," she says, slapping my shoulder.

"Is that a yes?"

I rise to my feet and place my hands on her hips, rolling my thumbs along her skin, exposing her midriff just above the band of her pants.

"I don't know," she teases. "Would *you* go out with *me* if I did something like that?"

"Is that your way of asking me out, Miss Marin?"

She tries to give me a flirty shove, but I hold her closer, touching the point of my nose to hers. She exhales and relaxes into me.

"Tell me more about this date."

I plant a kiss on her forehead and release her, stepping back into the hall.

"I'll pick you up at your place at seven. Look out for a limousine," I say softly.

Her eyes grow large and fearful.

"A *limousine*? Oscar, come on. Isn't that a little much?"

I keep stepping backwards toward the top of the staircase, grinning like an absolute idiot. An idiot in love.

"Seven o'clock," I say.

And with that, I turn away and march down the steps, leaving Lola confounded, yet undeniably intrigued.

CHAPTER
TWENTY-FIVE

LOLA

AUGUST 22, 2022

I don't get ready for dates. Not like this, anyway. The most I've ever dressed up for a man is by putting on my cleanest nylon pants (typically with a drawstring waist) and a less than clean fleece. I might even go crazy and accessorize with a carabiner.

Up until now, that is what Oscar has seen me in: what some might call *camping-chic*. And that thought makes me utterly embarrassed, especially considering he was dating an actress. I bet she wouldn't be caught dead with a sunburned nose and an ill-fitted booney hat. And yet, that is normal for me.

But tonight, I'm trading hiking boots for high heels.

Ruby stopped by to lend me some of her fashionable clothes, leaving me with a black cut-out jumpsuit that not only exposes the side of my ribs, but also has a plunging neckline that still accentuates my small breasts. That, coupled with skinny silver bars for earrings and a dainty silver necklace, make me feel like maybe I could walk the red carpet myself. It isn't so garish that I feel like a clown. It's comfortable, simple, and suited to me. At least, I hope it is.

I check my form in the mirror one last time before slipping on the sparkly, strappy heels that Ruby lended me. They remind me of dappled moonlight, and though they add an extra two inches to my height, they aren't so high that I'll instantly twist my ankle – not like Ruby's usual four-inch stilettos. I make a mental note to thank her for her mercy later.

I lock up my apartment and take the elevator downstairs to the lobby. The contrast between these clothes and the sullied carpet makes me second-guess myself. Maybe this is a bad idea. I forget that Oscar is this famous, high-society rock-star now. It's a far cry from the grease-stained t-shirts and broken-down acoustic guitar of our youth. Things change. But perhaps not *too* much.

I just hope that I am enough for him.

Through the rain-battered window, I watch as a long, black car pulls up to the curb. The backseat door swings open, revealing an elegant leather shoe, a tapered gray pant leg, and a slender thigh. I was once familiar with seeing those thighs in ratty skinny jeans. These slacks aren't as tight as those jeans, but the way it clings to Oscar has me worrying for the safety of his seams, and the sanity of every woman that looks at him with thirsty eyes, including me.

He enters the lobby with a gravitas that is entirely new to me, fame dripping from his gray suit and black tie. Still, beneath the glamor, I can sense the kind, humble man I've always known.

"Hey, Lo," he smirks. He doesn't approach me. Standing on the opposite side of the lobby, he slips his hands into his pockets and kicks his foot sheepishly as he eyes me down. "Would you like to go for a ride?"

The air between us crackles. Between me eyeing him in his tailored suit and his gaze gliding over me in my silver heels, it's a wonder that lightning doesn't strike right here in the lobby.

"In that old thing?" I tease.

Oscar looks back at the car and chuckles.

The limousine is far from old. It appears to be a brand new stretch Cadillac. Still, I am not accustomed to luxury. My car doesn't even have working air conditioning. So, to put myself at ease, I have to give him a hard time. Making jokes is the only way to level the field.

"Yeah," Oscar says. "Well, it's the best I've got. Are you ready?"

He outstretches his hand, beckoning me to cross the tiles and take it. I hardly have the chance to consider it before my feet are clumsily stepping toward him.

His fingers weave through mine like silk thread. In fact, they nearly dwarf my hands in his grasp. They don't release me until we pull up to the restaurant.

When we arrive, I am astounded to find that the restaurant isn't on the street level. Up until now, I was under the impression that all food establishments were always located on the street for easy access. And that may be true for somewhere like a café or a gastropub.

This is none of those things.

Instead, Oscar knocks on a big, metal door, which slowly creaks open for him, slow to move due to the sheer weight of it.

Taking my hand, Oscar leads me inside a narrow hallway that gradually opens into a wide, lavish foyer lined with sparkling elevators. Attendants stand near each elevator door wearing uniforms reminiscent of ones I've only seen on flight crews.

Fancy.

"You know, I'd be just as happy with a Big Mac," I think aloud.

Oscar chuckles. "You showed me your world. Let me show you mine."

An elevator attendant smiles at Oscar, gesturing for us to step inside. He holds the door to ensure my safety before following both of us into the elevator and pressing the button to the top floor.

"What is it with you and rooftops?" I tease.

"While you look down into the sea, I look up into the stars," Oscar says. "I enjoy being humbled by finding my place in infinite space. It's comforting."

"Doesn't it make you feel small?" I ask, fumbling nervously with my fingers the higher we ascend.

"No smaller than the ocean does. Inner or outer space, it's all the same."

I agree. In this world, I've never felt smaller.

The elevator dings, doors sliding open to reveal thousands of fairy lights suspended below a glass canopy to shield us from the rain. There is the faint, yet distinct sound of drops colliding with the glass, which soothes my anxiety just a little. It makes me feel more at home, reminding me that even though I have stepped into Oscar's world, I never left home at all. I am still here in Seattle. It's a feeling reinforced by each pat of the raindrops above.

When I look up, I can see the evening's first emergence of stars twinkling. Oscar is right. While I do feel small, strangely, I'm okay with it. Because within my reach is another galaxy, one with which I am desperate to merge – and I am trapped in his orbit.

We cross the open space of the rooftop as the host leads us to our table, moving through muffled voices as people with far more fame and money than I will ever know carry conversations which I will never truly understand.

Oscar pulls out a chair and urges me to take a seat before taking his place opposite of me.

"So, what do you think?" he says excitedly.

"It's lovely. But you know you don't have to impress me, Oscar."

His cheeks redden.

"I had spent so much time searching for you. And now that I have you… You can't fault a man for trying," he says, eyes lifting to mine. "I know you'd accept less, but you shouldn't have to."

Oscar reaches across the table, palms open and begging me to place my own palms in his. Muscle memory kicks in and I grant him my hands, as if the last decade never even happened. His touch is surprisingly natural, familiarity fusing us together with an electric current that, even now, sets my core ablaze.

The waiter comes to take our orders, which I accomplish with my usual lack of grace, unable to pronounce any of the French words on the menu. But Oscar doesn't judge. His gaze is only filled with admiration, and as the night progresses, it becomes harder and harder to ignore. Even harder not to reciprocate.

"Are you going to stare at me all night?" I ask, not accustomed to this level of attention. At least, not since I left all those years ago.

"Will you let me?"

"Why?"

Oscar's hungry eyes scan me up and down.

"I'm memorizing you. The new you. The *real* you."

My stomach flutters. "And what could possibly be real about me at this moment?"

Oscar simply laughs.

"I'm serious. What about me in fancy clothes and strappy heels screams authenticity?"

"Because," Oscar says. "You're not impressed by this, and I love you for it."

The flutter in my stomach moves to my chest. Oscar's deep and prolonged stare is piercing holes in my armor, and I am seconds away from waving a white flag in surrender.

Averting his gaze, I take a long sip of my wine and push

the lamb shank around on my plate.

"You're nervous," he points out. "Why?"

"Because you're making me nervous. This," I say, gesturing to my food, to the wine, to the restaurant, "makes me nervous."

"You want to leave," he says.

I nod.

"You want a Big Mac?"

I nod again.

"You want to get out of those clothes?"

I look up. Oscar is ravaging me with his focused hazel eyes. It sends a jolt through me, straight to my center.

"Let's go," he says, urgent and severe, as if continuing to watch each other from across this white linen table is going to make both of us combust.

I snatch my handbag and quickly rise to my feet. Oscar follows, his hand on my hip, propelling me toward the exit with burning haste.

When we reach the elevator, he slips the attendant a large bill and pats him on the shoulder.

"We've got this one," he says.

We step inside the elevator alone, and before the doors even finish closing, I am pressed against the wall with his mouth on mine. And it is everything I wished it to be.

The elevator begins to descend as Oscar weaves his fingers through my hair, tugging at the roots to tilt my head backwards, his lips and teeth scraping against the side of my neck.

"Oscar…" I breathe. "What if… the elevator…"

Words come out in waves, interrupted by kisses and moments of longing so severe that even Oscar can't help but moan against my mouth. The vibrations send a shock through my system, overloaded with desire.

Without even looking, Oscar slaps the emergency button on the elevator wall, just inches away from where I am pressed. The elevator comes to a halt, buying us at least a little bit of time before security comes to free us.

But Oscar's hands are already heavy at work to free me, at least from my clothes, slowly slipping the jumpsuit from my shoulders and peeling it down my frame until I am standing before him in only my underwear.

"Fuck…" he rumbles.

If I'm not mistaken, his eyes look a little glossy as they scan me up and down, absorbing every freckle, every angle, every pore.

His rough tenderness charges me, makes me overcome with want.

And I want him.

I have only ever wanted *him*.

Hastily, I clamber to get his suit off, tearing the jacket from his broad shoulders and fumbling with his belt so I may free his erection from his briefs.

Once it is liberated, I can feel the thick length of him move against my stomach. Oscar grips me by the back of my neck and growls in my ear.

"Please, Lola. Let me love you. Right here, right now. Please…"

His voice is low and almost sorrowful, but I understand why. I feel it, too. The love we thought we'd lost is right here, between our bodies. After all this time, after all that has kept us apart, we are here in this elevator together: trembling, vulnerable, and hot with lust.

And the clock is ticking. We don't have much time. But we need this – both of us – in order to mend the wreckage in our pounding hearts.

Oscar's hand falls to my breast. His fingertips capture my nipple and pinch so hard that I release a loud yelp. Then it falls lower, tracing the sides of my abdomen, and lower still until his fingers find my slit. Slipping between the skin, his finger presses and rolls around my center like a pearl bead.

I gasp. The friction of his callouses brings me to the edge, causing me to roll my hips and grind into his hand.

"That's it, baby," Oscar growls. "Good girl."

With those two magic words, I lose myself in his touch. The ache in me is growing, getting closer and closer to an inevitable crescendo with each caress of his thumb against my clit.

Then, he thrusts a finger inside, curling it against my inner walls, causing my legs to quiver. I buckle into his hand, which only drives his dancing finger deeper.

"Oscar," I whimper.

"Tell me what you need," he says, unsheathing his hand.

I feel like the elevator is spinning, and my eyes pinch shut as the world around me darkens. I can only squeal one word.

"Condom!"

Briefly, Oscar releases me to grab a condom from his pants pocket. He tears at the wrapper with his perfect teeth and slides the protection onto his cock. I can't stop watching, my mind flooded with memories of all the times we've been together, each time better than the last.

His mouth catches mine, hands cupped around my face and pulling me closer against him. I let out a soft, muffled cry against his lips, which he welcomes with a playful bite and a swipe of his tongue.

"Please," I beg. "Please fuck me."

He moans and shoves me harder against the wall, as if he was waiting for my explicit permission. Then, wasting no time, his tip slides against my slickness until suddenly, with one hard thrust of the hips, I am impaled by him.

"God, I've missed you," he roars.

I wrap my leg around his fit waist and throw my head back, squealing in ecstasy. The darkness lifts from my vision, and I am alive – so painfully and delightfully alive that each nerve ending in my body activates at once and I am aware of each curve, each vein of his length inside me.

Oscar's hand drifts along my raised thigh, gripping my ass as he sinks into me over and over, deeper and deeper, until we both feel my walls contract.

"Tell me what I am," I cry out.

"Mine," he says, his voice rich and thunderous. He repeats himself with each deep thrust, groaning with his lips resting on the shell of my ear. "Mine, mine, mine."

My toes curl and I cling to him even tighter.

"Oh, god! Oscar," I exhale. "Now. Please, now."

Instantly, I feel the pulsing in me and he cries out, so loud that I can't even hear the echo of my own shriek as I pull him in deeper with my clenched walls and bucking hips.

The storm gathers between my thighs as pleasure peaks, radiating from my core like tendrils of lightning flickering from my fingers to my toes. I'm caught in a vortex, whirling off the ground and into the clouds as I am consumed with all emotions at once: sad, glad, satisfied, and greedy. And loved. So very loved.

The vaulted door to my grief slams shut, and finally, I feel forgiven.

Oscar presses his lips to my forehead and holds my quivering bones in his stable possession. But he does not remove himself. We stand like this, panting and disheveled, for as long as we can bear the silence, which is soon interrupted by the sudden lurch of the elevator.

Before I begin to panic, Oscar leans down to retrieve my jumpsuit and offers his arm for balance as I dress myself as quickly as my shuddering limbs will allow me. He is barely able to tie off the condom and stuff his erection back into his briefs before the doors of the elevator inch open.

"It's okay, folks! Let's get you out of –" As the doors open, the security guard freezes at the sight of Oscar securing his loud, clanking belt buckle. "Oh, excuse me. Umm… that's, that's…"

Throwing his jacket over his shoulder and grabbing my

hand, Oscar pulls me out of the elevator. We sprint through the lobby, laughing and stumbling on wobbly legs.

When we are finally outside, we are greeted by a torrent of rain crashing upon the pavement. It is dark and the headlights of passing cars create a kaleidoscopic pattern of red and white lights in the splashing puddles.

"Where are we going?" I ask, catching my breath.

He squeezes my hand and twirls me around until I fall back into his chest.

"Still want that burger?" he smiles.

My cheeks burn hot against the cool rain. "You were serious about that?"

"Of course I was," he says, as if there was ever any doubt. He twists me around to face him and gently swipes the gathering rain from my lips with his thumb. "My girl gets what she wants, always."

My throat swells as I choke back tears. This is the man I left, and somehow, fate brought us back together. I didn't even realize how broken I was until he returned. Now that we are here, holding onto one another on this street, in this moment, I don't know how I ever let him go. The thought of losing him again is almost too much to bear.

He presses his lips to mine, tasting the rain drops that drip from my mouth, until we are interrupted by the flash of a camera. The light is blinding and the rapid click of photos from the growing hoard of paparazzi around us is overwhelming.

"Come on, I think there's a McDonald's on the next street," he says, gripping my waist and pulling me away from the commotion.

We dash away, kicking up our feet as we splash down the wet sidewalk.

I simply laugh, "Lead the way."

CHAPTER
TWENTY-SIX

OSCAR

AUGUST 23, 2022

A gentle dawn breaks, beams of light bursting through the small windows of Lola's apartment. Warmth from each raindrop prism caresses my skin as they move from one corner of the bed to the other. I can feel it through the weightless cover of the sheet that envelopes us. It smells like her. Everything does. Sea salt with a hint of vanilla – simply intoxicating.

Her arm drapes over my stomach with her head nestled against my chest. I try to still my breathing and the fierce pounding of my heart so I don't wake her, even though I am tempted to brush back the soft strand of golden hair that falls over her face, only made more beautiful in the delicate glow of sunrise.

Holding her asleep like this fills me with this strange feeling, both familiar and new, like the love we once felt for each other has grown. The difference that time and space has made, only to bring us back together, has created this overwhelmingly expansiveness in my chest – the chest where her head now lies.

My daydreams become too much, and my breath sputters. Water is pooling in my eyes and I pray the teardrops won't fall on her. But praying is useless when the goddess I worship is already here, wrapped around me. The tears swell, and like a dam breaking, once they fall, I cannot stop.

Lola's eyes blink open, but as she slowly wakes to understand what she is seeing, what she is feeling, my deity's hand cups my face and pulls me into a divine kiss.

"Oscar," she whispers. "What's wrong?"

I wipe my eyes. So fucking embarrassing.

"I never thought…" My throat constricts. "I never thought I would get to be with you like this again."

She smiles while her eyes scan me, searching for wounds. But all the wounds she is looking for can't be seen. They exist within me, and finally, they are beginning to heal.

"I didn't either," she says. "But we're here now. I don't want to keep thinking about the past. Not when I am happy with you in the present. It's okay."

She's right. The only way to move forward is to let go of our pasts. Still, there is this nagging inside me, a deep-seated anxiety I can't seem to release. In fact, I am beginning to feel sick from it, and I know the only way to ease the discomfort is to sit with it, suffering until it passes, or to turn to the substance that's been sustaining me.

Heroin.

I'll need to leave soon either way. It's not something that I would willingly expose Lola to, and while it is eating me alive to keep this secret, I can't risk losing her with the truth. But there is no future that includes her *and* the drugs. Eventually, I will have to choose. I just hope I'm wise enough to choose light over darkness.

I can't think about that now. It's too much. Instead, I cradle her head and pull her into my chest, trying my best to breathe.

"Remember when –" I start.

But Lola cuts me off.

"Don't," she says. "Please. It hurts. I'm not the same girl I was then, and you aren't the same guy. I love you, Oscar. I always have. But I can't just pick up where we left off. I need a new beginning. I need you to get to know the new me, and for you to let me know the new you."

My hand freezes on her bare, silky shoulder.

"The new me?" I say.

Thinking about dissecting my life that way, before she left and when I found her again, cuts through me. I know that she loved me then, even if she left. I don't think she would love the new me, not if she knew the truth.

"Yeah," she says. "You know what I mean. I want to take my time, peel back your layers."

My body turns from burning hot to frigid ice. She can peel back the layers, and I will let her, but what will happen when she finds the rotten center?

I am pulled from my fears when she places a soft kiss on my neck.

"Can I start with this layer?" she asks playfully, lifting the bed sheet away from my groin.

Nervously, I laugh, but sure enough, I am calmed as her fingers trail down my stomach, slowly and purposefully.

"Baby, you can start wherever you want," I whisper with shaky breath.

She traces the textures down my length. Sharply, I inhale.

"Want to know what I think?" she says.

"Yes," I moan.

"I think I already like what I see."

I look down at her through my fluttering lashes, overcome with desire, and caress the edges of her face.

"Keep digging," I dare.

She slides down the mattress, her gorgeous mouth sneaking into a smirk. And then, without wasting another second, it is wrapped around me.

My body quivers and I can't help but whimper, her name falling from my lips.

"Lola…"

I relax into her, but I am afraid to release.

She is determined to dig straight to my molten core. But I know once she does, it is her who will get burned. And I can't stomach the thought of it.

I need help.

Please, God. I need help.

I beg the heavens for strength, but Lola's tongue drags up my shaft, reminding me the true source of my faith.

"God damn," I murmur, guiding her head with my trembling hands.

And then, I am raptured.

CHAPTER
TWENTY-SEVEN

LOLA

AUGUST 25, 2022

"So, I've gone ahead and reserved the space at the Emerald," Dawn explains, licking her fingertips to turn through her stack of papers on the conference table.

"When?" Brandon asks sternly. "I hate to put a rush on this, but we are kind of running out of time."

He is sitting next to her with his head turned away from me. We've hardly exchanged words since the break up, and with Oscar here with his arm around the back of my chair, my thoughts are running rampant with all the possible ways Brandon wants to hurt him – hurt *us*.

I sip nervously on a cold glass of water. Anything to keep my hands busy.

Dawn peers through her reading glasses at one of the papers. "Looks like we are booked for September 29th."

I nearly choke on my water. Sputtering, I say, "So soon?"

Oscar smooths his hand on my back to soothe me.

"Dawn and I talked, and given the situation, we thought it best that we host the event as soon as possible," he says. "It was either a month from now or a year."

She nods. "Lola, honey. The funding for your research is nearly gone. We need to move on this or miss our chance entirely."

"But there's so much to do," I protest, even though I know in my gut that they are right. I don't have the luxury of time. "What about the guest list? The invitations? The catering? Oh, god. And the speech!?"

Oscar takes my hand and squeezes, urging me to look at him and collect myself. When I meet his eyes, my heart rate slows. But only a little.

"I am helping with the guest list. Dawn will handle invitations and catering. You and I can handle the presentations. We got this, baby. You and me," he coos, stroking circles into my palm firmly with his thumb.

Brandon rolls his eyes. I try to ignore it, but I can't. He and I were friends once – good friends – and now all of that is ruined. I wish I had never let Ruby talk me into crossing that line, because I should have known once it was crossed, there would be no returning to what we used to be.

Still, I try to allow myself to be comforted by Oscar, even in the presence of Brandon. Somehow, we all need to find a way to work together. It's no longer just my research. It's Brandon's, too. And I am not so selfish that I would take that away from him. He understands what is at stake as much as I do. It's not just one whale, but a global network of ecosystems. What affects one species cannot be isolated. It ripples, much like the ocean itself, until the impact reaches far beyond the local whale pods.

He might be able to find other work if we don't secure funding, but I know as well as he does that we need to finish what we started. Brandon may be jealous, but that's just it; I have never known him to bow out from anything. He always sees things through, right to the end, even if his pride is wounded.

"Okay," I say, releasing my held breath.

I smile at Oscar, struck by his handsomeness. Over the years, he lost much of the roundness to his cheeks and jaw. Now they're more rugged, more chiseled, and more...

hollow? There's something there, a pain I cannot place. I suppose I never learned the extent to which my leaving hurt him. Maybe the darkness under his eyes is because of me. I shrink at the memory.

Oscar plants a kiss on the top of my head.

"We'll need to get started writing those immediately," he says.

Brandon's fists clench on the table, in plain view. He makes no effort to hide his discomfort.

"I can help with the presentations," Brandon says through tight lips. "I can be useful, you know. This is my research, too."

Oscar's mouth tilts into his casual, cool guy smirk, almost as if he is taunting him.

"Any help is welcome," he says, though I hardly think he means it.

I wish they would stop covertly sparring when we are trying to plan something so important. It's too easy to chalk it up to men being men. This tense exchange is more than that. They are both trying to claim me. What they don't understand is that I refuse to be claimed. I am the one who made the decision, who chose between the two of them. If anyone is staking a claim, it's me.

This display of immaturity gives me a brief pause. I don't have any regrets. Being with Oscar is so much better than I ever imagined. He's smart, tender, and romantic. And while I admire his passion, I think it might destroy him someday if he isn't careful. Not that guarding my heart had been working out for me. We have to strike a balance, which we only seem to find in each other.

But that means we need to find peace with Brandon, too. I refuse to let our rekindled relationship come at the cost of my work. New beginnings should grow from fertile ground, not soil soaked in blood.

"I can work with you on the final presentations, Brandon," I say, offering him a smile like an olive branch.

"Whatever," he mumbles, unable to look at me.

Oscar must sense that we need to talk, because he abruptly rises from his chair.

"Excuse me. I'll be back, I just need to use the bathroom," he says. He exits the room hastily.

Dawn feigns surprise.

"Oh, look at the time! I have another meeting," She quickly gathers her things. "Call me if you need me, okay?"

I nod.

She leaves, and suddenly, I am left alone with Brandon for the first time since the breakup. I have no idea what to say. There's nothing I *could* say to make it better.

His name is all that I am able to offer.

"Brandon," I say gently.

"What?" he snaps. "Want to rub your thing with Oscar in my face some more?"

Blood drains from my face, leaving it shocked and cold.

"No, I – I just want to talk," I say.

Brandon's eyes finally meet mine, the eyes he's been actively avoiding for almost a week. It feels like I've swallowed a thousand needles, and when I see the pain and the strain in his stare, it's like they all pierce through me at once.

"There's nothing to talk about," he says, rising to his feet.

Before I even understand what I am doing, I am rising, too, rushing to block him. My hand presses to his chest.

"I really did like you," I say.

His eyes glimmer, but I can't ignore the faint flash of pain.

"But I loved you. I always loved you." Brandon clasps my hand and crushes it to his lips. "I know that I should just want you to be happy, but I can't help but be angry that it isn't with me. And now I have to watch, wondering what I did wrong."

I sigh, but my breath catches in my throat.

"You didn't do anything wrong, Brandon. Some things just weren't meant to be."

He avoids my searching stare.

"I must be pretty stupid for thinking it'd be me," he says.

I squeeze his hand. "Our destinies are just tangled with other people. Yours is out there waiting for you. I'm sure of it."

"I hope you're right."

He drops my hand, leaving it cold and vacant at my side. And before I find the strength to stop him, he's already gone.

CHAPTER
TWENTY-EIGHT

OSCAR

AUGUST 25, 2022

I tremble violently as I close the bathroom door and withdraw the small bag from my pocket. I have been trying so hard to resist, but withdrawals keep sending me right back to using. I tear at the seal with my teeth and scoop my finger in the white powder, bringing a small mound to my nose. Then, a frenzied inhale.

Still, I'm shaking. My fingers lose their grip on the bag, and almost in slow motion, I watch as the open bag swirls toward the dark tile floor, flinging powder as it falls. When it meets the tile, a plume of dust rises before slowly settling.

In my desperation, I crouch to the ground and try to sweep the powder into a pile with my hands, but as I do, I hear the unmistakable click of the door opening.

Shit, shit, shit!

A man stands in the doorway, and he's the last one I would ever want to catch me at this moment.

"Oh, sorry, my bad," Brandon says, turning away. But then, he does a double take. "Is that...? Oh my god. Is that cocaine? I'm telling Lola, I can't –"

"Wait!" I yelp. He halts. "I know how this looks…"

His body turns back toward me. His forehead wrinkles

and his brow twists in anger. "Really, Oscar? Because it looks like you're scooping drugs from the bathroom floor."

"Don't leave," I panic. "Close the door."

I am still kneeling, powder coating the palms of my hands.

Slowly, Brandon closes the door and locks it. His huge body looms over me, and for a second, I think I am about to get my ass beat.

"What the fuck are you doing, man?" he sighs. He doesn't sound angry. In fact, he almost sounds disappointed.

"I don't know!" I half whisper, half shout. My face is hot and red, and I feel like my chest is going to explode. "You can't tell Lola. Please! I'll do anything, just please don't –"

"You are out of your fucking mind if you think I would do anything to help you," Brandon says sternly. Then after a brief pause, he slaps the wall hard and turns away. "God damn it, Oscar. I thought as long as Lola is happy, then I could handle seeing you together. I was trying to be mature about this. But you make it fucking impossible. Drugs? Really? Are you so selfish that you would willingly drag Lola into that shit?"

He groans as if he'd been punched in the gut. But his words make it feel like a fist really struck mine.

"I'm trying to stop," I say meekly. My voice quivers in sync with my shaking body. "I can't. I'm trying, but I can't."

I hate groveling to anyone. The thought of begging on my knees to anyone but Lola makes me queasy. I never thought I'd find myself begging to Brandon, but I should know it's a lost cause. He'd feed me to the wolves the first chance he got if it took me away from her.

"I'm not doing this, man. I'm not your friend and I'm not keeping your secrets," Brandon says, tossing a handful of paper towels on the ground. "There is no way that this plays out with me not telling her. So, I suggest you clean yourself up."

He unlocks the door and steps out of the bathroom,

muttering under his breath, "Mother fucker, you're lucky I don't call security."

My heart is racing so fast that it feels like it's rising in my throat. I try to clean up the mess, but the room is spinning.

It's no use. Brandon is already gone. He's probably telling Lola what he saw right now, and when she finds out, it's over. But I have to be able to talk to her before she shuts me out forever. This is my last chance to fix things. I have to try.

Scrambling to my feet, I leave the powder and the paper towels on the floor and sprint on shaking legs out of the bathroom and to the conference room. But I can see through the glass walls that she is already gone. Brandon stands there alone, clenching his fists as he meets my panicked stare through the glass.

I tear down the stairs, out the front door, and through the parking lot. The second I step outside though, I am disoriented as the world becomes brighter and louder. The moody clouds, the severely green trees, the sound of insects near my ears. It's all too much. But I do make out one sound cutting through the noise: an engine starting.

I scan the rows of parked cars, looking for her beat-up Subaru. There aren't many cars parked, but it is enough to confuse me in my drug-addled state. I am losing time. She should be pulling out any second, and once she does, there's no getting her back – not while respecting her boundaries.

Suddenly, a car lurches forward in front of me. Without thought, I launch myself forward, planting myself firmly in front of the oxidized vehicle. It doesn't stop though, so I slam my fists onto the hood, startling the driver.

It's Lola.

She brakes. And when she brushes the hair from her face, I can see plainly that it is dripping wet with tears.

"Please!" I shout. "Stop! Let me explain!"

Lola rips the stick shift into park and climbs out of the car.

She is stomping toward me with a kind of fury that is reserved only for deceived women.

And I did it. I am the one who deceived her.

I feel the sting of her palm on my face before I even see her raise her hand.

"Cocaine, Oscar? Really?" she shouts.

"It wasn't cocaine," I try to explain, but I can feel the earth moving under my feet. I am only digging a deeper grave. "It was heroin."

"Heroin!? Jesus fucking Christ!"

She turns to get back in the car, but I gently grab her wrist.

"Baby, I'm trying to stop," I say, pulling her into me. I wrap my arms around her, pleading with her to stop. "Please, you've got to believe me. Don't go."

She clings tightly to my shirt with one hand and pounds on my chest with the other, sobbing onto my shoulder.

CHAPTER
TWENTY-NINE

LOLA

AUGUST 25, 2022

Oscar wraps his arm around me as I cling to him. I want to push him away and run away again, but it didn't fix anything last time I left. We are inevitably drawn together.

"How long has this been going on?" I ask.

I need to know if the man I love is the man I *know*. Was he an addict when I fell for him all those years ago? Or just now, when I fell for him again? How much of our relationship has been a deception?

"About a month," I admit.

"Before the day you found me at the conservancy?"

"Yes," I say.

I pause.

This entire time he was harboring two secrets: his girlfriend and his addiction. I wonder what else he has been lying about.

I peel myself away and stare up at him. "Are you keeping anything else from me?"

"No!" he says. He's panicked and frazzled, but so am I. I can't tell if he's being honest. "I swear, there's nothing else."

His arms twitch like he wants to reach for me but knows he shouldn't. And while the last thing I should want right now is for him to touch me, deep down, I wish he would try, even if I would just refuse him.

"Tell me one reason why I should stay," I say.

Give me a piece of the real you to hold onto.

His body softens in resignation. "You shouldn't. If you were smart, you would get as far from me as you can. I'm not a great man, Lola. I need help."

He's right. I should heed the warnings in my heart and get back in the car. I should drive away and cut contact.

But I can't.

I won't.

How can I leave someone I love when they need help?

"Then get help," I say. I squeeze his hand, though I cannot believe what I am saying. "Get help and I will stay."

His eyes light up. In a flash, he pulls me to him and wraps his arms around me, pressing his lips to the top of my head.

"I will," he cries softly. "I will, I will, I will. I promise."

"No more second chances," I say.

His breathing shudders in his chest. In a whisper, he agrees.

"No more second chances."

I lie awake at night, alone in my bed, with nothing but the all too familiar rainfall to keep me company.

My initial impulse is to blame myself, as if I sold him the drugs and forced it into his system when I left. But I can't do that. It isn't fair, and I know that.

Then, I want to be angry at him. I want to pretend that he did it on purpose, to spite me, in hopes that it will make me feel justifiable in my rage. But that isn't fair to him. He's sick. Addiction was not something he chose.

So, if I can't blame Oscar or myself, who is left? Do I blame the universe for dealing such a shitty hand and binding us to it? Or do I let go and stop searching for answers where there are none?

I suppose the only logical choice is letting go, and choosing love and support over anger and pity.

Oscar doesn't have anyone else. And though his recovery does not rely on me, he still needs someone. There's no clawing his way out of that hole all by himself. The most I can do is offer my hand to hold when he feels like he can't keep going. It's a kindness that I would want for myself, too.

I fear that this could kill him. And that would weigh far heavier on me than this. So, I will stand by him.

In the morning, he'll be sick. And the morning after that. And probably the one after that. But once the withdrawals pass, we'll start going to meetings. We'll write our speeches and hold a gala. We'll move forward because I can't keep living my life looking backwards. We'll heal from this the same way we have healed from everything else.

I don't know if all of that is true. But I have to hope.

That's all we have to cling to.

Hope.

CHAPTER
THIRTY

OSCAR

SEPTEMBER 5, 2022

Over the past week, I have never thrown up so much in my life. And the pain. Don't even get me started on the pain. I guess that's why it's best to detox under medical care.

They say the first few days without heroin are the worst pain imaginable. Now that I have gone through that myself, I can say with absolute certainty that is true. But Lola stuck by me, visiting me at the detox center daily.

Today, she is taking me back home – back to the penthouse.

The car ride through downtown Seattle is a solemn one. The traffic agitates me, I agitate Lola, and then Lola simply shuts down.

I won't downplay my misery – coming down off the drugs was horrible – but Lola's experience with this was also anything but pleasant. And while I want to console her, what I really need is for her to console me. But when the oxygen masks drop from the ceiling of a plane, we have to secure our own masks before helping others, right?

Lola accidentally drives the car through a pothole, jerking my body side to side.

"Sorry," she whispers, taking in a sharp breath as if she

had just ripped a bandage from her own skin. "I really tried not to hit that, I swear."

"It's okay," I say, but my stomach is lurching.

I must look sick as hell, because she does a double take when she looks at me.

"Are you feeling okay? Do I need to pull over?"

I shake my head.

"No. I'll be fine. Thanks, baby."

The truth is that, for the most part, I feel a million times better – at least better than I did a few days ago. The worst of it has passed and for the time being, I can sit up without vomiting before lying back down and rolling in pain. Still, I am not fully recovered, and this car ride is testing my strength.

"Just let me know if that changes," she says, turning down the music to see better. It's so funny she does that.

I reach my hand over the scratched console and set it on her thigh. Her car has seen better days, but that's actually true for both of us.

"Thank you," I say again. "I mean it."

Timidly, her fingers wrap around my hand. It's like she is afraid of me, like everything between us has shifted, and now I don't know where we stand at all.

"I'm just glad to see you doing better," she smiles. At least that appears to be sincere.

"You didn't have to do any of this, you know," I say, bringing the back of her hand to my lips. I kiss it lightly, but find myself leaving it there as I remember the touch of her soft skin. "You could have left me, but you didn't. Why?"

She shoots me a quick, pained stare.

"Because," she says. "I don't abandon the people I love."

"But you didn't owe me that. I show up out of nowhere, wreak havoc on your life – and you still feel convinced that you love me. That doesn't seem very fair."

She withdraws her hand.

"Look, Oscar. I know you feel like you deserve to suffer, and I know you pity me for sticking around. But please don't let whatever shame you feel affect the way you see me – or the way you see yourself. I don't know why you started doing drugs. That's none of my business, and it's not my place to condemn you for it. As far as I'm concerned, you did what you felt you needed to do to survive. I'm not mad at you for that. I'm mad because you lied."

My chin dips toward my chest as I crumple under her scrutiny. I've been apologizing for the wrong thing this whole time. It's not the drugs that scared her, it was the dishonesty.

I guess I thought she cared more about the stigma of substance abuse, but she has never been one to care what others think. I also definitely underestimated how deep her empathy goes. I'm so used to being around shallow rich people that I forgot that Lola is nothing like them. They all care so much about how anyone might affect their reputation. But when you aren't in the spotlight, you're more likely not to care about all of that.

Lola knows what it's like to be an outcast. Her past – growing up with all of the rejection, the bullying, the loneliness – has built a protective shell around her, to the point where she will bear the brunt of any negative perception if it spares someone else the pain or humiliation she already knows too well.

And she knows she's doing it. She's happy to make that stand. So, I guess I really should stop pitying her. If she wants to shield me from all of the ugliness, both within myself and out there in the wide world, I have to let her. She's *asking* me to let her.

"I'm sorry I didn't tell you," I say solemnly. "I guess I didn't know how to. Not when I was trying so hard to win you back."

Her mouth clenches into a half-smile.

"I understand why you did it. But it doesn't make it hurt

any less," she says. "Just promise me you're done keeping secrets, okay?"

She won't look at me. And though my entire body is begging her to look my way, to meet the sincerity in my gaze, her eyes stay glued to the road.

"I promise. Nothing but honesty," I say.

The car slowly brakes at the curb, but Lola doesn't turn off the car or shift into park. Her foot stays firmly planted on the brake, ready to depart as soon as I get out.

"You don't want to come inside?" I ask.

She still won't look at me.

"No. You go ahead. I've got a lot of work to do," she says.

"Are you sure?"

My hand lingers on the door handle.

"Yeah. Go on, get some rest. I'll call you later."

"Okay," I sigh. "I love you. Thanks again for the ride."

I swallow the lump in my throat and open the door. My limbs feel too heavy to move, but somehow I manage to swing my legs out onto the sidewalk.

"I love you, too," she calls out, too late.

I've already shut the car door.

***

The penthouse is empty when I enter. I don't know what I expected. Certainly not a welcome home party, but maybe at least Jacob would be here?

I toss my keys onto the counter and heave my body onto the leather couch. I spent so much time wishing I was home during my detox, that now that I am here, I'm a little disappointed. I thought I might feel instant relief, like everything would be better and I could immediately move forward with my life, but the entire floor is eerily quiet, to the point that I can hear the air circulating around me.

And this rift with Lola makes everything even harder, like

a ten-ton weight is pressing against my chest, making it impossible to breathe.

I tap my fingers anxiously on my knee, waiting for a sign of what to do next. But the only thing that calls to me is coming from the bedside table in my bedroom.

Don't do it, Oscar. Never again.

How could I be so stupid to leave a bunch of drugs here? As if I could just come home and simply forget about it? Not a chance. I can feel its presence in these walls like a phantom, a piercing wail prompting me to find it.

Suddenly, I feel like I am crawling out of my skin, and the only way to relieve myself is to answer its call. My legs lift me from the couch and carry me down the hall, each step echoing against the concrete walls. I pause in the doorway, but the call only grows louder, until finally I am sliding open the drawer beside my bed and removing several small bags of white dust.

My hand shakes as I hold them.

Don't do it.

Fingers trace the seal. It would take no effort at all to pinch it open and bump a hit.

Oscar, no...

I grip the bags tighter, remembering my promise to Lola. I said no more lies, but I can't bring myself to get rid of these. Pretty sure there are protocols for safely disposing of heroin anyway. I can't put it in the trash. I can't wash it down the drain. But it can't stay here either.

I rush to the kitchen, drugs in hand, and whip open the pantry. Scanning the contents of the cupboard, I search for somewhere to store it, somewhere out of sight that I can keep it until I can make the responsible choice. I grab a box of valerian root tea and empty the tea bags into the trash. No one likes the stuff anyway, and they won't think to look inside the box.

Quickly, I stuff the drugs into the tea box with trembling hands and place it on the top shelf behind the other teas.

It should be safe there. At least, I hope it will.

But I can't stay in the penthouse with it, not when I am alone. It will be the end of me, of this band, of my relationship with Lola – and I can't live without any of those things. So, I grab my keys and dash to the elevator.

Anywhere is better than here.

CHAPTER
THIRTY-ONE

LOLA

SEPTEMBER 7, 2022

"Your slides look great. You probably just need to practice your speech a bit more, that's all," Dawn says.

I hang my head in my hands and groan.

"I've been practicing it a dozen times a day! Can't Brandon do it?"

Brandon shakes his head.

"You've had a lot going on lately," Dawn says, coddling me with her words. "Just give it time and keep trying. We've still got a few weeks."

It's true. With Oscar detoxing, I have been distracted to say the least. Between visiting him every day, checking in on Ruby and Tino, and showing up for work every day, it has been a lot to handle at once. I already struggle to manage everything under normal circumstances.

In fact, sometimes I'll have a meltdown just because it's a typical Monday. Even though I love my job, it can be difficult to leave the house and start a new work week. In the end, I guess I hate doing things purely because of the obligation.

But no one has tasked me with taking care of the people I love. I *want* to do it. Love is always a choice, never an obligation.

I choose to be here for Oscar. Maybe other people would

walk away, but not me. Addicts deserve care and love as much as anyone else – even if they lie. I have to believe that he can come back from this... that he can come back to *me*.

The man I love is still in there, and he deserves a chance.

"You can run it through with me if you want," Brandon offers.

It's a nice offer. A sensible one, even. But given all we've been through lately, I think it's best that we spend as little time together as possible.

"That's okay," I say. "I'll get it eventually. Oscar can help."

"Can he?" Brandon says. I scowl at him for his skepticism. "I just mean that he hasn't exactly proven to be dependable lately. Maybe relying on him isn't the best idea."

"Brandon!" Dawn gasps. "Don't be rude."

"I mean it. All he's done since he showed up has cause problems," he says defensively.

"Maybe for you," I snap.

He tilts his head and scoffs.

"Excuse me?"

My mouth cinches shut. I've already said too much; I really don't want to get into this with Brandon.

Brandon sits up tall.

"No, really. Explain. I'd like to know."

"Brandon, I don't think we should –"

"Tell me. Tell me why you're so content leaving me for *him*."

The way he says that, it's like even mentioning Oscar is like biting into a rotten lemon.

"Can you even hear yourself?" I say. My face feels hot, and my eyes prick with tears. "You're not the nice guy you think you are."

"Oh, and Oscar is?"

"Yes!" I cry. "He actually is! Oscar doesn't need to do any of this! He came here on his own accord because he cared about something more than he cared about being rich or famous. Don't you dare think for a second that he isn't a good person just because you are jealous. You have no idea what kind of man he is."

Brandon scrunches his face, the skin mottled red and angry.

"I know *exactly* what kind of man he is," he simmers.

"Oh yeah?" I taunt. "And what is that?"

"He's only pretending to care about this to get to you. He doesn't care about the cause, and he doesn't care about you. He only cares about himself."

"That's not true," I whimper. But part of me wonders if it is true. Suddenly, the conference room feels smaller, colder, darker…

"Keep telling yourself that," Brandon scoffs, rising from his seat.

As he walks away, I want to say something – anything – but he gets the last word. The longer I sit with it, the more it hurts.

I don't want to believe it.

I choose not to.

Someone has to have faith in Oscar if he's going to recover. And that someone is going to be me. No matter what Brandon thinks, I know there is a good person in there, and that person loves me.

Oscar believes in me. It's only fair that, this time, I believe in him.

SEPTEMBER 29, 2022

"Are you ready?" Lola says.

She's wearing the blue tiered gown I bought her just for tonight, each sheer layer fringed in white lace to resemble the crashing of ocean waves. God, she looks pretty.

"I think the real question is, are you?" I quip.

Lola laughs, but it's strained. I know she is excited about the gala. How could she not be? But there is a lot riding on the event, and I see the moment that it dawns on her when her eyes flash and the laughter abruptly stops.

"Baby," I coo, gently running my hands up and down her arms. "It's going to be great. There's no need to worry."

"But we hardly had time to prepare!" she yelps. "Shit, Oscar! I'm kinda freaking out here. What if we *lose* money? What will happen to my job? My family? Oh god…"

"Lola, I need you to listen, okay?" I say softly. She looks up at me with glossy eyes and hesitantly nods. "We have spent the last month writing and rewriting our presentations. We've rehearsed a million times. Dawn and Brandon have taken care of everything else. Now, take a deep breath with me."

I breathe in, filling my chest as full as I can. She follows by inhaling a shaky breath. Together, we hold it there – clinging to the possibility that this could end in disaster – but then we release, letting air escape our lungs with all of our doubts and fears and negativity.

"Thank you," she says. "I was spiraling a bit there, wasn't I?"

"We all spiral sometimes," I chuckle. But deep down, the thought fills me with dread; how I almost ruined everything with her with my secrets and my addictions. Still, she stuck by me during the withdrawals, and even now in recovery.

I hate to admit it, but some days, I am resentful of my newfound sobriety. I resent myself for not understanding moderation, or avoiding certain substances altogether. I resent Lola for forcing me to choose. And then I resent myself again for thinking that.

Jesus, what a shitty thought to have.

Lola kisses my cheek, and then the thought escapes me as if it was never there at all. *This.* This is my true addiction – and not one from which I ever hope to recover.

My hands meet her waist, fingers digging into her hips as I pull her closer. Nose to nose, we stand in a trance as she gently tugs on the ends of my bow tie.

"Thank you," I say. And I mean it.

Her brow twists as she pulls away. "Thank you for what? I didn't do anything."

"Like hell you didn't." My hand travels down her thigh and gathers up her dress until I find my way under. I want to feel her. As my hand meets the heat between her legs, she inhales sharply. "I wouldn't be here right now if it weren't for you."

Her warm breath flows against my neck.

"I'm really proud of you," she says in a sweet whisper.

I tease along her slit and she opens for me, soaked and shaking, as she clings to the arms of my suit.

"Baby, look at you," I growl, slicking my finger and

plunging it inside. "I'm going to spend the rest of my life making it up to you."

Like I said, I have a problem with moderation.

Lola tilts back her head and moans.

"Oscar…" she breathes.

"Yes, baby?"

"We shouldn't – oh god!"

Her squeals vibrate in my ear as I press my finger against her walls.

"We shouldn't what?" I whisper playfully.

She melts into my hand like chocolate.

"Later," she wheezes, barely able to make out the words. "After the gala… Please…"

"Promise me," I say, pumping her harder.

I feel her tighten as she lets out the breath she's been holding, and suddenly, her entire body is quaking. "Yes!" she yelps. "I promise!"

I hold her in my hand until the convulsing stops, hugging her tight to my chest. When I withdraw my hand and softly nibble on her ear, she whimpers.

"Damn it," she says. Her dizzy eyes scan the room as she collects herself. "Now I have to go fix myself up again."

I can't help but smile. She looks absolutely radiant.

"I don't know, Lola. You can really rock that post-O glow," I tease.

She tries to give me a stern look, but the laughter sneaks through.

"Yeah? Do I rock it well enough for everyone to give me a few thousand dollars?"

"Shut up and take my money," I say.

Lola swats at me and smooths down her dress before turning to touch up her hair and makeup.

She leaves my line of sight, but I can still hear her mumble playfully, "Asshole."

My stomach flips and it's like there is a flicker in my veins.

I would walk through hell and back all over again for this woman. Yes, I may be an asshole, but I want to be better, and she is my reason – my purpose.

It's as if these past few weeks, I expelled all of the emptiness that was consuming me (along with all of the sweat, shit, and vomit). Now, all that is left is Lola, and perhaps that was all I was ever really missing.

And I have the opportunity to make it up to her.

Faint laughter sounds from the elevator in the penthouse before it dings and the doors open. It's no longer faint, but boisterous. A woman's voice, and a man's, and the unmistakable sound of stumbling heels.

Madison.

I peek out of the bathroom and down the dim lit hallway to see Madison in a red gown clinging to the shoulders of Tyler's tuxedo as they sway and laugh, lurching toward me.

Of course, they are together now.

"Oscar!" Madison sings. "We were looking for you. Oh! Is that a new suit? Looking fresh."

The remark makes Tyler scowl, and he grips her shoulder tighter before challenging me with his gaze.

"What do you want?" I sigh.

"Tyler wrote a new song," Madison slurs. Her skin is flushed and her pupils are small as pin-pricks. "It's about me. Want to hear it? It's basically perfect."

Seeing her in his arms doesn't bother me. But the fact that they are barely tolerable when they are separated makes them a nightmare when they are together, especially now that they don't have to hide their affair. Especially now that I am sober.

"Please, go," I say in an aggressive whisper. I try to shove them down the hall to Tyler's room, but their bodies resist. Even though Madison wobbles on four-inch heels, she plants them firmly into the ground, making it impossible to move her.

"What crawled up your ass and died?" she snarls.

Tyler chuckles. "Didn't you hear? Oscar cleaned up for that boring, old bitch of his."

My fists clench at my sides and I feel a fire ignite in my chest. Under any other circumstances, I would have driven my knuckles so hard into his jaw that he would be laid out on the floor in a matter of seconds. But tonight is the gala. I can't bust up my hand and start shit. It's Lola's night.

I halt Tyler with my hand pressed firmly – too firmly – against his chest.

"Watch it," I say sternly. "Don't *ever* talk about Lola like that. I love her."

"Oh, is that what it is? Love?" Madison says. "Wow, you really are boring. Can't wait to see you get all washed up with that white picket fence, *has-been*."

Her words slice deeper than they should. If there's one thing I am not willing to accept, it's the end of my career. It has always been about the music, but I'd be lying if I said it didn't feel good to be relevant. If anything, it means people are listening. And if people are listening, then I can still support myself with music. I don't know how to do anything else.

Madison cocks her eyebrow, like she knows she's struck a nerve.

"If you're not going to be fun anymore, then at least let us have the rest of your stash," she says, taking a step down the hall towards my room – towards Lola.

I grab her arm and pull her back.

"No, it's not in there," I say.

I realize what I've just admitted. Even though Madison and Tyler are high, they realize it, too, and suddenly, my sobriety seems like a big, fat joke. Why else would I still be hiding it?

Tyler smirks.

"Where is it?" he says.

Madison shakes off my grip and pulls Tyler's hand, trying

to take another step to my bedroom. "Come on, I know where he keeps it."

I block the hall with my body.

"Stop," I whisper. "It's not there anymore. I… I moved it."

I know that I have to get rid of the drugs. If Lola found out I still had some, I would lose her forever. It's one thing to have hidden it from her once. It's another to hide it twice.

"Show us," Madison says in a seductive, hushed tone.

Tyler nods excitedly.

"Follow me," I say.

I lead them away from the bathroom and into the kitchen. They pursue me with lethargic, clumsy footsteps. My hands are shaking, knowing that Lola could appear any moment. And then what would I do? How could I possibly explain myself?

Quickly, I open a cupboard and retrieve a crumpled box of valerian root tea, except there's no tea inside. No one in the band would touch the stuff, including me. It's nasty, and the fact that it tastes like a lingering fart meant that the box was safe. No one would ever think to look inside. If they did, then they would find several small bags of heroin – in no small amount.

"Take it," I say, thrusting the box into Madison's hands.

She smiles and hands the tea box to Tyler.

"So fucking boring," she says.

"Whatever. Just get the fuck out of here, will you?" I snap.

Lola's footsteps sound down the hall, and I can hear her calling out to me, searching for me.

I hiss at Tyler and Madison, urging them to scatter like roaches when the light turns on. They turn on their heels to leave, but as they round the corner to the hall, Lola bumps into them.

"Excuse you," Madison barks.

Then they disappear, tea box in hand, and my secret still intact.

Lola staggers in, face flushed and flustered. She is not used to wearing heels, so her stance is less than secure.

"Was that who I think it was?" she asks.

"Yeah," I say nonchalantly, as if having my ex in our penthouse is totally normal and not at all concerning. I'd rather Lola fear Madison than fear my potential relapse. "Don't worry. She's with Tyler now."

"Oh," she says, gears turning in her head with the lilt of her voice. "Okay. Well, umm… I guess I'm ready. Do I look okay?"

I step to her and pull her close to me.

"Baby, 'okay' doesn't even begin to describe how gorgeous you look," I say. "Whether you're in a gown or in cargo shorts, you're perfect."

"That doesn't mean much," Lola teases, tapping the tip of my nose. "My ass looks amazing in cargo shorts."

I chuckle and kiss her cheek. I don't disagree.

But although I got rid of the drugs, there's a residual ache in my gut. I've betrayed her for the last time.

CHAPTER
THIRTY-THREE

LOLA

SEPTEMBER 29, 2022

Cameras flash as we step out of the limo and onto the blue carpet – because of course there's a special carpet. It's very short, measuring only about ten feet, but everything is a spectacle with these people. It's disorienting, and I have enough trouble walking in heels as it is, but Oscar holds me by the waist as we slowly make our way to the entrance.

I feel his breath on my ear.

"You're doing great," he whispers.

I hide my blushing face from the flashing lights and duck inside. When I look up and clear the spots from my vision, I see tons of A-list celebrities scattered in the lobby, chatting amongst other rich folks as they queue for the elevator. And while the gala is on the rooftop, I am stunned to see the elegant decor extended to the ground floor.

Several small tables are littered throughout the white marble lobby topped with little glass bowls filled with water lilies. The plush blue carpet leads the way to the host of elevators against the towering wall, but few people are in a hurry to make their way to the roof. It appears Dawn anticipated this, or perhaps Oscar, because servers in white tuxes carry shiny silver trays of champagne to distribute among the lingering guests.

Oscar retrieves one of the champagne flutes and hands it to me. My eyes roll back into my head after I take the first sip.

"That good, huh?" Oscar teases.

I nod emphatically.

"This is the best champagne I have *ever* had," I say. And I mean it.

Best of all, a massive statue crafted from driftwood in the shape of a humpback whale stands in the center of the room, slabs and branches of gray wood smoothed by the pull of ocean tides arranged so skillfully that it feels alive.

I'm rarely moved by art, but this... all of this... it's overwhelming. I want to dance around the room to shake off this excess energy, but I still myself, settling for smoothing my fingers over the silky thread of my dress.

"Come on," he says, squeezing my hand. "I want to show you the roof."

I giggle.

Up until now, no one would let me see the gala space. While I insisted on total control, this was one piece that I was willing to relinquish to Dawn and Brandon with complete trust. Oscar had looked earlier in the day – on my insistence – just to make sure everything is as it should be.

The elevator doors roll open, and I step inside. But as it ascends to the rooftop, it feels like it left my stomach on the ground floor. I pinch my eyes shut, unable to take the anticipation.

Oscar takes notice of my fidgeting foot and caresses the skin on my bare back, causing a ripple of goosebumps.

"Breathe, baby," he says.

Together, we fill our lungs until the doors open and the air is forced from me in astonishment.

I am first struck by the incredible display of colors covering the full spectrum of the ocean: white for frothy waves on the table linens, aquamarine for sunny shores draping over the rooftop, and of course the star-scattered night sky a shade of navy reminiscent of the depths of the sea.

Small lanterns sit atop the tables, each containing a silhouette of a whale, and fairy lights twinkle overhead, making it seem like the stars are just within reach.

"Oscar…" I whisper.

"Do you like it?" he asks. His voice breaks, as if he's nervous that I will say no.

"I love it," I say, turning to him and kissing his cheek. "Thank you."

Dawn and Brandon emerge from the light crowd around the bar, her face beaming and his attempting to disguise a scowl.

"You guys!" I scream. "I can't believe this! How? How did you make it so perfect?"

Brandon relaxes a little and raises his glass to me to triumph.

"The revenue from tickets covered it. The rest is up to you," he says. "You'll kill it."

I wrap my arms around both of them and pull them close. I am not much of a hugger, but the swell of emotions I feel right now has me wanting to kiss the entire world!

Of course, that isn't possible, so I kiss Oscar instead.

I feel light on my feet, as if a heaviness has been lifted from me. All these months spent worrying about my future, and now it is finally coming to a conclusion. If the guests are as pleased as I am by everything, then this might actually work. With enough funding, my research could even expand.

Oscar and I mingle as the remainder of the guests arrive. Soon, the presentations will begin, dinner will be served, and then, hopefully, checks will be written. The entire time, I am starstruck. I think I even see Shane Silver through the crowd, though Oscar seems to want to keep his distance. I still confess that I love Shane's movies though, much to Oscar's annoyance.

I check the time obsessively, and with each passing minute, I grow more and more anxious. Public speaking is not my strong suit, but I am hoping that having Oscar at the podium before and after my presentation will make it seem more interesting than I am able to. He brings the charisma, I bring the clumsy hyperfixation. Together, we might come across as passionate or inspirational.

"It's almost time," Oscar says, taking me aside. "Are you feeling okay?"

I shake out my hands and bounce, the heels sending a twinge of pain through my calves.

"Yeah," I breathe. "I think I'll be okay."

He gently grips the back of my neck and pulls me into him, planting a kiss on my forehead. "You got this. If you can sing Poison at karaoke, talking about what you love will be a thousand times easier. Just be yourself."

Oscar takes his place at the podium and clinks his water glass into the microphone to get everyone's attention. I stand behind him, but as they slowly catch on and take their seats at the tables, my heartbeat quickens.

"Esteemed guests, welcome!" Oscar says. "I'm Oscar Kelly from The Unadored. Some of you may know me."

This gets quite a few laughs from the guests. He needs no introduction.

"What you might not know about me is my love of the ocean. I imagine you all love it, too. The health of that wondrous ecosystem, though, depends on a keystone species – one which we would like to talk about with you tonight."

He turns and winks at me, his eyes flashing green and gold in the spotlight.

"Now, I love humpback whales. But this incredible woman standing behind me loves them so much more. So much that she has dedicated her life to saving them. Every morning, you can find her gathering sounds here in Washington to analyze in her lab and inform policy change. And all of us are fortunate enough to listen to her today."

Extending his arm toward me, he urges me to the podium.

"Please join me in welcoming the *goddess* of marine biology and acoustics, Lola Marin!"

The audience erupts in applause and my body stiffens.

I feel a slight sense of relief though when Oscar walks to my side and offers his arm.

He leans in and whispers, *"Ain't lookin' for nothin' but a good time,* baby."

His fingertips brush my arm, sending a tingle down my spine that takes me out of my head as I slowly step to the podium. Each step is overly cautious as I try to make sure my heels don't snag on the end of my gown.

This is so much scarier than drunk karaoke.

A gradual hush falls over the audience, with only the sounds of traffic below and a distant shore to comfort me. Everyone is staring, expecting brilliance and inspiration, and I just don't know if I have the charisma or confidence to give it to them. But then I look over at Oscar, and I am overcome by the power he instills in me.

I take a deep breath and begin.

"Hello everyone, and thank you for coming out tonight for such an important cause," I say. "Please join me for a moment of silence. Close your eyes and listen to the sounds around you." I pause and together, we all shut our eyes and listen to the pulse of the city: honking cars, laughing pedestrians, an airplane soaring overhead. Teeming with life, the sound is deafening, even when it is dulled by the height of the rooftop.

"Loud, isn't it?" I continue. "Now imagine everything you hear, but amplified as you try to call out to friends and family thousands of miles away. Not tens. Not hundreds. *Thousands.*" One woman near the front audibly gasps, to which I must hold back a smile. "A low-frequency humpback whale song can travel up to ten thousand miles away, when the circumference of the earth itself is just under twenty-five thousand. Imagine shouting and shouting halfway across the world over the din of all the boats in the ocean, but your message is never received. What effect does this have on the whales, or the ocean at large? How can we be part of the solution instead of the problem?"

The audience is stunned silent – well, all but two drunk guests cackling at the bar. I try to ignore them, to center myself and collect my thoughts, before I continue.

"Connection is –" I begin again. But the laughter gets louder and they shout at each other, or maybe at me. From here, it is hard to tell. Regardless, I am immediately unnerved.

Soon, the attention is torn from me, and the audience has all turned to observe them. Unsure what to do or how to proceed, I look over at Oscar. His jaw is clenched and his eyes narrowed as he unbuttons his suit jacket and marches off the platform. He makes a beeline toward the boisterous guests, one of whom is a tall blonde in a red dress. She looks an awful lot like his ex-girlfriend, Madison.

Before he reaches them though, the loud man accompanying the blonde woman loses his balance and falls to the floor, convulsing on impact. The woman screams.

Oscar's pace quickens to a sprint. The guests rise to their feet, either with the intention to help or get a better view, and I lose sight of what is happening. The last I see is Oscar's head dipping below the surface of the standing audience, many of whom are cupping their mouths and wincing as they witness what I cannot see.

When my limbs unfreeze, I force my way through the crowd toward the bar. Then, I finally see Oscar. Madison shrieks at his side as he kneels on the ground, clutching the paling, lifeless body of his bandmate, Tyler.

And just like that, I am frozen again. I cannot breathe

through this. I cannot breathe at all. At my feet lies a celebrity, dead from an apparent drug overdose, with a dense crowd pressing into me as they try to get a better look.

Oscar's eyes meet my own as tears fall down both of our cheeks. There is so much we need to say, but can't. But I cannot mistake the guilt in his stare as he releases his grip on Tyler.

"I'm sorry." He mouths the words, but I can't hear them.

Security guards appear and try to force the crowd back, one of whom starts performing CPR. But it's clearly too late. The man is dead.

Besides the roar of panicked murmurs, the world falls silent.

The only sounds that cut through are the blare of sirens and the drumming of my own heartbeat rising in my throat.

CHAPTER
THIRTY-FOUR

OSCAR

OCTOBER 12, 2022

I may appear calm, yet I am anything but that.

Though I am sitting in what appears to be a perfectly comfortable chair in a perfectly comfortable rehab facility, my leg is bouncing wildly as I wait for her to visit.

It has been thirteen days since the gala – an event the news is calling "an unavoidable tragedy." But I know it could have been avoided. I could have kept my heroin stash away from Madison and Tyler. I could have flushed it down the toilet. I could have been honest with Lola about everything from the very beginning instead of keeping secrets.

But I didn't.

I lied. I lied so many times, and now I have destroyed *everything*.

Tyler is dead.

The band is done.

The gala was an extravagant waste.

And Lola won't talk to me. Rightfully so. This is all my fault. My negligence killed a friend and destroyed the life of the woman I love.

After that night, the only thing I could think to do is to check myself into rehab. I needed to understand why I kept the drugs at all, and why I gave them away – why I did everything but the responsible thing. It could have been Madison that died. It could have been me.

And now I feel an extra layer of guilt as the man that slept with my girlfriend behind my back, the man that I already didn't particularly like, is dead because of me. I wonder if it would be any easier if I hated him. I wish I did, but I don't. He was just misguided. Same as me.

And then I wonder, maybe I could properly grieve if I liked him.

Instead, I am caught in this torturous middle, where I *have* to blame myself, because if I don't, the destructive path will continue until it has claimed everyone and everything I have ever loved until it takes me, too. That isn't how I want to live my life. This isn't the legacy I wanted to leave.

I feel a shadow cast over me, and the hairs on my arm raise.

"*Lola...*" I whisper.

The shadow shifts as she moves in front of me to take a seat. She immediately busies herself by picking at her cuticles, which are already swollen and raw.

"You actually came," I say. I can't look at her, even though I sense her intense stare boring into me.

"I didn't want to," Lola says. "I don't know whether to yell at you or to cry."

"I'm sorry..."

"Sorry doesn't fix things, Oscar. I was pleading for my future while your friend died writhing on the floor from the drugs *you* gave him." She buries her face in her hands. "Do you have any idea how fucked up that is? How does someone move on from that?"

"I'm sorry..."

"I'm losing my job." Her voice breaks. "Now I have to find something new, somewhere else, far away from the family that needs me."

"*I'm sorry...*" My body begins to shake.

"Stop fucking saying sorry!" Lola shouts, slapping the arm of the chair with a loud *thud*. "You don't get to be sorry. I trusted you, Oscar! After Brandon told me about your problem, I should have just walked away, but I didn't. I was so blinded by our past that it clouded our future. I thought you would help me, but instead you pulled me down with you. And now I have nothing. You took that from me, and I won't give you the forgiveness you want."

I sit there, stunned silent and still shaking. I can't even produce the tears I need for release, so the pressure keeps building and building until I feel like my body will combust.

"There's nothing I can say or do to make things right," I say over my broken breathing. "All I have is sorry – too little, too late."

Finally, I look up at her face. Her cheeks and nose marble into a mosaic of red, and her eyes well with tears. She is gripping the side of the chair, digging her fingernails into the sterile beige fabric.

"I know it will never be enough," I continue. "But you came here for something. Not an apology, but something. I will give whatever I can."

She tears her eyes from me, twisting her head in defiance, but I can see her conflicting with herself, wondering why she came at all.

"What is it?" I ask calmly. "Money?"

"Not from you," she snaps. "If you think I'll let *you* save me from the mess *you* made…"

She doesn't finish her sentence. She doesn't need to because she is right. What is the sense in treating a wound that I inflicted? It would be like countering poison with more of the same poison.

"Where will you go?" I say, defeated.

Lola sighs.

"I don't know," she says. "Whatever ocean will have me."

Her voice is weary, and it sends a shooting pain, a sucker

punch to my beating heart, to hear her so discouraged. I want there to be something in my power to do, but I have done enough. Each effort of mine to help is undermined by my seemingly innate need to destroy.

"I think I came here to make you see what you've done to me," she mutters. "I needed you to see my pain."

And I do see it. Its presence hovers over us like a dark cloud, the air charged and static with her resentment. Except it seems like she resents herself more than she resents me.

I reach out to touch her knee, but she immediately recoils, retracting deep into her seat as if I were a venomous snake attempting to strike.

"I see your pain," I say. "But I need you to direct that hatred towards me, not yourself." Lola chokes into a sob. She knows I am right, and maybe hearing it from me is even more painful. "I did this. Not you. Every mistake, every lie, has been my own. Don't carry that burden. Put it on me where it belongs."

"Don't do that," Lola says. I blink at her, unsure of what she means. "Don't try to make me feel sorry for you. You did this to yourself."

"Keep going," I say. I want her to blame me, to shout at me, to tell me how rotten I know I am. It's as if I need her anger as penitence.

She thins her lips into a tight, stern line.

"You're a piece of fucking work, Oscar. You deceived me from the very beginning. I wish you had never come back to Seattle. I wish you had let me be."

"More."

"I wish I had never met you!"

She gasps, startled by the words that passed her lips. But I won't make her put them back. It's out here in the open now, where it belongs.

"Good," I say. "If you hadn't met me, I wouldn't have to live knowing how much I hurt you."

She simply nods.

"I wish..." she says. "I wish I could still love you. But I can't. And that hurts worst of all."

And there it is, the thing that she came to say. And it's the thing I think I need to hear most if I am ever going to change.

To make matters worse, a blonde demon appears in the distance behind Lola, scooting her feet down the corridor. I try not to make eye contact or draw attention to myself, as I have been since I discovered Madison had checked into the same rehab, but I can feel the moment that she sees me, as if I am about to be struck by lightning. She skates along the tile in her grippy socks, heading in our direction, but I still won't acknowledge her – not until she is standing beside us and clears her throat.

Lola looks up at her in horror.

"What the fuck!? You're here with her?" she seethes, getting up abruptly from her seat.

I reach for her, but she flinches at my touch.

"Lola, it's not like that. We haven't even spoken –"

"Oscar," she whispers through bared teeth. "I don't know how many more of your lies I can take. Explain why your ex, whom you gave your secret drugs to, is here at the same place as you. Explain it in a way that makes sense, because I swear, I am about to snap."

Madison opens her mouth to speak, and for an instant, I wish words were bullets so I could dive in front of hers and save Lola from impact. Whatever she has to say can't possibly help matters.

"I knew he was here," Madison squeaks, her voice soaked in shame. "I didn't know where else to go, what else to do. I had hoped he had answers for me, but he's been dodging me this whole time. Don't be mad, please. Either of you. Please, don't be mad..."

Lola turns to me, puzzled and outright disgusted.

"Are you joking? I am so far past mad right now," she says, poking her finger right at Madison's face.

Madison's pouting lip trembles and I try to step between them.

"For fuck's sake, stop passing around blame and just put it on me, both of you! Madison didn't do anything. You need a villain? Well, I am standing right here," I say.

Lola aims her finger at me and shoves it into my chest like a spear pointed straight at my heart.

"Then take responsibility, asshole!" she shouts.

She turns on her heel and before I can say another word, she is storming off down the hall and out of the exit doors.

Madison swipes a tear rolling off her face with her baggy, long sleeve. My instinct is to comfort her, but I can't, because Lola is right. I need to take responsibility for what happened, and until I stop resenting Madison and accept the full blame, I'm just living out another lie. Not only lying to them, but to myself, as well.

I pat Madison on the shoulder hesitantly, but it just makes her cry harder.

"It's my fault," I say, as if that will fix anything. My hope, however, is that it will make her recovery easier.

"No," she says so quietly, I can scarcely hear it. "No. Tyler and I brought you into this. And now… now he's gone."

Her face falls into her hands as she lets out a wailing sob.

"You actually loved him, didn't you?" I say.

She nods, unable to make a single sound.

"Then I understand why you did it," I sigh. "I'm no better than you. I'm sorry if I ever kept you apart. I can't be upset with you over that. Not after…"

I can't force myself to say it, to tell her what she is already all too aware of. Her lover is dead, and if it weren't for me, maybe he'd still be here with her.

Madison holds her breath and pinches her eyes shut, as if she is trying to project herself into another realm, anywhere but this ice-cold reality. She manages to steady herself, and then releases all of the air she has been holding in one slow, controlled exhalation. Her eyes blink open and pierce through me.

"I thought I loved you once, too, Oscar. But love doesn't do what *we* did, and nothing either of us can say will change that. We both killed Tyler, and we have to find a way to live with that," she says.

She touches my arm hesitantly and walks away, leaving me alone in my guilt.

Like fire on gasoline, the messy thing between us blew up. The news is right; tragedy was inevitable. We'd been stoking that flame for too long, and now, we stand on scorched earth, desecrated with the lives we collectively destroyed.

CHAPTER
THIRTY-FIVE

LOLA

OCTOBER 19, 2022

I don't even get the chance to open my door before I hear Ruby's key slip into the lock. She has called me at least five times a day since the gala to check in on me, and while I suppose I should be grateful, she's already taking care of Tino. It isn't fair to have to take care of me, too. I have to learn how to be independent, especially if I have to leave Seattle. Wherever I go, Ruby can't follow.

Ruby swings open the door and slams it shut.

"You didn't answer your phone," she scolds.

I shrug and return my attention to my laptop. "I was busy."

"Too busy to talk to me? Come on. You can't spend all day doom scrolling and consider that busy," she says.

She removes my blanketed legs from half of the couch so she can take a seat, clumsily dropping them to the floor.

"I'm not doom scrolling. I'm job-hunting," I tell her. "You know, considering I won't have one soon."

After ripping the laptop from my hands, she begins to look through the listing page I already had open. It doesn't take long for her brows to knit together in dismay.

"Five jobs? There are only five jobs in the U.S.? How is that even possible?"

I try to massage the tension out of my head and neck.

"That's just how it is," I say. "I'd be fortunate to get any of them considering how many applications they get."

Ruby twists her mouth as if she is piecing together a puzzle.

"Well, you're kinda famous now, right?" she offers. "That has to count for something."

"I'm famous for having a rockstar die at my fundraiser. I'm not sure that's going to help me," I say.

She squirms in her seat. "You know what they say: All press is good press?"

I scoff and retrieve the laptop from her hands to continue filling out applications. Ruby leans in to watch, which would be unnerving if it were anyone else, but she is my sister so I suppose the familiarity dulls my anxiety.

"What about that one?" she says excitedly. I freeze, the cursor hovering over a listing. "Yeah, that one! It's in the Virgin Islands!"

I sigh. "That's so far away. I don't know if I should apply to that one."

"Why not?" Ruby says. "It's St. John! That's like a dream come true."

Shaking my head, I try to scroll past it, but Ruby smacks my hand.

"Ruby, it's not even relevant to my research! Look, it's a junior position and it's studying sea turtles!" I protest. "Here, studying humpbacks, is the dream come true. Not thousands of miles away."

She falls silent, but I can feel her stare burning into me.

"What?" I say, slightly annoyed.

"We'll be okay without you," she says. "There's no need to feel so guilty. It's temporary, right? You'll come back eventually and when you do –"

"But what if I don't? What if I end up stuck on an island

far, far away, and something happens? It's not like I can just get in my car and come visit."

Ruby sets her hand on my shoulder.

"Then we'll figure something out. You can't save everyone and everything, Lola. I can manage, and Eva is here, too. We'll be okay."

My chin quivers as I hold back tears.

"I guess I don't have much of a choice. Oscar ruined everything."

Even uttering his name sets my veins on fire as I spiral into a blind rage.

It must be plain to see, because Ruby sneers, "I still can't believe that happened. What an asshole."

While it's cathartic for me to think ill of Oscar, hearing it from her kind of irks me. It turns out I am still protective of him. Only I can call him that because he was *mine.*

And yet, he wronged me.

But I suppose that's why I feel like only I can pass judgment. It's so hard to cling to my anger though, because deep down, part of me will always care for him. He was my first love. And some days, it feels like he will be my last.

So, I ignore Ruby's remark. With my emotions as foggy as they are, I don't want to confirm that it's okay to talk about him like that. When I allow myself to think clearly about it, I know that he is sick and deserves compassion. The only thing I can't decide is whether he deserves my forgiveness.

"Apply to the St. John job," Ruby says. "Just in case."

"You just want to get rid of me," I joke.

She playfully shoves me over.

"Yeah. You're the *worst.*"

Ruby stays the night – something I didn't know I needed. When I ask if we can order food, she agrees, but only under the condition that I eat something healthy (which is honestly fair, my body probably needs greens more than pizza).

Then we each curl up under our respective blankets and binge watch *Crazy Ex-Girlfriend* until we fall asleep. We're too somber to sing along.

It hurts knowing that these comforting nights with my sister will soon come to an end. All these years, they have been a source of comfort. When I move, I won't have anyone. The thought is enough to jolt me out of my sleep in a panic.

Starting over is never easy. But for the first time in my life, I will be truly alone. I'll need to learn how to be more independent and it terrifies me. Without Oscar, without Ruby and Tino, without Dawn and Brandon, who am I? What am I actually capable of?

The future is full of unknowns, and it stretches out before me like an endless sea, with both a sparkling horizon and storm clouds overhead. Anything can happen, and whether I like it or not, change is coming.

CHAPTER
THIRTY-SIX

OSCAR

OCTOBER 21, 2022

The point of the colored pencil in my hand crunches under the pressure I place upon it as I fill in the space between these lines. There's not much we can do in rehab, not without our phones, our stuff, or for that matter, our autonomy. So, most of the time, when we aren't spending time outdoors with kayaks or horses, I am drawing in the common room by myself.

The idea was to keep drawing until I could focus enough to write a song, but something's blocking me. My brain and my heart are broken, and I don't suppose I will be able to write anything at all until I can fix them.

Part of me thinks I don't deserve to get better, like maybe I should continue to spiral, but then sometimes there is a small moment that gives me hope – hope that I can be better and help others, not just myself – and that gives me the strength to fight another day.

A woman clears her throat behind my shoulder, causing the point of the pencil to break.

"Mind if I have a seat?" she says.

A little annoyed, I whip myself around only to see Madison standing there, fidgeting with her fingers.

"Sure," I sigh.

Madison pulls out the chair beside me and takes a seat, retrieving a blank piece of paper from the center of the table. I move the box of pencils closer to her, retrieving one for myself. She cracks a smile and withdraws a blue pencil.

"Sorry they're not sharper," I say.

"No need to apologize," she replies softly. "I probably would have dulled them regardless."

I try to let out a little laugh, but it comes out as a single grunt.

"Fair enough. How are you doing?" I ask.

She shrugs and blows out a breath.

"Oh, you know. One day at a time." I understand the indifference. It's hard to keep catastrophizing for this long without the shame losing its edge. "It's getting easier, but then I just feel guilty about that, too."

"Eventually, we have to work through this," I say. "That guilt will fade in time, I'm sure."

She pauses, her blue pencil frozen on the page.

"How?" she asks sorrowfully.

"How what?"

She stammers. "How do we work through it without escaping punishment?"

"Not sure either of us are at that step yet," I chuckle dryly. "Pretty sure at some point we have to make amends though. You aren't supposed to suffer forever."

"I'm not?" she asks, genuinely surprised.

I look up at her.

"No, Madison. You're not."

Her chin quivers. "And what about you? Are you going to suffer forever?"

"Probably," I joke, turning my attention back to my drawing. It's nothing special. Just patterns and doodles as I try to get my head right.

Still, I can sense Madison scowling at me.

"I'm not going to get better if you don't," she says. "Doesn't seem very fair."

"Wouldn't it be easier to leave me behind?" I say. "That's what you do, isn't it? Put yourself first?"

She hangs her head. I didn't mean to let the bitterness slip like that. I knew it would wound her before I said it, and yet, I said it anyway. I really am an asshole...

"Sorry," I say. "I didn't mean that."

"Yes you did." She sniffs and sets down her pencil. "And you'd be right. That is what I do, but I don't want to be like that anymore."

It's weird seeing this side of Madison: so self-aware, so gentle, so... kind?

"I don't either," I mutter.

"I was awful to you, Oscar. Don't think I don't know that. But I am so, so sorry – for everything I put you through. You don't have to forgive me. I don't expect you to, it's just –"

"I do forgive you," I interject.

She blinks in disbelief.

"What?"

"I do forgive you," I repeat. "Maybe I shouldn't, but holding onto resentment won't do me any favors. Consider me your first correction."

I flash a smile to assure her of my sincerity. I want her to recover, and I refuse to stand in the way of that.

Her eyes pool with tears and she clasps my hand tightly.

"Thank you," she says, as if she were accepting a heartfelt gift. "I forgive you, too, you know."

I squeeze her hand in mine and release, picking up my pencil again and continuing to scribble.

We are both so entangled in this entire mess, that it's impossible to know where to shift the blame. Some days, I am so sure that everything that has happened is her fault. But I always know that isn't true. Tyler's blood is on both of our hands. There's no sense in figuring whose hands are bloodier.

"I hope someday you are able to forgive yourself," she says.

It's as if she can read my thoughts. I guess being together for a few years will do that.

"Me too," I say. "But I'm not there yet."

"Me neither. I think we'll get there though." She rises to her feet. "Hang in there, okay?"

I nod as she lingers for a moment longer, and then she walks away.

It's so easy to forgive others, but it's not so easy to forgive ourselves. After I do the work I need to do on myself and I am ready to make amends, I hope that I can make things right with myself, too. Other people might not accept my apologies, and they will disappear and I will be left with the one person I can't seem to forgive: *myself.*

Life is too long to spend hating who I am, and I am deserving of love and joy. Maybe I don't feel that way now, but when the day comes that I accept that, maybe I can truly live again.

CHAPTER
THIRTY-SEVEN

LOLA

AUGUST 16, 2023

Ocean waves ripple in front of me, lapping at the shore, crystal blue. I reposition my weight to still the squirming green sea turtle in my hands. It's nesting season.

"Hold her steady," my boss, Tom, says.

I try to prevent her from twisting and writhing as she attempts to escape with only moderate success. It's fine though. Tom manages to adhere the radio transmitter to its shell, allowing me to release the critter. Her nest is somewhere closeby, but she won't be returning to it. Once the eggs are buried, she is done. I give her a bittersweet wave as she slips back into the water, the tide pulling her toward her next journey – which could be anywhere. That's what we are trying to find out.

Tom offers up his hand for a high-five. Reluctantly, I accept it and slap his hand.

"Good work today," he says. He scratches at the white hair on his chin and readjusts his khaki booney hat, the latter of which looks uncomfortably similar to my own. "When I retire, you'll be leading these yourself in no time."

Tom is a fine person, but he often comes off a little patronizing. While I did accept the available junior position in St. John, I am anything *but* junior. He seems to forget that.

"Thanks," I laugh, following the script in my head. "I'm learning from the best."

I say that, but I don't mean it.

I just hope that the mask I wear at work works well enough for me to advance quickly. I spent nearly all of my money moving to St. John for a job that pays much less than my previous one. And while I love all creatures of the ocean, I would rather continue my study of humpback whales.

"That's kind of you to say," Tom chuckles.

I remind myself that this is the option available to me right now. Hopefully, soon, I can make some connections to try to hold another fundraiser for my whale research. For now, I guess day in and day out, it's going to be me and Tom.

And while that makes me incredibly sad, it's sadder to be completely alone. And considering that it's Wednesday, I should prepare for that.

"Are you heading home?" I ask. I avoid eye contact and dust the sand off my knees.

"Sure am. The missus has got dinner waiting for me," he says.

I pause, wondering if I am desperate enough to ask him to stay. Or worse – for me to ask to join his family dinner. Ultimately, I shake out my hands and rise to my feet.

"Sounds good, boss. I guess I will see you again tomorrow," I say, so professionally that it feels almost robotic, "Drive safe."

The script never stops.

Tom simply smiles and nods before turning on his heel and leaving me alone on the beach.

Acute loneliness emerges instantly. Not a slow creep, but a swift pounce. It's been nearly a year since I've been on a date, months since I've seen my family, days since I have spoken with Ruby, and now, minutes since I saw my milquetoast colleague.

I knew adjusting to this new reality would be difficult. I

just never for a moment thought about how I would fare out here, all by myself – how I would suffer alone.

So, I lean on my old habits, and call Ruby as I watch the ebb and flow of the shoreline. She answers almost immediately.

"Hello?" her voice cracks.

Damn this signal.

"Ruby, hi. It's me," I say, trusting that my cell service improves for just long enough to subdue my depression. "Can you hear me? Is this a good time?"

The sun peeks from behind a cumulus cloud, shining golden light through slivers of palm leaves and onto the top of my head.

"Of course. Is everything okay?

She sounds clearer, but I don't expect it to hold for very long.

"Yeah, just wanted to hear your voice – or any voice for that matter," I say.

"Wow, you know how to make a girl feel special," Ruby laughs. "I miss you. When am I going to see you next?"

I press my fingers into the sand, relishing the feeling of it on the most sensitive parts of my skin.

"Not anytime soon, unless you've got a cool million lying around to fund my old research," I whine.

"Just plan another gala, but in St. John!"

I roll my eyes. "Yeah, right! It wasn't easy before, when I had help. Now it would be impossible."

"I'm serious, Lola. You've got to at least try."

"How's Dad?" I ask, quickly changing the subject.

"He's doing well! I'm actually with him right now, I'll put him on," she says, but her voice gradually crackles and I know that I don't have much time before the call drops.

"Dot! Hi, how are you?" Tino answers jovially.

"Dad, I am so happy to hear you! I'm doing okay, work is okay – "

"Lola, are you there? Hello?"

I try to repeat myself, speak more clearly, but then the phone beeps. The call has dropped.

And now, I'm still here in the Virgin Islands, by myself, wondering how to get back to my family without walking away from my career.

Maybe I *should* host another fundraiser. Maybe not an entire gala – I won't go down that road again – but maybe a summit for politicians, scientists, and whale enthusiasts? I don't know. I guess I can look into just renting a space for some presentations and see what happens.

I need *something*.

St. John is beautiful, don't get me wrong, but it's not my moody Pacific Northwest. I can't stay here, and I am reminded of that each time the sun is beating down on me, like it is right now.

If I don't try, how is anything supposed to change? Isn't that what I have been preaching about my whole career?

Turning my back to the ocean, I walk back to my car.

There is a lot of work to do.

SEPTEMBER 7, 2023

I sip at the foam of my nonalcoholic beer in peace. People don't stare as much anymore, not since the band broke up. Now, we're hardly recognizable, and completely irrelevant by the media's standards. But honestly, I'm okay with that. I still get to play music and live comfortably. And, from time to time, I still get to see Jacob. He's even less recognizable than me now that he's let his beard grow.

Bars don't make me uncomfortable anymore, so it's fine that I am still meeting Jacob at our favorite pub in Seattle. At least they have good food.

Jacob sees me at the small table in the corner and waves, picking up his step as he squeezes between the people swarming the bar.

"Oscar, hey!" he says, slapping the back of my shoulder as he takes a seat. "What piss are you drinking? I'll join you."

I push my pint glass toward him, offering a taste. He picks up the glass and takes a much-too-eager swallow.

"This." He picks up the glass and holds it up to the light. "This is *shit*. I'm gonna get a real one, if you don't mind."

I laugh. "Go right ahead."

Jacob flags down the server, who takes our orders before disappearing into the rowdy crowd. I continue to drink my nonalcoholic beer. Not savoring it, but enjoying it never-theless.

"So, what's new?" Jacob asks.

"Not much," I say. "Working on the solo stuff. Should be recording in a few months. What about you? Any other bands lining up to take you on?"

Jacob has been touring with other bands as their live bassist. Not just popular rock bands, but jazz groups, too. He's really been broadening his talents.

"Yeah, actually, might be joining another band permanent-ly," he says. There's a cautious edge to his voice though, as if he isn't sure how I will react.

But I honestly couldn't be happier for him.

"Congrats, man!" I say, clinking my glass to his. "That's really awesome. What band?"

"I'm not at liberty to say. It's uhh... It's more like a music collective –"

"What, like one of those anonymous masked bands?" I tease. Jacob shields his eyes. "Oh my god, it *is* one of those masked bands! Is it Sleep Token? If it's Sleep Token, you legally have to tell me."

"I think that only applies to cops, not bassists," Jacob says.

"Actually, I don't think it even applies to cops. But I would hope you would tell me all the same."

Jacob rubs the back of his neck. "You don't think that's stupid?"

"Definitely not," I say. "It's all about the music that way. Kind of makes me wish we had done things differently."

He squirms uncomfortably in his seat. Talking about the past makes both of us feel strange, like we were once part of this fever dream together. One minute we are famous, the next, we are having drinks in public without drawing any attention whatsoever. I guess we couldn't ride the waves of fame forever.

"We can't change the past," Jacob says. "And that's okay. We had a hell of a run."

A small twinge of guilt still creeps up, as it often does, knowing that I was the one who ended our reign. But I've learned to make peace with these feelings, because he's right – we can't change the past. All we can do is move forward with the lessons we learned and hope to do better.

Jacob's face suddenly lights up, as if he's just remembered something important.

"Speaking of the past," he says, withdrawing his phone, "are you talking to Lola at all?"

A bigger twinge of guilt hits this time. Not even a twinge. A sharp, shooting pain straight from my brain to my heart.

"No," I say solemnly.

"Have you even tried?"

"She doesn't want to talk to me."

The server places baskets of fish and chips in front of us, as well as two fresh beers. Jacob pops a fry into his mouth, gnashing open-mouthed as he tries to cool it down.

"Did she *say* that she doesn't want to talk to you?" he says, washing it down with his double IPA.

"Not exactly. I just don't want to reach out until I know how I can make things right, you know?"

He nods emphatically, shoveling a fork full of fried fish. "Well, I know you're not on social media anymore, but she posted something interesting recently."

I tilt my head, both puzzled and intrigued.

Jacob hands me his phone, illuminated with an image she posted to promote an event in the Virgin Islands.

St. John Humpback Whale Fundraising Summit. September 15th, 2023. Keynote speaker: Lola Marin.

"Bro, that's like next week!" I say.

"It is," he says calmly. "But I have an idea."

Usually, I am the one with schemes. I guess now that I

check my impulses more often, Jacob assumes the throne of hijinks.

"Okay, spit it out," I say.

"What if we invite a few dozen people to this thing? Give her a little fundraising boost?"

My heartbeat quickens, and suddenly, I feel a little dizzy.

Holding my head and leaning my elbows against the table, I sigh. "That didn't exactly work out well last time."

"Hear me out," Jacob says. "With the right people, it could be a way for you to try to mend things with her. Last time was a spectacle, and it attracted the wrong people. This time, it's just her in a small venue, presenting her shit. No frills. No drama."

The room feels like it's spinning, and I briefly wonder if I was given alcohol by mistake. The thought of seeing her again, of making things right, makes my stomach flip a million different ways.

"I don't know, Jacob," I say. "If I fuck up again, she will never talk to me again."

"She's already not talking to you, dude. At least try to fix things."

My hand trembles as I pick at my food. Embarrassed by my tremors, I decidedly set the fork down and place both palms firmly on the tabletop.

"I only have one chance, man. One chance to earn her forgiveness. If this doesn't work –"

"It will work," he says. "Trust me."

My muscles tense everywhere in my body. "How can you be so sure?"

"Because I already started a list," he smiles.

The tension releases and a wave of lightness washes over me, like a sudden surge of cool rain on a hot day.

"You sneaky bastard," I say. "Show me this list!"

And he does. In his notes app, he's drafted a list of

affluent people – not just musicians and actors, but also tech giants, philanthropists, and politicians.

I audibly gasp. "How the fuck do you know these people?"

"Living in California has its perks," he says. "And I've been volunteering during my off-time on tours. Let's just say you inspired me."

"And you really think you can get these people to come to her event?"

Jacob grins widely.

"Buddy, I know I can."

CHAPTER
THIRTY-NINE

LOLA

SEPTEMBER 15, 2023

I shift uncomfortably on my feet. The day is finally here, and though I didn't have much time to make arrangements, I've had this presentation ready for more than a year.

In truth, I am actually kind of astonished by how many people are present. Each time I see a famous face, I chew my bottom lip into oblivion. However, nothing prepares me for when I glimpse both Dawn and Brandon at the registration table, which is generously being manned by some interns I met at Tòti Research Lab.

"Oh my god, hi!" I say, approaching the table.

Dawn lets out a high-pitched squeal and squeezes me into a tight hug. I look over her shoulder as she gives my body a shake to see Brandon look up from scribbling his name on the sign-in sheet. His mouth curls into a gentle smile.

When Dawn releases me, she not-so-subtly shoves me towards Brandon. But what I expect to be an awkward hand-shake is dismissed when he wraps one arm around me, pulling me close. It's timid and almost apologetic, the way he holds me here, just a few seconds longer than he should.

"It's good to see you," he says.

"Likewise," I say, stepping back. "I didn't think I would ever see your face again, let alone here in St. John."

He averts his eyes and rubs the back of his neck.

"Yeah, I didn't think so either."

Silence swells between us. There's so much I'd like to say, but this is not the time nor place. He must know that.

Luckily, he breaks the silence.

"So," he laughs nervously. "This is really cool, this summit thing. Damn good turn out, too. Pretty sure I saw the governor of California."

"Yeah?" I ask, doubt seeping into my voice. "It really isn't much. I just kind of threw this thing together last minute."

Brandon's eyes snap back to me.

"Hey, don't do that," he says.

"Do what?"

"Sell yourself short. This is a good thing you are doing. You'll be great."

I forgot how supportive he always was. It should still make me feel guilty about everything that happened between us, but actually, I'm touched. When I think about it, he's actually the most genuine friend I've ever had.

Before I can thank him, Dawn tugs at his t-shirt (no tuxes this time, thank god), pulling him into the moderately sized conference room. Still, seeing them here so far from Seattle makes me feel reassured.

Left alone in anticipation, I inhale deeply and join the volunteers in welcoming the attendees. Each guest is surprisingly informed when they make their introductions.

"Thank you for putting this together, Ms. Marin," one man says. "Your research is precisely the kind of thing we need to be talking about on Capitol Hill."

"Thank you," I say. "It's nice to hear that."

I don't ask how he already knows about my research. Instead, I opt for false confidence, as if there's no scenario in which any of these people wouldn't have a clue who I am or why I am here. The universe gives. I suppose I must graciously accept.

The man shakes my hand before striding away, carrying himself in a way that only those in positions of power seem to.

"We've got this, Lola," says Chloe, one of the interns. "*Go. Enjoy your event.*"

"Alright, alright," I chuckle. "I'll stop hovering. But promise me you'll take a break soon."

Chloe laughs. "Seriously, we're fine. Don't you have to present soon?"

I glance at my phone to check the time.

"Shit. You're right," I mumble, hoping the guests don't hear me. One woman clearly does though. I catch her amused smirk as I turn back toward the conference room.

The guests all talk to each other as if they are close friends. The warmth in their voices, the proximity of their bodies, the frequency of their laughter, all feels as if I am on the outside of some kind of inside joke, making it difficult to breathe.

Hastily, I make my way to the corner of the room to do discrete breathing exercises. Since arriving in St. John, it's the only way I can seem to steady my rapid pulse and ward off tunnel vision. I suppose I should thank Oscar for teaching it to me.

Despite everything, when I think of him now, I am comforted by who he used to be. And I often wish I knew the man he became after I left him that day in rehab. I was angry then. But it must be true what they say: time heals all things.

And it did take time, but now, there's no bitterness in my heart for him anymore. I sincerely hope he's doing well.

I wish he could see me now. Would he be proud?

My heart rate stabilizes just in time for my presentation to begin as Chloe appears beside me.

"Are you ready?" she whispers, soft and dove-like.

"Yeah," I say. "I think I'm ready."

She smiles, albeit with an edge of concern. "Okay, I'll get the lights."

Chloe dims them slightly as I slowly make my way to the microphone at the front of the room. It crackles the moment I touch it.

In response to the sound, everyone finds a seat and a reverent hush fills the room.

"Hello and welcome, everyone. My name is Lola Marin, and I am a marine biologist and acoustician," I say. "Today, I want to talk to you about the importance of humpback whales as a keystone species, as well as the impact of their migratory habits and communication. All of you are probably already familiar with whale songs, but what you might not know is their purpose and complexity."

A muffled cough echoes, throwing me off just enough to forget what I want to say next. My eyes dart toward the exits, and I briefly consider just running away or forgetting this whole thing.

Instead, I opt for an uncomfortable laugh.

"As I was saying, whales use songs to communicate with one another. The purpose of these songs ranges from, umm…" It feels like my brain is short circuiting. "Locating food, or uhh, a mate…"

The door in the back of the room creaks open, shining light from outside so that all I can see is the silhouette of a man. And while the room is not exceptionally large, the dimmed lights make it impossible to make out any of his features – except I swear I see a top hat.

"This slide shows some of the popular past theories, all of which have now been debunked," I continue, getting my bearings. "While no theories have definitively proven why these songs exist, my research looks into how they spread from one population to another, and how human-caused noise pollution gets in the way."

The presentation slide projected on the wall illuminates the room enough that I can more clearly see the faces of the attendees, including the man still standing in the back.

I notice his crossed arms, his long, curly, dark hair, and…

I swallow.

His familiar, dreamy, hazel eyes gazing at me.

Oscar.

Oscar dressed as… Slash?

Oh my god…

My mouth is suddenly dry and it feels as though I might faint. But Oscar smiles encouragingly, exaggerating the rise and fall in his chest as he breathes, supporting me in the best way he knows how.

So, I inhale. I exhale. I imagine singing my heart out in a dive bar.

And then, like a lost spirit, a sudden confidence possesses me. I speak as if it were just me and Oscar, out in the Puget Sound on the old research boat, and I finish the rest of my presentation without a hitch.

I only return to reality when I am jolted by the roar of clapping hands. One by one, the attendees rise from their seats, lining up eagerly before Chloe at the donation table.

Oscar, unsurprisingly, is the first in line.

CHAPTER
FORTY

OSCAR

SEPTEMBER 15, 2023

I step to the table at the back of the room, the sound of applause still echoing in my ears. But this time, it's not for my vain acts on stage, but for something true and good.

For Lola.

"Would you like to make a contribution?" the small woman asks.

"Please," I say.

She withdraws a clipboard and clicks her pen.

"And how much would you like to donate today?" she says.

"One-hundred thousand," I say softly, leaning over the table just slightly so she can hear better. I'd like to keep this discreet. I'd give more if I could, but without the band, finances have been complicated.

"One-hundred thousand!?" she repeats, far louder than I would like. "Dollars?"

My cheeks redden and I try to hide beneath my hair.

"Yes," I whisper.

The girl must notice my discomfort, because she immediately puts her hand to her mouth, as if she had just exposed my secret. She had, but I can't fault her for it. Lola would never willingly accept money from me, but it feels wrong not to help.

Suddenly, I smell the familiar, subtle scent of sea salt and vanilla as a presence grows behind me like a waxing moon.

"One-hundred thousand, huh? Is that what I'm worth to you?" Lola teases.

I turn to face her standing there, vibrant and poised in her navy blue suit. She looks so smart, so professional, so… sexy. Meanwhile, I look ridiculous in my Slash costume.

"Hi," I say nervously, unsure if we stand on solid ground. "You're probably surprised to see me. Sorry, I promise I'm not stalking you, it's just –"

"Just a random visit to the world's smallest whale summit in the Virgin Islands? Wow, my Instagram ads must have worked better than I thought," she laughs. "Nice costume. You look like you belong in Paradise City."

I laugh, too, but it carries far longer than normal. I am still uneasy, and while I can be relieved that Lola is joking with me, I can't tell if it's friendly or resentful.

"Relax, Oscar," she says. "*Breathe.*"

My eyes widen. It dawns on me how our roles have reversed. Now, *she's* supporting *me*. She never needed saving. But I did.

I crack a sheepish smile.

"I did come here for you, I just… I couldn't come empty handed, so…" I gesture around the room. "I invited some friends."

Her amused smirk turns into beaming tenderness.

"You did this?" she asks.

I shrug. "I had some help."

Before I even have a second to blink, her arms are wrapped around me, gently tugging me against her.

"Thank you," she says. "It means a lot that you're here."

"Yeah?"

She pulls away, releasing me. A chill descends upon my body despite the warmth of the Caribbean air.

"Yeah," she says. "Finish up here and come find me, okay? I've got to mingle, but I'd love to catch up."

I didn't expect instant forgiveness, but it's painful to watch her walk away. Still, a hug is more than I expected from her. I am thankful for that much.

I sign my check and hand it to the young woman at the donation table and move out of the way. The last thing Lola needs is a further barrier to donate. She can go mingle, and I'll kindly step out of the way. This is her moment. I want her to relish it.

After a full hour of her shaking hands and laughing at old men's jokes, the venue has emptied, leaving only myself, the donation woman, and Lola.

I anxiously wait outside the venue, wondering if she forgot. She probably has, and it would be understandable. I've been out of her life for the last year, never reaching out to her even once. Of course her mind would move onto other things.

That's just one of the many consequences of my actions.

Wringing my hands in my lap, I listen as I sit outside the doors, only hearing the faint murmurs of their voices.

All of a sudden, I hear Lola shriek.

"No way!"

More shrieking, apparently from joy.

"Oh my god! Chloe! Thank you, thank you, thank you!" she cheers, followed by a quick succession of footsteps heading my way.

The door swings open, revealing an exasperated Lola looking around frantically. Tears are streaming down her face, and when she doesn't see what she is looking for, they seem to turn sorrowful.

I clear my throat, and her head snaps towards me, a visible wave of relief washing over her. She races to me, and without wasting a single moment, she pulls me to my feet and kisses me right on the mouth.

Then, she lightly slaps me.

"You son of a bitch," she says.

"It's about time," I say, gently rubbing where the faint sting of her palm fell on my cheek. She laughs excitedly, clearly vibrating out of her skin. "While I am sure I deserve worse than a slap, I have no idea why you're smiling. What's going on?"

She jumps up and down and squeals in delight.

"We did it! I can't believe we actually did it!"

"*We*? What did we do?" I ask cautiously, unable to fathom how I could have helped do anything at all.

"You and me," she says. "We raised the money!"

Then, without warning, her face pales and her feet give out beneath her. Just before she comes crashing down to the ground, I grab her by the waist and gently lower to the floor with her.

After a minute or two, her eyes, woozy and clouded, flutter open. Holding her in my arms, my hand frames her cheek and smooths her soft hair out of her face. Dreamily, she looks up at me.

"I can't believe it," she whispers.

"You did it, Lola," I say with a smile, but the words catch in my throat. I don't even try to hold back the swell of emotion. I am so damn proud. "Are you okay? Do you need water or…" I look around helplessly. "Just water, I guess."

Lola slowly tries to lift herself. I guide her up with my hand on her back, ensuring she doesn't collapse again.

"I'm fine," she says. She searches my face for something, a hint of unmistakable affection in her blushing cheeks. "I could go for some shaved ice though. It's just next door. Want to join me?"

"Yeah. I'd like that."

I help her to her feet, clasping her hands tightly in mine.

But when she is finally steady, I find myself unable to let them go. It's as if dropping them will pull her from me permanently, and that is something I am not ready to accept.

Much to my surprise, she doesn't let go either. She simply squeezes and urges me toward the exit door, never letting her eyes off me for even a second.

All the while, my stomach flutters frantically and my legs feel an absence of gravity. I am genuinely concerned that she will be the one picking *me* up off of the pavement – that is, if I don't take her down with me. Her hand just grasps mine tighter.

Draped in a strangely comfortable but tense silence, we approach the rainbow shaved ice hut in the parking lot, surrounded by mostly empty picnic tables. Maho trees sway along the perimeter, casting just enough shadow to shade us from the explosive orange sunset as the slow, gentle sound of the tide coming in and out echoes behind the treeline.

We take a seat with our sticky cups of shaved ice. Hers is cherry red, and mine is berry blue. Only then does she release my hand.

The absence of her touch is agonizing, not knowing if or when I might feel it again.

Lola digs her spoon into her scarlet dessert.

"I don't even know how to begin to thank you," she says.

"Please don't thank me," I sigh. "Not after what I put you through."

She freezes.

"You went out on a limb for me, you supported me, you believed in me. I don't think you understand how much you've helped me. I hit my fundraising goal because *you* cared. Now I can follow migration routes and collect the data I need with my own boat and my own equipment. That's a really big deal, Oscar. Don't let the mistakes of your past color your future."

"It was all you," I assure her. "You were great up there. I didn't make them sign their checks. You inspired that."

She waves her hand at me, dismissing the compliment. Though it doesn't go unheard. I can tell by the flush of her cheeks, red as the syrup coating her shaved ice.

"I'm sorry," I say. "For everything."

Her midnight eyes pierce through me as her spoon dips into her sultry mouth.

"I'm not mad. Not anymore anyway," she says softly. "I wanted to hate you forever, I really did. But it wouldn't have changed anything – not what happened, and not how I feel about you…"

My heart hammers in my chest.

"Oh? And how is that?"

She looks away, turning her attention back to her cup. She doesn't take a bite though. She just scrapes at it nervously, stirring until the syrup and ice cream mix into a milky shade of pink.

We don't speak, we dare not to, afraid of what will happen if we speak the truth.

So, I decide to break the tension.

"I half expected you to break out into song during your presentation," I chuckle. "Seemed like a good time to bring back sexy Bret Michaels."

She snorts, nearly choking on her last bite.

"Oh my god," she pants, catching her breath. "I still can't believe you're wearing that. You look ridiculous. Why would you bring that up?"

"Bring what up? That you're sexy, or that you were Bret Michaels?"

"All I heard is that you think I'm sexy. I refuse to acknowledge the rest. It *never* happened, got it?" she says, pointing her spoon at me.

I put my hands up in surrender.

"Loud and clear," I say.

She laughs, pushing her cup aside. With nothing to occupy her hands though, she gets restless.

Then, she reaches across the table, beckoning me to offer my hand. I obey without hesitation.

"I do love you, Oscar," she says. "Always have. Always will."

I open my mouth to speak – to tell her how much I love her too – but she hastily rounds the table and drops into my lap, wrapping her hands around my neck and dragging me to her lips.

My heart stops.

Greedily, I open for her, taking her cherry-flavored tongue into my mouth, pawing at her. My hands wander up her arms, through her hair, along her throat, and this time, I refuse to let go.

"Please, take me home," she moans into my mouth, her voice vibrating throughout my entire body, down my spine and into my groin.

"Show me where, baby," I growl. "I'll take you anywhere you want."

Her keys are in my hands before I can catch my breath.

EPILOGUE

LOLA

JULY 10, 2024

The TV blares, casting a colorful reflection on Tino's smiling face. Since I returned to Seattle, I stop by and sit with him for a few hours as often as I can. Whenever I do, his face lights up, even if he doesn't recognize me every time. If he forgets my name, it hurts – but the unmistakable love in his eyes tells me that deep down, I'm still in there. I'm there, and he loves me. For now, that is enough.

Eva sits on the opposite side of the room, smoking her usual cigarette and scowling at me. I pay her no mind. This is my time with Tino, not hers. I won't let her ruin what we have left, not since I found the strength to visit.

It's hard watching the people you love slowly sink from your reach, and I guess I thought that if I just ignored it – if I didn't have to see him decline – I could remember him as he was.

But that isn't fair to him. Grief is difficult to navigate, but avoidance wasn't the answer. Being here, clutching his hand as he watches the screen because conversation is too challenging, is the best thing I can do – for both of us.

Tino looks over at me, a softness in his stare.

"What is it, Dad?" I ask.

His smile widens. "Just happy to be here with my Dot."

My eyes prick. *He recognizes me.*

"I'm happy to be here, too," I whisper, squeezing his hand.

In five minutes, he might forget again. But for now, I cling to this moment. It's just a simple acknowledgement, but who knows when it will be the last.

"Hey, Dad," I say.

He turns his head back to the TV.

"What is it, Dot?"

A lump rises in my throat.

"I love you."

He closes his eyes and rests deeper into the couch.

"I love you, too."

I try not to stare at Oscar as he helps load the equipment onto the catamaran, the name *What the Fluke?* painted on the back in bold, blue letters. He is shirtless, revealing more tattoo ink than bare skin, which always puts me in a frenzy. I bite my lip, unfocused on untying the knots of rope that tether us to the dock.

Oscar notices me staring and smirks, setting down the black duffel bags and sauntering over to the starboard side where I fuss with the knot. He wraps his arms around my bare waist from behind, his fingers tracing the edges of my green bikini. Soft kisses tickle my neck.

Twilight fades away as the sun creeps farther and farther from the horizon. We have to get going if we want to see the whales breach.

But the feeling of his lips skating along my skin makes it hard to tear away.

"Oscar…" I whisper breathlessly.

He squeezes me tight and bites my ear.

"Sorry," he says. "It's hard wanting you all the time. I'll let you get to work."

Bringing his hand to my mouth, I lightly kiss the tips of his fingers.

"To be continued," I promise.

"Deal. Here, let me help you with that."

He retrieves the rope from my hands and undoes the knot that I inadvertently added when my attention was solely focused on the deep, muscular lines running from his hip bones to his pelvis.

Handing me the rope, he smacks my ass and steps aside.

"I'll let you do the honor, Captain."

And with that, I unwrap the rope from the dock cleats and push us away by just a foot or two. I rush to the helm and start the motor, navigating our familiar, gentle path out into the Puget Sound.

The water is calm, and we drive out slowly, the miniscule waves simply bobbing us along the surface. When we reach our favorite spot, the sun has begun to set, hovering along the horizon, painting fiery strokes of red and orange across the sea. I kill the engine and toss the new hydrophones into the water.

And now we wait.

I am able to listen to their calls on the boat now, making it easier to locate them in the Sound. And while a network of other boats will typically communicate the whales' locations on the radio, it's too late in the day for that. But that's okay. I know where they like to go. They should be close.

Oscar and I sit side by side, fingers entwined as we scan the surface, our legs dangling off the edge of the bow.

"You know, every day I think it won't get better than this, and every day I am proved wrong," I say. "I feel like for years, we were calling out to each other, but we just kept getting lost in the noise. I'm glad you finally found me, Oscar. I really am."

Oscar smiles, flashing his perfect teeth.

"You made this happen. Don't forget that," he says. His shoulder nudges me.

My cheeks flush, probably made all the more red by the glow of the setting sun reflecting off the water.

Suddenly, a column of mist blasts out of the water just a few meters from our feet, followed by the fanning fluke of a whale. It's mottled with white and slate-gray, with a saw-like trailing edge – a classic characteristic of humpbacks.

I push up to my feet and rush to the radio, cranking up the volume to the microphones below the surface.

We are met with the low, melodic groan of a nearby whale.

Oscar appears at my side, cupping his ear to hear better.

"What do you think they are saying?"

"I don't know," I admit. "Probably just searching for a familiar song, to find where they belong."

"I know I found mine," Oscar says, pulling me close.

I smile up at him, grazing my fingers along his sharp, stubbled jaw.

"You know, I think I did, too."

His hand brushes through my windswept hair, and I press my lips to his, opening myself to a brighter future – and if there's one thing I know for certain, it's that Oscar is in it. Not as a distant memory or a past regret, but as the present bliss I hold onto again and again, never tiring of the comfort it brings.

He and I belong together.

And together, I believe we can change the world.

One song at a time.

ACKNOWLEDGMENTS

What a strange year this was. I wrote this book after my own autism diagnosis, after allowing myself to explore my hyper-fixation on humpback whales, after teaching myself to play the guitar. Writing this story was the amalgamation of so much personal growth, all at once.

It also allowed me to express the love I hold for the recovering addicts in my life. My heart breaks for the judgment and stigma they faced on top of the monumental battle they already faced within themselves. They are so deserving of love and second chances. I hope I communicated that clearly in this story.

I continue to learn and grow from my own experiences with neurodivergence and substance abuse, and each day, I try to make the right decisions for my mental health by offering myself and others endless compassion, forgiveness, and understanding.

If you know anyone fighting for their lives, offer an ear to listen if not a hand to hold.

This book is for you.

ABOUT THE AUTHOR

Sara Wetmore is an award-winning contemporary romance novelist. When she isn't penning stories about neurodivergent heroines and their broken heroes, she's playing guitar or practicing modern witchcraft.

This is her last book under the name of Sara Wetmore. Moving forward, she will be writing as *Sara Scully*.

ALSO BY SARA WETMORE

The Christmas Script